THE ENGINEER

BOOK 4 IN THE BACHE LOFTT SERIES

NICK ADAMS

Elliptical
Publishing

PROLOGUE

A meeting, outside GDA space

EIGHTY-SEVEN THOUSAND LIGHT YEARS DISTANT, deep in the uncharted regions beyond the furthest GDA outposts, a very unusual kind of gathering was taking place.

In a vast chamber carved from living crystal, twelve figures gathered around a pool of swirling liquid metal. Their bodies were tall and sinuous, covered in iridescent scales that caught the light from the bioluminescent growths adorning the walls. Six-fingered hands gestured over the pool as it shaped itself into a perfect replica of GDA space.

'The Dimioi fleet has been destroyed,' hissed the tallest of the figures, its voice like stone grinding against metal. 'The entire race, cleansed in a matter of moments.'

'They called it the Extermination War,' another replied, touching a scaled finger to the pool. The liquid metal rippled and formed a perfect image of a decimated fleet of a thousand ships.

'Just as the prophets foretold,' a third voice joined in, deeper than the others. 'The cycle continues as it will.'

The leader, distinguished by the elaborate crest of spines that ran from its forehead down its back, moved closer to the pool. Its vertical pupils narrowed as it studied the image.

'For a thousand years we will wait, hidden beyond their reach, rebuilding our strength,' it said. 'The Extermination War was merely the beginning. They believed they had destroyed us, the Dimioi, greatest of all species. They believed wrong.'

The tall figure reached forward, clawed fingers extending towards the pool. The liquid metal responded to its touch, reshaping into a new image – the surviving GDA fleet moving through space.

'Our physical fleet failed us,' it hissed. 'But we are patient. We have waited a millennium already. What are a few more years?'

The leader's vertical pupils narrowed to slits.

'We will revert to the infiltration procedure. Humans are so very gullible and fragile.'

The liquid metal rippled again, forming a perfect replica of a planet. The leader extended one claw, piercing the miniature globe. The metal flowed around the intrusion, resealing itself as if nothing had happened.

'Our agents are already in place on Dasos,' the leader continued. 'The Klatt will also serve our purpose too by keeping the humans busy, as they have for centuries without knowing it.'

'And if they fail?'

The leader's scaled lips parted in what might have been a smile, revealing rows of needle-like teeth.

'They most likely will, but it will be too late by then… as we shall emerge from the shadows ourselves. The objective to secure our influence on every human planet and on every vessel will already be in place.'

The twelve figures raised their arms in unison, a low humming filling the chamber as their voices joined in ancient harmony.

'For the glory of the new Omada,' they intoned. 'The true inheritors of the stars.'

The liquid metal pool shimmered once more, resolving into an image of the galaxy…with a wave of darkness spreading slowly across its spiral arms.

1

———

ELEVEN HUNDRED YEARS LATER.

Bache Loftt's cabin, *Katadromiko 2*, docked with Vasi
Stathmos Station

The summons arrived at 0400 hours, jarring Bache from a sleep so deep he'd been dreaming of interstice tube calibrations.

"Lieutenant Loftt, your presence is required at the Dresse inquiry, Kentro GDA Council chambers. 0900 hours today." The message repeated until he called for it to stop. He opened one eye and peeked at the glowing message on his wall screen with the unmistakable GDA high-priority encryption border.

Bache sat up, blinking away sleep as he ran a hand

through his short dark hair. Council chambers? That couldn't be right. He hadn't set foot in a GDA council meeting since Dresse, and that was three years ago. Three years since the affair on Dresse and the hidden battle fleet. Three years since he'd been promoted to chief engineer on the *Katadromiko 2*.

His cabin felt suddenly cold. Bache checked the authentication codes on the message twice, then a third time. Legitimate. Direct from the president's office.

'Why now?' he muttered, swinging his legs over the edge of the bed. The metal floor chilled his bare feet, grounding him in the present and making him shiver. 'What could've possibly changed, that they want me again?'

The *K2* had been on routine patrol for months, monitoring the shipping lanes near the Serris agricultural colony. Nothing remarkable had happened…exactly as it shouldn't. He was looking forward to some leave, a visit home to Tyraan City on Deelatayne and a few beers with his father, Tirexion.

He grabbed his dress uniform from the storage compartment. The stiff fabric felt foreign in his hands after years of wearing the more practical engineer's boiler suits. He hadn't expected to need it on this rotation.

Two hours later, he stood in the small capsule of the Kentro space elevator, watching the huge space station shrink to a speck above him. The transparent walls of the elevator offered a panoramic view of Dasos and the sparkling city of Kentro growing larger beneath his feet. His stomach lurched slightly as the capsule accelerated, though whether from the descent or the upcoming inquiry, he couldn't be sure.

The capsule slowed as it entered the atmosphere, the gentle hum of the stabilisers increasing to a low whine. Clouds parted around the wide tube, revealing the sprawling governmental complex below. Kentro was massive, the administrative heart of over sixteen hundred worlds of the GDA and home to the GDA's central council chambers.

'*Chief Engineer Loftt, please confirm identity for final clearance,*' the automated customs system requested.

'Loftt, Bache. Chief engineer, *Katadromiko 2*,' he said, pressing his palm against the seat scanner. The light pulsed green.

'*Identity confirmed. Welcome to Kentro.*'

He checked the time: 0835. Plenty of time to reach the chambers, but not enough to gather any information on why they'd summoned him. His reflection in the glass looked tired. The premature grey at his temples had spread slightly over the past three years, an unwelcome reminder of the stress that came with his position.

The capsule touched down with a slight bump, and Bache stepped onto Kentro soil, his polished boots reflecting the cold morning sunlight. The Council Chambers loomed ahead, a massive structure of gleaming white stone and glass that dominated the central plaza.

Bache passed through the security checkpoint, where his credentials were scanned again. The guards' faces betrayed nothing as they waved him through. Inside, the chambers were hushed, the vaulted ceilings amplifying even the smallest sounds. His footsteps echoed as he followed the directions on his tablet to the assigned meeting room.

He paused outside the ornate double doors, straightening his uniform, and took a deep breath. Whatever this was about, he'd face it head-on. Just as he reached for the handle, a familiar voice echoed behind him.

'Chief Engineer Loftt. Still punctual to a fault, I see.'

Bache turned, his heart skipping a beat. Zaphir Mye, ex-colleague, ex-lover, stood a few metres away, her dark brown eyes studying him with the same intensity he remembered. She wore the uniform of a senior systems specialist now, with new insignia he didn't recognise.

'Zaphir,' he managed, surprised by the dryness in his throat. 'They called you in too?'

She approached, her tall lithe figure still carrying that efficient grace he'd always admired.

'Apparently someone thinks we need to relive old nightmares together,' she said, ruefully.

'I see you're both here.' The deep voice came from behind them as the chamber doors swung open.

Bache turned to find Admiral of the Fleet Zeers standing in the doorway, his weathered face expressionless. The man's silver-streaked beard was longer than regulation permitted, a privilege of rank Bache supposed.

'Sir,' Bache and Zaphir said in unison, straightening to attention.

'At ease. Come inside.' Zeers stepped back, gesturing them through.

The council chamber was smaller than Bache expected, an intimate oval room rather than the grand assembly hall he'd imagined. A semicircular table dominated the space, behind which sat five figures. Bache recognised President Xutan at the centre, his face more lined than when they'd last met. The other four were strangers to him, though their uniforms indicated two admirals, a civilian councillor, and a systems intelligence director.

Most surprising was the solitary figure sitting to the side, a man in plain civilian clothes, his back partially turned. Even from this angle, Bache would know that profile anywhere.

'Dad?' The word escaped before Bache could stop it.

Tirexion Loftt turned, his face haggard in a way Bache had never seen before. The renowned engineer and ship designer's eyes were bloodshot, his normally immaculate appearance dishevelled.

'What's going on?' Bache whispered to Zaphir, who looked equally confused.

President Xutan gestured for Bache and Zaphir to take the two empty seats at the centre of the room. 'Please, sit down. We have matters of grave importance to discuss.'

Bache lowered himself into the chair, his eyes never leaving his father's face. Something was deeply wrong. Tirexion wouldn't meet his gaze, his fingers fidgeting with a small data chip – a nervous habit Bache hadn't seen since his mother's funeral.

'Three years ago,' Admiral Zeers began, 'the two of you uncovered a Gata plot involving illegal battleships and mining rights. Your actions prevented a catastrophe.'

'With respect, sir,' Bache said, 'we've been through this debriefing multiple times. Has something changed? And why is my father here?'

A heavy silence fell across the room. President Xutan exchanged glances with the other council members before leaning forward.

'Chief Engineer, your father came to us voluntarily three days ago with…disturbing information.'

Bache's stomach tightened. He looked at his father again, who finally raised his eyes…red-rimmed and haunted.

'Tell him, Tirexion,' Xutan said quietly. 'He deserves to hear it from you.'

Tirexion's shoulders slumped as he stood, the movement stiff and mechanical.

'The ships, Bache. The Gata battleships you destroyed.' His voice cracked. 'They were mine.'

The words hit Bache like a physical blow. His mind refused to process them, even as his body reacted…heart hammering against his ribs, palms suddenly sweaty against the polished table surface.

'What?' The word emerged as barely a whisper.

Tirexion's eyes were fixed on some invisible point on the floor. 'I designed them. The basic schematic. The hull configuration. The drive systems.'

Each confession emerged with visible effort, as though the words themselves were causing him physical pain.

Bache's vision narrowed, the faces around the table blurring at the edges. He felt Zaphir tense beside him but couldn't look at her. His entire focus was locked on his father – the man who'd taught him everything he knew about ship design, about integrity, about doing what was right.

'That's not possible.' Bache shook his head. 'You've

dedicated your life to GDA vessels. You wouldn't…' His voice caught. 'You couldn't.'

'I didn't know what they were for.' Tirexion finally looked up, his eyes pleading. 'Not at first. They came to me fifteen years ago. Said they needed transport vessels with enhanced defensive capabilities for dangerous sectors. Mining support ships, they called them.'

'Who?' Bache demanded, leaning forward. 'Who came to you?'

'A private contractor. At least I thought it was private.' Tirexion's voice dropped to barely a whisper. 'It was Flast Enterprises, operating through a shell company. I had no idea at the time.'

'Ah, crap,' Bache grunted. He felt as if someone had sucked all the oxygen from the room. His father – the man who'd taught him the ethics of engineering, who'd insisted that every design choice had moral weight – had designed weapons for Ystolion Flast? The woman responsible for thousands of deaths?

'You worked for Flast?' The words scraped from Bache's throat. 'For fifteen years?'

'No.' His father's hands trembled as he placed the data chip on the table. 'The initial designs, yes. But they were modified extensively after I delivered them. I discovered the truth during a routine systems analysis three months ago. They used my basic framework but weaponised it far beyond what I'd imagined possible.'

Bache's mind raced, connecting pieces he'd never thought to examine. The familiar look of the Gata ships' array systems. The sound of the antigrav drives that had reminded him of GDA vessels. The subtle elegance of the hull design that had struck him as strangely familiar even as he was fighting for his life.

'Why didn't you come forward sooner?' Zaphir's voice cut through, sharp and accusing.

His father flinched. 'I didn't know. Not until recently.

2

Council meeting room, GDA Central Chambers, Kentro, Dasos

BACHE STARED AT HIS FATHER, his mind spinning between disbelief and a mounting sense of betrayal. The man who had lectured him about engineering ethics since childhood had designed warships for Ystolion Flast? The same woman who'd nearly killed him on that fractured moon?

'What happens now?' Bache asked, his voice sounding strange in his own ears. He looked directly at President Xutan, deliberately avoiding his father's gaze. 'What becomes of him?'

The weight of the question seemed to press down on the entire room. Xutan's lined face remained carefully neutral as he leaned forward, steepling his fingers.

'That's partly why we've brought you here, Chief Engineer. Your father's cooperation has been invaluable in identifying potential security breaches. The designs were accessed through classified GDA databases…databases that should have been impenetrable.'

'You're using him,' Bache said, the realisation hitting him like a physical blow. 'As bait? Or an informant?'

Admiral Vesten cleared his throat. 'Your father faces serious charges, Loftt. Treason being the most severe. However, his continued cooperation could significantly mitigate his sentence.'

The word "treason" landed like a punch to Bache's gut. He'd seen what happened to traitors in the GDA. Military prison on Kaltos IV was notorious – a frozen hellscape where inmates rarely survived their full sentences.

'I deserve whatever punishment they decide…'

Tirexion's voice trailed off as President Xutan raised his hand. Something shifted in the president's expression…a calculated look that made Bache's skin crawl.

'Before we continue discussing your father's fate,' Xutan said, his voice lower than before, 'there's something else you both need to understand.'

The president pressed something under the table, and a soft hum filled the chamber. Security field. No recording devices would work now.

'Tirexion was led to believe he was designing ships for a private contractor, yes. But the trail we've uncovered suggests a more troubling origin for those orders.' Xutan's eyes narrowed. 'They came from within the GDA itself.' He pressed his palm against the table's surface, and a holographic display flickered to life between them.

Bache's breath caught. The display showed a series of encrypted communications, timestamps, and transfer records. Names scrolled past…many he recognised from the highest echelons of GDA leadership.

'Your father was a pawn,' Xutan continued, his eyes never leaving Bache's face. 'A convenient scapegoat, should this ever come to light. Which, thanks to his conscience, it has.'

Bache's blood ran cold. He glanced at his father, whose expression had shifted from shame to confusion.

'Sir?' Bache managed, his throat tight.

'We have evidence that someone on the Naval Defence Council authorised the initial designs through back channels. Someone with access to our most secure systems.' Xutan's gaze swept across the room. 'The same person who likely helped Desulet install the sabotage protocols on the *K2*.'

Bache leaned forward, scanning the data. 'These are authorisations. Command-level clearances for…' He stopped, the implications hitting him like a physical blow. 'These are approvals for the transfer of almost all the classified ship designs, propulsion designs, weapon designs. Not just my father's work.'

'Exactly.' Xutan's voice hardened. 'For the past twenty years, there has been a shadow council operating within our government. People with access to our most sensitive technologies, selling them to private interests…including Flast.'

Zaphir's sharp intake of breath beside him mirrored Bache's own shock. 'How deep does this go?' she asked.

'Admiral Henns was openly…let's say, unappreciative of your father…and, it seems, set him up for the fall. Henns, as we know, disappeared just before the treachery was discovered, his wife too. But we don't believe he was acting alone.'

'You think they're still operating, don't you?' said Bache.

'We do,' said the president, leaning back in his chair and getting nervous glances from the others either side of him. 'It could still be Henns for all we know. With Flast's money, I'm sure he'll have had surgery and have a completely different appearance now.'

Bache couldn't remember his father ever looking so vulnerable. It was as if someone had taken all the self-belief out of the man. He looked over at him again. Tirexion sat slumped in his chair, staring at the marble floor with a haunted look in his eyes.

'If Henns rubber-stamped all this, you're not going to be blaming my father,' Bache announced, surprising himself with the forcefulness of his tone.

The president took a deep breath and stared back at Bache.

'Chief Engineer, remember who you're talking to,' Xutan growled in reply. 'But I understand your frustration and of course your allegiance.'

'Where do we fit into all this?' Zaphir asked.

Bache turned to look at Zaphir, struck by the directness of her question. Her dark eyes held that familiar intensity…the look that had always cut through complications to find the core issue. Even after three years apart, she still possessed that uncanny ability to voice exactly what he needed to ask but couldn't find the words for.

The council members exchanged glances, and Bache noticed the subtle shift in their body language. President

Xutan leaned forward slightly, his weathered hands clasping together on the polished table.

'You two are uniquely qualified,' Xutan said, his voice dropping lower. 'You've encountered Flast's operation first-hand. You've seen what she's capable of. And most importantly, you've already proven you can survive their attempts to eliminate you.'

'Only by pure luck,' Zaphir countered.

Bache's stomach tightened. 'You want us to go after this group of whoever they are?'

It wasn't a question. The realisation settled over him like a cold weight. Three years of relative peace…of rebuilding the *K2*, of establishing his reputation as chief engineer…and now they wanted to throw him back into the fire against that psychopathic woman.

'Not exactly,' Admiral Zeers interjected. 'We need you to investigate something…unusual. A pattern we've detected that may be connected to this group.'

The admiral activated a holographic display, revealing a star chart of the Frontier Worlds. One system pulsed with a soft blue light: Serris Adelaine.

'Agricultural world,' Bache said automatically. 'Major food producer for the Carina Arm.'

'I'm impressed,' said Zeers. 'You know your systems. Serris has reported unusual yield patterns in their crops over the past six months,' Zeers continued. 'Widespread failures in some regions, while others show unprecedented growth rates.'

Bache frowned. 'Agricultural anomalies? With respect, sir, that sounds like a job for environmental specialists, not engineers.'

Zaphir shifted in her seat beside him.

'Or is it the AgriNex system?' Her voice had that edge Bache remembered…the one that meant she'd seen something everyone else had missed.

The president's eyebrow rose slightly. 'Very astute, Specialist Mye.'

'The AI farming system,' Bache murmured, connections forming rapidly in his mind. It made sense now. The AgriNex was cutting-edge technology, integrating planetary sensor networks with robotic harvesters. Perfect for a world like Serris Adelaine.

'The system was implemented eighteen months ago,' Zeers said. 'Initially, production increased by thirty percent. But the recent fluctuations have been…unpredictable and concerning.'

'You think someone's tampered with it,' Zaphir stated flatly. She leaned forward, eyes narrowed. 'But what does this have to do with Flast's operation or the stolen ship designs?'

Bache watched the silent exchange of glances between the council members. There it was…the question he'd been about to ask himself. Where did they fit into this tangled web?

'We believe the AgriNex software may have been reprogrammed,' said the man sitting to the president's left and wearing the insignia of the systems intelligence director.

'Reprogrammed?' Bache repeated, his mind immediately racing through the implications. 'You think someone's deliberately sabotaging the food production on Serris Adelaine?'

The systems intelligence director nodded grimly. 'We need you both to investigate…quietly. Your engineering expertise combined with Specialist Mye's systems analysis skills make you uniquely qualified.'

'Serris has been experiencing…irregularities,' Zeers continued. 'Crop failures in regions where our agricultural AI systems predict peak yields. Communication disruptions. And unusual power fluctuations across their primary settlement grid.'

Bache glanced at Zaphir, catching the subtle tightening around her eyes that he still remembered so well. She leaned forward, her shoulders squaring in that familiar way they always did when she was about to challenge someone.

'With respect,' she said, her voice controlled but edged with impatience, 'what on Dasos does an agricultural colony's technical problems have to do with a GDA conspiracy and Bache's father? Where exactly are we going with this puzzle you're constructing?'

The question hung in the air. Bache felt a surge of gratitude towards her for voicing the obvious question.

Xutan's expression hardened slightly. 'The AgriNex AI system that controls Serris Adelaine's agricultural production was also designed by your father, Tirexion.' He gestured towards the slumped figure. 'And the system's recent…modifications were approved by the same authorisation codes that signed off on the stolen ship designs.'

Bache's head snapped towards his father. 'You designed AgriNex too? Is there anything you haven't had a hand in?'

'I was busy…what can I say?' Tirexion muttered with a shrug. 'One of my later projects. A fully integrated agricultural management system. It was meant to revolutionise food production across the frontier worlds.'

'When do we leave?' Zaphir asked, her voice cutting through his thoughts.

'Immediately,' President Xutan replied. 'A transport is waiting.'

3

―――――

Western Division Agricentre, Central Flatlands, Serris
Adelaine

THE JOURNEY to Serris Adelaine passed in an uncomfortable silence. Bache spent most of the three-day trip reviewing technical specifications of the AgriNex system, avoiding both his troubled thoughts about his father and the palpable tension between him and Zaphir. She'd barely spoken to him outside of mission parameters since they'd left Kentro.

The agricultural monitoring centre in the western division of Serris Adelaine's central flatlands was a sprawling complex of low, white buildings surrounded by test fields that stretched to the horizon. Bache stood at the observation window, watching the automated harvesters move with precision through rows of tall golden grain. After two days on the planet, something felt profoundly wrong…but he couldn't put his finger on what.

'You've been staring at those fields for twenty minutes,' Zaphir said, coming to stand beside him. Her presence still unsettled him, familiar yet distant after their years apart. With his early promotion to chief engineer three years ago, and her surprise posting as a systems specialist on another ship, they'd barely had a private conversation in all that time.

'Something's off about the harvester patterns,' he muttered. 'They're too…perfect.'

She handed him a tablet.

'Look at this. I've been analysing the system logs from the past six months. There are these odd patterns in the data distribution. It's like…' She trailed off as the main entrance door behind them slid open.

Bache turned, his mouth falling open as a tall figure strode through from the agricultural centre's atrium. The newcomer moved with a casual confidence that Bache recognised instantly, despite not having seen her in nearly eight years.

'Tyrett,' Bache whispered, hardly believing his eyes.

Bache had met Tyrett Shazz just before he joined the navy. She was already a lieutenant and a navigator and pilot for the GDA.

Tyrett spotted them and grinned, the same crooked smile that made her popular with everyone she came across. She'd grown her hair longer since Bache had last seen her, and her once immaculate regulation pilot's uniform had evolved into something more casual, but there was no mistaking those deep green eyes.

'Loftty…I heard you were poking around my systems.' Tyrett closed the distance between them in a few long strides, enveloping Bache in a bear hug with almost enough force to break ribs.

'Your systems?' Bache croaked, confusion momentarily displacing his shock at meeting an old friend.

'I'm the lead systems architect for AgriNex implementation on Serris,' she said proudly, tapping the ID badge clipped to her lapel. 'Two years now. Though no one bothered to tell me the GDA was sending their most handsome engineering prodigy to inspect my work.'

Bache felt Zaphir stiffen beside him. She and Tyrett had never really gotten along. Zaphir had always been convinced Tyrett had wanted more from Bache than just friendship.

'It's been a while, Tyrett.' Bache managed a smile, stepping back from her embrace. The familiar scent of her perfume – something with citrus notes – brought back memories of the Flast episode that had nearly cost them their lives.

Tyrett kept her hand on his arm, her fingers giving a light squeeze. 'Too long. You've grown up since I last saw you. Chief engineer suits you.' Her eyes travelled appreciatively over his uniform, lingering a bit longer than necessary. 'I always knew you'd go far, but breaking up Gata conspiracies? That's impressive even for you.'

Bache felt his neck grow warm. Tyrett had always been effortlessly charming, but there was a directness to her attention now that hadn't been there before. He became acutely aware of Zaphir's rigid posture beside him.

'We're here on official business I'm afraid,' he said, clearing his throat. 'The yield anomalies…'

'Oh, those.' Tyrett waved a dismissive hand, stepping closer. 'Minor calibration issues. Nothing that requires GDA intervention, though I'm certainly not complaining about the company.' She smiled, her eyes crinkling at the corners. 'Maybe we could discuss it over dinner? There's a place in the settlement that serves actual imported wine. Not the synthetic stuff.'

The brush of her hand against his was deliberate, and Bache instinctively took a half-step back. He glanced at Zaphir, whose eyes had darkened with unmistakable irritation.

'I think the yield anomalies warrant more than dismissal as "minor calibration issues,"' Zaphir said, her voice cool as she stepped forward, positioning herself slightly between Bache and Tyrett. 'Especially considering the pattern of failure matches precisely with the implementation dates of your software updates.'

Bache felt the tension in the room spike. Tyrett's smile remained fixed, but something flashed behind her eyes.

'Zaphir Mye,' Tyrett said, extending her hand with exaggerated politeness. 'Still following Bache around like a faithful shadow, I see. How…dedicated.'

Bache winced. This was going south quickly.

'We work well together,' Bache said quickly, trying to ease the sudden tension. He could feel the air between the two women practically crackling. 'We've been assigned to investigate the yield irregularities. Official GDA inquiry,' he said, quickly. 'The GDA takes food security very seriously.'

'Of course they do and so do I.' Tyrett moved closer to Bache again. 'And I'd be happy to show you everything you need to see. Personally.' She looked across at him through her lashes. 'Starting with the system core, if you'd like. It's quite impressive...not many people get the private tour.'

'The crop failures are hardly minor,' Zaphir interjected, stepping forward. 'According to the reports we've seen, entire sectors have experienced complete yield collapse while others are showing growth rates that defy biological possibility.'

Tyrett's fingers brushed against his arm again, lingering.

'Well, I'm all for...thorough investigations,' she said. 'Just like when we were together before isn't it, Bache?'

The memories flashed through Bache's mind...he'd been just a teenager, fuelled by caffeine and the excitement of solving a galactic conspiracy. But the way Tyrett described it now carried implications that hadn't existed then.

'That was a long time ago,' he said, taking another half-step back.

Tyrett opened her mouth to respond when the monitoring station's alarm suddenly blared, cutting through the tension between them. Red warning lights pulsed along the ceiling, bathing the observation room in crimson.

Bache turned towards the main console as it flashed with multiple system warnings.

'What's happening?' he asked, turning to Tyrett.

'That isn't supposed to happen,' Tyrett said, her flirtatious demeanour instantly replaced by professional concern. She rushed to the nearest terminal, fingers flying across the interface. 'We've got a critical failure in the eastern quadrant irrigation systems. The whole bloody network's shutting down.'

Zaphir was already at another terminal, her expression intense as she scrolled through code. 'This isn't a malfunction. Someone's executing a shutdown protocol in a server room to erase the data.'

Bache joined her, scanning the cascading data. The shutdown sequence was sophisticated…not a crude hack but a precisely engineered backdoor. As he watched, irrigation systems across three agricultural sectors went offline simultaneously.

'Can you trace the origin?' he asked.

'Working on it,' Zaphir mumbled through her concentration, her fingers flashing across the interface. 'There… sub-level three, server room G.'

Bache was already moving, his hand instinctively reaching for the sidearm he wasn't carrying.

'Security override on the lifts,' he called back to Zaphir. 'Authorisation Loftt-delta-seven-nine.'

The elevator responded to his command and crept annoyingly slowly downward towards sub-level three.

The lift doors opened finally on the lower level and Bache sprinted down the dimly lit corridor. His pulse hammered in his ears as he rounded the corner towards server room G. The door was ajar…someone had definitely been here.

'Halt…don't move,' he shouted as he sprang into the room.

A figure in a maintenance jumpsuit whirled around,

eyes widening in recognition. Not security personnel or a technician – it was Elden Voss, the deputy systems administrator who'd greeted them upon arrival a couple of days ago. The man's fingers still hovered over the keyboard, a data extraction device blinking red on the server tower.

The terminal he'd been working on was still active with lines of code scrolling rapidly across the screen. The acrid smell of fried circuitry stung Bache's nostrils. Voss had physically damaged the hardware…a small device was melting into the main data core, eliminating evidence completely and permanently.

'Chief Engineer,' Voss stammered, his hand sliding towards his pocket. 'This isn't what it looks…'

Bache lunged forward, but Voss was quicker. The flash of a stun baton arced between them. Bache twisted, feeling the crackle of energy as it narrowly missed his shoulder. He grabbed for Voss's arm, but his fingers closed on empty air and he tripped and fell over an adjacent chair, as the man darted past him towards the door.

'Zaphir,' Bache yelled into his comm unit as he clambered off the floor. 'Voss is our saboteur, he's heading for the elevators.'

Voss slammed a hand against the emergency panel as he fled. Blast doors began descending throughout the sublevel, compartmentalising the underground facility. Bache ducked under the nearest one before it sealed, the metal edge scraping his back.

The corridor blurred as Bache sprinted after Voss, his pulse drumming in his ears. Another blast door was descending ahead of him. He dropped into a low slide, scraping under it with centimetres to spare. His uniform tore at the shoulder as he scrambled back to his feet.

'Lockdown protocol engaged,' announced the facility's automated system. 'All personnel remain at your stations.'

Voss was nowhere to be seen. The row of closed elevator doors greeted Bache as he arrived and he stabbed the call button hard in frustration.

'The system's locked down the elevators,' Zaphir's voice said through Bache's comm unit. 'He's triggered some kind of cascade failure in the irrigation systems. Tyrett's trying to contain it.'

Bache burst through the emergency stairwell door and discovered he could hear Voss's boots clumping upwards around the stairs and landings above. He attacked the stairs three at a time, heart pumping, lungs burning.

'The emergency stairs are still open,' Zaphir called.

'I know, he's heading for ground level,' Bache gasped into his comm. 'Probably has transport waiting somewhere.'

The stairwell ended at a maintenance exit. Bache shouldered through the door into blinding daylight. He squinted, raising a hand to shield his eyes as he scanned the sprawling equipment yard. Rows of agricultural machinery stretched before him – harvesters, soil analysers, irrigation drones.

He stopped and listened. Nothing. Not a sound. Voss had completely vanished.

4

Western Division Agricentre, Central Flatlands, Serris Adelaine

AN ENGINE ROARED to life somewhere to his left.

A sleek red agricultural skimmer shot out from behind a row of harvesters, kicking up a cloud of dust. Voss was not visible through the skimmer's darkened screen as he accelerated towards the perimeter fence.

Bache swore under his breath and sprinted towards the nearest vehicle, a bulky maintenance crawler with over-sized tracks. He slammed his palm against the ignition panel, silently thanking the engineers who'd designed these machines with standardised GDA security protocols. The crawler's control panel lit up and its engine rumbled to life beneath him.

'He's heading east on a skimmer,' Bache shouted into

his comm. 'I'm in pursuit, but this thing moves like a drugged Dasonian sloth.'

The crawler lumbered forward as Bache pushed the throttle to maximum. The engine protested with a rattling roar, clearly not designed for high-speed chases. Through the dust cloud ahead, he could see Voss's skimmer already approaching the perimeter gate.

'Cut him off at the eastern access road.' Zaphir's voice was clearer now he was above ground. 'Tyrett says there's a security checkpoint there.'

'Is it manned?' he asked.

'Tyrett says it's automated, his skimmer will have to stop because she's shut down the automation. He won't be expecting that.'

Bache yanked the steering column hard left, taking a shortcut between rows of dormant harvesters. The crawler's treads crushed the smaller irrigation pipes beneath, sending water spraying across his windshield. He squinted through the streaks, keeping the red blur of Voss's skimmer in sight. It was pulling away, despite the crawler's engine screaming in protest at being pushed beyond its design limits.

'Come on, you piece of...' Bache muttered, slamming his palm against the dashboard.

Through the dust-streaked windshield, he saw the eastern checkpoint ahead – a simple electronic shield gate with flashing red warning lights. Voss should have been slowing down, but instead, the skimmer accelerated.

A blinding flash erupted as the skimmer collided with the barrier. The explosion ripped through the morning air, the shock wave hitting Bache's crawler seconds later. He instinctively ducked, though the reinforced windshield protected him from the worst of it. Metal fragments pinged against the crawler's panels like deadly hail.

'Zaphir,' Bache shouted into his comm. 'How could he have missed the red lights? That wasn't supposed to…'

Bache slammed on the brakes and the crawler slid to a halt twenty metres from the burning wreckage distributed widely around the gate. 'Surely he would've known that barrier was lethal?' His stomach knotted as he stared at the flaming debris. No one could have survived that.

Movement caught his eye…not at the crash site, but inside the perimeter fence. A cloaking field dissolved, revealing a small spacecraft nestled between two massive harvesters. Its engines were already cycling up, the distinctive high-pitched whine of antigravs cutting through the air.

'Zaphir…there's a ship,' Bache shouted into his comm, opening the door of the crawler. 'East of me, inside the fence.'

The military-issue stealth gunship's landing struts retracted with mechanical precision, it pivoted to face the crawler. Two missiles streaked out from its side-mounted weapons pods.

'Ah, skata,' Bache swore, as he leapt down from the machine and dived under a nearby auto-plough.

The explosion was immense and he felt his ears pop as the crawler erupted. Bits of it fell around the plough and he had to wedge himself behind one of its tracks to avoid the hailstorm of shrapnel.

The gunship, seemingly happy with its work, turned to face straight up and just launched skyward as if fired from a gun. A sonic *boom* was closely followed by the unmistakable metallic *ding* as it jumped from inside the atmosphere.

'Bache…Bache,' Zaphir called, obviously panicking. 'Are you there?'

Bache climbed out of his improvised safety zone to find the ground on fire and began stamping out the burning patches to stop them spreading to the nearby machines.

'I'm all right, apart from being deaf…do we know where they went?' he called.

'Oh, thank the ancients… Tyrett says the only arrays are at the main space port, so we have absolutely no idea who it was or where they went. Is Voss dead?'

'That's a good question,' he said. 'Was he in the skimmer? Or on that ship?'

'Isn't there a body from the skimmer?'

'It was vaporised, it hit at such a speed there's virtually nothing left.'

A distant hum cut through the ringing in Bache's ears. He squinted up at the smoke-filled sky, expecting more trouble. Three sleek dark grey vessels descended through the clouds, their distinctive profile unmistakable…military-grade GDA interceptors. The kind absolutely not assigned to agricultural colony protection.

'We've got company,' Bache called into his comm, backing towards the shelter of a nearby harvester. 'Three ships, GDA markings, but I don't recognise the squadron insignia.'

'Are they friendly?' Zaphir's worried voice crackled through the static caused by the antigravs.

'We'll find out soon enough.'

The lead interceptor touched down twenty metres away, kicking up a cloud of dust that stung Bache's eyes. Its landing struts absorbed the impact with practised precision as the other two vessels took up flanking positions, hovering protectively.

The airlock on the lead ship cycled open. Six figures emerged in formation, clad in matte-black tactical armour that Bache had never seen in a standard GDA inventory. Their helmets concealed their faces completely, and each carried what looked like prototype laser rifles.

Bache tensed, calculating his odds if they were hostile. Not good.

The lead figure removed their helmet, revealing a woman with short silver hair and a face lined with experience. She scanned the burning wreckage before her eyes locked onto Bache.

'Chief Engineer Loftt?' Her voice carried the unmistakable authority of someone used to commanding respect. 'Don't panic…we're not here for you.'

Bache opened his mouth to respond when a loud crack split the air. The silver-haired woman jerked sideways, a spray of crimson erupting from her shoulder. She crumpled to one knee as her team instantly formed a protective circle around her.

'Sniper,' one of them shouted, raising his weapon over Bache's head and scanning the vehicles behind him.

Bache flattened himself against the ground as laser fire erupted from several hidden positions among the agricultural machines. The harvester beside him pinged with impacts, chunks of metal flying off dangerously close to his head. His heart rate went through the roof as he crabbed sideways behind the harvester's huge tracks, trying to put himself behind something substantial and make himself as small a target as possible.

Four figures in full armour emerged from the smoke, their faces hidden behind black tactical helmets. Not GDA issue…these were different, with jagged red markings across the visors. They moved with military precision, firing as they advanced, their suit joint servos whining. Bache realised this was not a random event. Whatever this was, it had been carefully orchestrated.

'Mercenaries,' the silver-haired woman shouted, her voice clipped and strained with pain as her team returned fire. 'Loftt, stay in cover.'

Bache didn't need to be told that might be a good idea. He scrunched himself into the fetal position under the harvester, his mind racing. Who were these people? The mercenaries weren't wearing any insignia he recognised… not Klatt, not Gata, not even GDA separatists, or the usual pirate markings either.

A bolt sizzled through the air inches from his head, leaving the acrid smell of ozone in its wake.

The two airborne gunships joined the fray and moved sideways to enable their cannons line of sight on the armoured figures. This however enabled them to be targeted too, as all of the armoured figures suddenly swung their heavy lasers upwards. One of the gunships went down almost immediately, slamming onto the top of the landed one. The resulting explosion was substantial and blew all the GDA soldiers flat on their faces.

Seemingly encouraged by the way things were going, the armoured suits all thudded forward, all four of them now targeting the remaining gunship, which slewed sideways and dropped down behind the shielded gate and smoke from the burning gunships.

'Shit,' Bache spluttered, realising it wasn't going well for the GDA contingent.

He peered across from under the harvester, realising there was an undamaged harvester parked about ten metres away and now hidden from the advancing suits. He rapidly crawled the length of his own machine, emerging out the back right behind the enemy suits. Jumping up, he sprinted over to the other harvester, acutely aware there was still a sniper hidden somewhere further afield.

He quickly climbed the ladder, opened the door to the tiny cab and ducked down inside, slamming the door behind him.

The harvester's control panel lit up as Bache slammed his palm against the ignition panel. Huge engines roared to life, sending vibrations through the entire cab. He grabbed the steering yoke with sweaty hands and scanned the basic driving controls. Utilitarian…nothing fancy, but right now all he needed was forward momentum and mass.

'Come on, you monster,' he muttered, ramming the throttle forward.

The huge hundred-tonne machine lurched ahead with a low whining from the gearbox. Through the dusty front screen, Bache could see the four armoured figures still advancing on the remaining GDA personnel, their backs to him. Perfect.

A laser bolt sizzled through the cab window, showering him with safety glass. The sniper had spotted him. Bache ducked lower but kept his eyes on the controls, his heart hammering against his ribs. Another shot punched through the metal above his head, leaving a glowing orange hole in its wake.

'Not today you don't,' Bache mumbled through clenched teeth, swerving the harvester to make himself a harder target. The machine's treads dug into the soft soil as it picked up speed…not fast, but faster than the armoured suits and unstoppable.

The nearest armoured figure turned at the sound of the approaching behemoth, but too late. Bache braced himself as the harvester's massive front cutting blade hit it with a sickening clatter. The suit went down, quickly disappearing under the treads with a series of metallic pops as the armour burst.

The second suit went the same way only seconds later, but the third and fourth had time to trudge sideways and just avoid the wide cutting blade. Bache slewed to the right, swinging the blade around and knocking the third suit over. The laser weapon dropped out of its grasp, enabling all the GDA soldiers to pop up and target him. His suit shielding and armour were soon overcome by the sheer weight of fire. It exploded in a mist of blood and servo fluids.

The fourth suit was retreating now, stomping away back the way it had come and occasionally turning to fire at the oncoming harvester. This allowed the remaining gunship to swoop in and turn the suit into another cloud of pink mist. It then gained height and went in search of the sniper's lair, along with the uninjured GDA soldiers, who spread out and advanced machine by machine.

The sniper, realising he was about to be surrounded and his concealment days were numbered, attempted to exfiltrate as quickly as he could. He only managed to sprint a hundred yards before being hit in the leg by one of the soldiers.

5

Agricentre medical facility, Central Flatlands, Serris
Adelaine

BACHE PACED OUTSIDE the medical centre's observation window, his boots clunking up and down on the polished floor. Through the transparent panel, he watched the medical team work on the silver-haired woman. Her tactical gear had been cut away, revealing the angry red wound in her shoulder where the sniper's bolt had burned through flesh and muscle.

She looked older than before, but it was probably the grimacing that created all the lines across her face.

She hadn't lost consciousness once during the transport back to the facility. Even now, she remained alert, her jaw clenched as the medics worked to repair the damage. Whatever pain medication they'd given her didn't seem to be doing much, as she glared upwards at the ceiling.

'She's going to be okay,' Zaphir said, appearing at his side. 'The medic says it missed anything vital.'

Bache nodded, unable to shake the feeling that everything about this situation was wrong. 'Did you see her team? That's not standard GDA issue armour. And those new weapons…' He trailed off, shaking his head.

'Gotta be a black-ops set-up,' Zaphir whispered, leaning closer. 'Has to be. The kind of operation that doesn't exist on any official manifest.'

'Well, neither the president nor the admiral of the fleet told us they'd be here and if they didn't know, then whose black-ops team are they?'

A commotion from the adjacent medical bay drew Bache's attention. The captured sniper was strapped to a bed, thrashing against his restraints as two of the black-clad soldiers stood guard. The medical staff had stabilised his leg wound, but made no effort to make him comfortable beyond that.

'I need to know what he knows,' Bache muttered, as he turned and walked towards the door.

He brushed past the guards without asking and entered the medical bay where the captured sniper lay. The man's leg was wrapped in a thick regrowth gel pack, the medical android hovering nearby monitoring his vitals. Even with the wound stabilised, pain etched deep lines across his face.

'Leave us please,' Bache ordered the guards, who exchanged glances before reluctantly stepping outside.

The sniper's eyes followed him as he dragged a chair to the bedside. Up close, Bache could see the man was younger than he'd expected – maybe early twenties, with a military-style haircut and the lean, hardened look of someone who'd seen combat.

'Let's keep this simple,' Bache said, leaning forward. 'Who exactly are you working for?'

The sniper's lips curled into a tight smile. 'Get fucked.'

Bache sighed and reached for the medical control panel. With a few quick taps, he turned off the pain medication flowing into the man's system. The effect was almost immediate, the sniper's face tightened, sweat beading on his forehead.

'That's just a taste,' Bache said, his voice low. 'I can make this considerably worse and if you decide not to chat with me, then you'll just be disappeared like your rather flat friends out there.'

'You GDA types,' the sniper grunted through clenched teeth. 'Always pretending to be on the moral high ground…better than everyone else. But when it matters, you're just as dirty.'

'At least eight people died out there today,' Bache countered, the memory of the exploding gunships fresh in his mind. 'I'm not asking for a confession,' he continued, leaning closer to the sniper. 'I'm asking for information that might save lives…yours included.'

Something flickered across the sniper's face…doubt, perhaps. Bache pressed his advantage.

'I can make this easier or harder,' he continued. 'Right now, you're facing charges of assassination and attempted assassination of GDA personnel. That's a guaranteed death sentence on most worlds.'

The young man turned his head away, jaw clenched

against the pain. His military-style haircut was matted with sweat, and a muscle twitched in his cheek.

Bache studied him carefully. Not a common mercenary…the training was too evident in his bearing, even while injured. His tactical gear had been top-grade, and his Makrys sniper rifle wasn't the kind you picked up on some backwater black market, military issue only.

'Look, I know you're not talking because you're loyal. I respect that,' Bache said, softening his tone slightly. 'But whoever sent you and your team here left you behind. They had the ship you came in nearby. They could have extracted you…but they decided to abandon you all and jump away.'

A flicker of something crossed the sniper's face again before he masked it.

'They'll come back for me,' he said, but there was the slightest waver in his voice.

Bache leaned back in his chair. 'No. They won't. Not a chance. You know how this works. You're a liability now. They might send someone to kill you…but it won't be to save you.'

The medical panel beeped, showing the man's elevated heart rate. Bache reactivated a small dose of pain medication, just enough to take the edge off without dulling the sniper's mind.

'What's your name?' Bache asked.

'Fuck you and fuck off.'

'Fine. I'll call you Mr Shit Sniper then. Seeing that you couldn't even hit me at two hundred metres with the most accurate rifle in the galaxy.'

The sniper's expression darkened, his jaw clenching so tight Bache could see a muscle twitching in his temple.

'We weren't permitted to hurt you or the girl...just scare you away.'

'That went well didn't it?'

'You can mock me all you want,' the man snarled, straining against his restraints until the bed creaked. 'But at least *I* don't betray my people.'

Bache leaned forward again, resting his elbows on his knees. The antiseptic smell of the medical bay filled his nostrils, mingling with the metallic scent of blood and burnt flesh from the sniper's wound. Outside the window, he could see Zaphir pacing, occasionally glancing in his direction.

'Traitors like my father, you mean?' He watched the sniper's face carefully, again looking for any reaction.

There it was – a slight widening of the eyes, quickly masked. The man knew what he meant.

'I don't know what you're talking about,' the sniper said, but his voice lacked conviction.

'You mention your people...who are your people exactly?" Bache asked, keeping his voice level. 'You're not Gata. Not Klatt. Not wearing any insignia I recognise.'

The sniper's eyes flicked to the door, then back to Bache. His breathing had quickened slightly.

'You should be more concerned about your own people,' he said finally. 'The traitors in your ranks.'

A chill ran through Bache's spine. 'Traitors like Voss, you mean?' He watched his reaction again, looking for any giveaway tic.

There it was once more – a slight widening of the eyes. This man knew plenty.

'I don't know what you're talking about,' the sniper said, too casually.

'Let's try something else,' Bache said, leaning back. 'Look at your situation.,' Bache continued. 'Your team is dead. Your employers abandoned you. Your leg is shot. And the only people who know you exist want you to disappear.' He gestured towards the door where the black-ops team waited. 'Those aren't regular GDA troops out there. They don't file reports. They don't process prisoners of war. They clean up and at this precise moment, you're making quite a mess.'

The sniper's eyes narrowed. Bache could see the calculation happening behind them…weighing loyalty against survival, pride against pain. He'd seen it before in cornered operatives, that moment when self-preservation starts to erode training.

The sniper's jaw worked silently, his gaze darting between Bache and the door. A thin line of sweat trickled down his temple.

'You've got a couple of minutes before they come back in,' Bache said, checking the time. 'After that, it's out of my hands, bye bye Mr Shit Sniper and no-one will ever know what happened to you, or care for that matter.'

'Denaillion,' the sniper finally muttered. 'Corporal Rena Denaillion.'

Bache nodded, keeping his expression neutral despite the small victory.

'Military background, Corporal?' he asked, as he turned to increase the pain relief again.

'Ex-GDA black ops, like them. Discharged three years ago.' Denaillion shifted, wincing as the movement sent pain through his injured leg. 'Look, I don't know the whole operation. We were compartmentalised.'

'Who hired you?'

'Handler called Vex. Never saw a face, just tablet comms. Payment came through untraceable accounts.'

They both glanced over at the medical android as it suddenly stepped closer. Before Bache could react it had thrust a needle into the corporal's neck and injected something.

Bache thrust the android away, sending it crashing across the small room. Surprisingly, it picked itself up again and with a half-full hypodermic still clutched in its hand, it lunged back at Bache.

There was a pulse of a laser weapon, the android stopped suddenly and collapsed across the corporal's bed, half its head missing. The needle clattered harmlessly across the floor. The black-ops soldier in the doorway lowered his rifle as Bache turned back to Denaillion. He was convulsing and staring at Bache, a frightened look in his eyes.

'Where do we find this Vex person?' Bache shouted.

Denaillion's mouth opened as his eyes fixed on Bache's.

'Pan...pan...pan...'

The corporal slumped, convulsed one last time and went still. His eyes still staring at Bache, pleading.

6

———

Agricentre medical facility, Central Flatlands, Serris

Adelaine

'Vex,' Bache whispered, staring at Denaillion's lifeless body. 'And what did you mean by "pan."' The man's final words echoed in his mind as he stepped back from the bed. Whatever had been in that hypodermic had worked with terrifying efficiency.

He turned to find the silver-haired woman standing in the doorway, her injured arm in a sling, face pale but composed.

'That was unfortunate,' she said, glancing at the destroyed android. 'But not unexpected.'

Bache's head was spinning. He needed to talk to Zaphir, needed to process what had just happened.

'Your team should secure this room,' he managed, stepping past her. 'That android was compromised. There could be others.' He paused and turned. 'And don't you disappear off anywhere either. I'll want to know what you're doing here and why.'

'I expect you do,' she said.

In the corridor, he found Zaphir waiting, her face full of concern. Without a word, he took her arm and led her towards a small maintenance room at the end of the hallway. Once inside, he locked the door and leaned against it, exhaling heavily.

'The sniper's dead,' he said. 'Killed by that bloody android before he could tell me much.'

'I saw.' Zaphir's voice was quiet. 'It happened so quickly…did you get much from him?'

'A name. Vex. Apparently their handler.' Bache rubbed his temples. He was bone-tired after the events of the day and was trying to organise his thoughts. 'The sniper… Corporal Denaillion, he was ex-GDA black ops. Said they were compartmentalised. Never saw Vex's face, just tablet messages and untraceable payments.'

Zaphir leaned against the maintenance room wall, eyes narrowed in concentration.

'Vex. And the word "pan" at the end. What do you think he was trying to say?'

Bache paced the small space, his mind racing through possibilities. The maintenance room smelled of lubricant and cleaning solutions, the low lighting casting shadows across Zaphir's concerned face.

'Could be anything. "Pan"…pandemic? Panacea?' Bache stopped pacing. 'Or it could be a location. Panacea Station in the Rigel sector? Pan Quadrant?'

'Or Pankillit,' Zaphir suggested. 'The old mining colony?'

Bache shook his head. 'No, that's been abandoned for decades.' He rubbed his forehead, feeling the tension building behind his eyes. 'Was Denaillion saying "PAN" like the initials of a company or business?'

He sat down on an upturned crate, the events of the day weighing heavily on his shoulders. His uniform still smelled of smoke from the harvester explosion, and his ears continued to ring faintly from the blast.

'Vex, Vex, Vex,' he muttered. 'Something about that name has to give…'

'Hang on,' said Zaphir. She pulled out her tablet, fingers flying across the interface. 'Running it through GDA personnel records. Nothing obvious is coming up.'

'Try cross-referencing with AgriNex.'

'No…nothing,' she said, after a few seconds.

'Try V E X as initials?'

'What, in the GDA personnel?'

'No…in everything. All human worlds affiliated to the GDA and known people from unaffiliated worlds too.'

'Bloody hell,' she said, glancing up. 'That's a big pool. Might take a while.'

'He's our only lead.'

'Might be a she,' she said, with a smirk and set the tablet on its mega search.

Zaphir sat down too. She exhaled and let her tablet slip into her lap as she ran her hands through her hair.

They both jumped as only a few seconds later, the tablet chimed. She snatched it up and stared at the screen.

'Ventor Elit Xaam,' she said, glancing up at Bache. 'Holiday resort entrepreneur.'

'Whereabouts?'

'Dasos, Hellamaine and Panemorfi,' she said.

Bache's eyes opened wide.

'That's it,' he spluttered.

'What is?'

'Pan…it's Panemorfi.'

'Fuck the ancients…so it is,' she exclaimed. 'He's the owner of one of the islands there.'

Bache grinned.

'Fancy booking a holiday, Mrs Loftt?'

'Why can't we be Mr and Mrs Mye?'

'Actually, I believe a pseudonym would be better.'

A knock at the door interrupted them.

'Mye, Loftt? You two in there?' It was the silver-haired woman's voice.

Bache exchanged a glance with Zaphir before unlocking the door. The woman stood there, her arm still in a sling but her posture ramrod straight despite the injury. Two of her team flanked her, their faces still obscured by tactical visors.

'Commander Shrell, Special Operations Division,' she said without preamble. 'I believe we need to have a conversation.'

'Special Operations? I guessed as much,' Bache repeated. 'I wasn't aware the GDA had deployed special forces to Serris for this enquiry.'

'That's rather the point of special operations, Chief Engineer.' A hint of wry humour crept into her voice.

'President Xutan sent us as your backup. We've been monitoring the situation since you arrived.'

Bache felt his eyebrows rise. 'The president didn't mention that when he sent us here.'

'Need-to-know basis. The president suspected a leak in his inner circle.' Commander Shrell gestured with her good arm. 'Let's find somewhere more private to continue this discussion.'

Ten minutes later, they sat in a secure room deep within the facility. Commander Shrell had dismissed her team except for a single guard at the door. It had taken a lot of persuasion to get rid of Tyrett as well. She was obviously extremely agitated about what had happened and all the damage to her installation.

'I apologise for the theatrical entrance,' she said, wincing slightly as she adjusted her position. 'We had to maintain our cover until absolutely necessary. I'm going to cut to the chase,' Commander Shrell said, leaning forward despite her injured shoulder. 'We're Xutan's personal intelligence unit. Off the books.'

Bache exchanged a glance with Zaphir. The revelation wasn't entirely surprising after what they'd witnessed, but hearing it confirmed made his pulse quicken.

'How many of these special units does the president have?' he asked.

'Enough,' Shrell replied with a tight smile. 'The important thing is we've been tracking Flast's operation for months. We believe she's expanding beyond simple resource acquisition into something more dangerous.'

'The AgriNex system,' Zaphir said.

Shrell nodded. 'Food control is power. Especially on frontier worlds.'

Bache's mind raced, connecting pieces. 'And my father's designs are central to both operations. First warships, now agricultural systems.'

'Precisely.' Shrell winced as she shifted her injured arm. 'We believe Flast is working with someone high in GDA command to systematically exploit your father's technologies.'

'Henns has to be involved somewhere,' Bache muttered.

'Possibly. But we suspect he's just another pawn.' Shrell's eyes narrowed. 'This is bigger than one corrupt admiral and we know she'll quickly get rid of him if he shows any sign of pointing the finger. Look what happened here today. Her influence and organisation is spread extremely wide and until we know who is on her payroll, we'll always be on the back foot.'

They turned as shouting in the corridor outside took their attention. Tyrett burst into the room without warning or knocking, her face flushed with anger.

'Three of my technicians are dead, my facility's in lockdown, half the eastern quadrant's irrigation is fucked and seventeen of my machines are destroyed. Just…just who the hell are all these people, Bache?' Tyrett demanded, her eyes wild as they darted between him and Commander Shrell. 'And what in the ancients is going on?'

Bache glanced at Zaphir, who met his gaze with a slight nod. They'd gotten what they needed. Panemorfi. Ventor Elit Xaam. It was time to move.

'They're GDA Special Operations,' Bache said, rising from his seat. 'And they're here to help clean up this mess.'

'Clean up? They caused most of it.' Tyrett's voice rose an octave.

Commander Shrell shifted in her seat.

'Ms Shazz, I understand your frustration, but this facility has been compromised at the highest level. Your deputy administrator was working for hostile interests.'

'Voss? He said that too,' Tyrett scoffed, jabbing a finger at Bache. 'It's ridiculous. He's been with AgriNex for three years.'

'Which is exactly when the system was implemented here,' Zaphir interjected. 'Perfect timing for a saboteur to get nicely integrated and trusted.'

Bache stepped forward, placing a hand on Tyrett's shoulder. She flinched slightly at his touch, but didn't pull away.

'Tyrett, Commander Shrell and her team will handle the investigation from here. They'll help restore your systems and provide security while repairs are made.'

Shrell raised her eyebrows at the last comment, but refrained from commenting.

'We need to get to Panemorfi,' Bache said, lowering his voice as he steered Tyrett towards the door. 'The lead might get cleaned up if we loiter too long.'

Tyrett's eyes widened. 'You're going to piss off? Now? After all this? Are you?'

'As I said, Commander Shrell and her team will handle things here,' Bache repeated, though he wasn't entirely sure that was going to be true. 'You must realise this goes way beyond Serris.'

'I'll arrange transport,' Shrell said, her eyes meeting Bache's with an understanding nod. 'Civilian vessel, unmarked. You'll need to maintain low profiles and have alternative ID.'

Tyrett scoffed and shook her head in disbelief, but Bache had already turned away, his mind racing ahead to what they might find on Panemorfi. He felt Zaphir's hand on his arm, her fingers giving a light squeeze.

'We should go now,' she whispered. 'Before anyone else comes out of the woodwork and decides to try killing us.'

They exited the room and began the journey to the space port.

'Actually, Denaillion told me they had been instructed not to harm you or me,' Bache whispered back.

'That's weird,' she said. 'If it is Flast involved in this, she would have had us killed in an instant and danced on our graves.'

Three hours later, Bache stood in the small cabin of their chartered civilian transport vessel, watching through the viewport as Serris Adelaine's blue-green atmosphere gave way to the darkness of space. His ears still rang faintly from the explosions, and his muscles ached from the day's exertions.

'Coordinates set for Panemorfi, sir,' the pilot Shrell had provided called back. 'If you'd like to go and relax, we'll be jumping in five minutes, ETA approximately seventy-eight hours.'

7

Vex Island Resort, Panemorfi ocean planet, Trelorus
system

THE SCREAM of the antigravs peaked as the small chartered ship descended smoothly towards the private landing pad at the resort. Bache gazed out at the sparkling waters surrounding Vex Island, the deep blue stretching to the horizon in all directions. Panemorfi certainly lived up to its reputation as one of the most beautiful holiday locations in the galaxy.

Zaphir appeared beside him, her face illuminated by the soft blue glow of the control surfaces.

'Ready for this, Mrs Spindaker?' Bache asked, adjusting the collar of his expensive white Falaxion silk shirt. The rare natural fabric felt strange against his skin after years in uniforms manufactured probably by the lowest bidder.

Zaphir smoothed the front of her flowing sundress, a garment so unlike her usual attire that Bache had done a double take when she'd emerged from the transport's small walk-in wardrobe.

'As ready as I'll ever be, darling,' she replied, the endearment sounding awkward on her lips. She leaned closer, lowering her voice. 'Remember, we're madly in love newlyweds. Try to look like you're actually thrilled to be married to me.'

Bache forced his face into what he hoped was a besotted smile, though his mind was racing through their cover identities. Daaken and Lissa Spindaker – wealthy industrialists from the Dasos sector on their honeymoon. Commander Shrell's team had constructed the identities meticulously, complete with digital footprints going back years.

The ship touched down with barely a whisper. Bache, impressed with the pilot's skill in an unfamiliar vessel, nodded his approval as the airlocks slid away to reveal a beautiful beach of white sand and gently swaying palms.

The ocean breeze carried the scent of exotic flowers as they stepped onto the pristine sand of one of Panemorfi's most exclusive and expensive resorts. The humidity felt thick against his skin after the climate-controlled environment of the transport vessel. Zaphir walked beside him, her hand resting lightly in the crook of his arm as they played their roles of newlyweds.

'Welcome to Paradise Cove, Mr and Mrs Spindaker,' the concierge beamed, his white uniform tight against his tanned skin. 'We're absolutely delighted you've chosen our humble establishment for your honeymoon,' he gushed.

Bache returned the smile with practised ease. 'We've heard wonderful things about your resort. My wife has been especially looking forward to the cocktails and private beaches.'

The word felt strange in his mouth, referring to Zaphir as his wife. He'd spent the journey memorising their cover identities and preyed he didn't have any slip-ups.

'Mr Xaam prides himself on providing the ultimate in privacy and luxury,' the concierge continued, gesturing towards a waiting cart adorned with fragrant flower garlands. 'Your oceanfront villa awaits. Mr Xaam himself selected it for you when he heard it was your honeymoon.'

Bache felt Zaphir's hand tighten on his arm as the concierge mentioned Xaam's personal attention to their reservation.

'How thoughtful,' Bache said, keeping his voice casual despite the alarm bells ringing in his head. 'I wasn't aware our stay had garnered such high-level attention.'

'Oh, Mr Xaam takes a personal interest in all our honeymoon guests,' the concierge replied, helping them into the flower-adorned cart. 'He believes the beginning of a marriage should be unforgettable.'

The electric cart hummed quietly as it carried them along a winding path bordered by lush tropical vegetation. Bache studied their surroundings, mentally mapping the layout of the resort. Security cameras were discreetly positioned at regular intervals, their tiny lenses almost invisible among the foliage.

'Isn't this just perfect?' Zaphir cooed, leaning against

his shoulder in a convincing display of newlywed affec-tion. Her lips brushed his ear as she whispered, 'Security everywhere. We're being watched.'

Bache nodded slightly, wrapping his arm around her waist.

'Nothing but the best for you, my darling,' he said loudly enough for the driver to hear, then lowered his voice to a whisper. 'At least twelve cameras on this path alone.'

The cart rounded a bend, revealing a secluded crescent of private villas nestled along the shoreline. Under different circumstances, Bache might have appreciated the beauty of the place.

'Your villa is one of our most secluded,' the concierge continued, gesturing towards the most private building at the far end of the beach. 'Complete ocean access, a private infinity pool, and of course, our signature amenities.'

Bache squeezed Zaphir's hand as they approached the villa. The structure was stunning, all glass and polished wood, perched on stilts that extended partly over the water. A perfect honeymoon retreat – and perfect for a trap.

'Darling, it's even more beautiful than the brochure,' Zaphir said, leaning into him with familiar ease.

'Nothing but the best for you," Bache repeated, planting a kiss on her forehead that felt oddly natural despite the circumstances and brought back memories of when they were lovers some years back.

The concierge showed them around the villa, pointing out luxury features that would have impressed Bache under different circumstances. Now, all he could think about was how isolated they were…the nearest villa was a good three hundred metres away, hidden by a curve of the beach and thick tropical vegetation.

'Mr Xaam has invited you to the welcome reception this evening at the main pavilion,' the concierge said as he prepared to leave. 'Seven o'clock. Formal attire is provided in the wardrobes.'

'We wouldn't miss it,' Bache said, tipping the man generously to maintain their cover as wealthy newlyweds.

As the cart hummed away, Zaphir hugged him close.

'This place is…' she began.

'Completely monitored,' Bache finished in a whisper, squeezing her hand in warning. He pulled her closer, his lips close to her ear. 'Assume everything we say and do is being watched.'

He felt her nod against his shoulder before she pulled back with a dazzling smile that didn't quite reach her eyes.

'It's absolutely perfect, darling,' she said loudly, twirling around the spacious living area. 'I can't believe we're finally here.'

Bache moved to the large windows overlooking the ocean, scanning for surveillance devices while appearing to admire the view. The villa was stunning – open-plan with polished hardwood floors, a massive four-poster bed draped with thin white chiffon swaying in the light breeze just visible through an arch.

Bache leaned against the window frame, letting the warm sea breeze wash over him. He kept his expression relaxed, the picture of a contented newlywed while his eyes methodically scanned the surroundings. The villa jutted out over crystal-clear water that revealed a vibrant reef below. Perfect for snorkelling, but unfortunately there wouldn't be time for that on this trip.

'Darling, we should prepare for the reception,' Zaphir called from beside the enormous wardrobe. 'Look at all these beautiful clothes they've provided.'

He crossed to her side, playing the devoted husband, and whispered against her hair. 'Let's sweep the place first.'

She squeezed his hand in acknowledgment.

'I need a shower after that long journey,' Bache announced loudly, pulling Zaphir towards the bathroom. Once inside with the water running, he placed a finger to his lips and began a methodical search of the tiles, fixtures, and vents.

He found the first listening device behind an ornate soap dish. Small, sophisticated...military grade. The second was embedded in the shower head itself. Both far beyond standard resort security measures.

Zaphir pointed to the running water and mouthed, 'Will it mask our voices?'

'Only partially,' he whispered back. 'Wait just a moment and don't say a word.'

He pulled out his tablet and connected it up to his illegal dermal data chip, selected something from a menu and touched an icon as it appeared.

'Okay...should be fine now,' he said. 'Local jammer... will mess up any signals within about fifty metres.'

'Still got that dodgy data chip then?' she said. 'Haven't you had to have that removed?'

'Nope...there's only a couple of people who know about it and it's saved me on more than one occasion.'

'Xaam personally selecting our villa?' she said. 'D'you think he knows who we are?'

'Possibly.'

She nodded, her breath warm against his neck. 'Or he's suspicious and paranoid enough to want us isolated and watched.'

'This evening's reception gives us a chance to see the layout, identify him and check out his personal security.'

'I'll wear something that draws attention,' she whispered back with a slight smirk. 'Give you cover to have a poke around.'

8

Vex Island Resort, Panemorfi ocean planet, Trelorus system

THE RECEPTION PAVILION glittered with light as Bache and Zaphir approached arm-in-arm. Crystal chandeliers hung from the vaulted ceiling, casting prismatic reflections across the polished marble floor. The evening air carried the scent of flowers and expensive perfumes, mingling with the salt tang from the nearby ocean.

'Ready?' Bache whispered, adjusting the cuffs of his tailored jacket.

Zaphir squeezed his arm. 'I'm always ready, as you well know.'

They passed through the wide entrance where a uniformed attendant checked their names against a holographic guest list before waving them through with a professional smile. Inside, at least sixty guests in formal attire mingled and chatted, the soft murmur of conversation broken by occasional bursts of laughter.

Bache scanned the room, cataloguing details with a trained eye. Three exits, security personnel positioned discreetly at each. Serving staff circulating with trays of sparkling wine and overly fancy nibbles. He accepted a flute of something bubbly from a passing server, using the motion to survey the crowd.

'There,' Zaphir murmured, her lips barely moving.'

Ed's eyes landed on a tall, lean man with silver-streaked dark hair who was moving purposefully in their direction.

'The newlyweds,' he exclaimed, arms spread wide in welcome.

Ventor Elit Xaam closed the distance between them with the smooth confidence of a predator. He grasped Bache's hand in a firm handshake, his smile never quite looking sincere.

'Mr and Mrs Spindaker, how delightful to welcome you to our little slice of paradise.' His voice was rich and cultured, carrying just a hint of an accent Bache couldn't place. 'I trust the villa meets your expectations?'

'It's absolutely stunning,' Bache replied, maintaining his cover with ease despite the tension coiling in his gut. 'Your personal attention to our accommodations was unexpected but very much appreciated.'

Xaam's eyes flickered with something…amusement?…recognition?…before he turned to Zaphir, taking her hand and bringing it to his lips. 'And the new Mrs Spindaker. The holographs don't do you justice, my dear.'

Bache fought to keep his expression neutral. Holographs? Their cover identities had been created mere days ago.

'You're too kind,' Zaphir replied, her voice laced with false adoration while her fingers tightened almost imperceptibly on Bache's arm.

'Please, enjoy yourselves,' Xaam said, gesturing towards the lavish buffet. 'The night is young, and I insist you try the seafood. Caught fresh this morning.'

As Xaam moved to greet other guests, Bache guided Zaphir deeper into the crowd, keeping his expression relaxed while his mind raced. Something about Xaam's manner set his nerves on edge.

'I don't like this,' he whispered, leaning close to Zaphir's ear as they moved through the crowd. 'He knows something.'

Zaphir nodded slightly, her eyes scanning the room as they strolled.

Bache froze mid-step. The crystal flute nearly slipped from his fingers as he spotted a familiar figure across the pavilion. Commander Shrell stood near one of the side exits, dressed in an elegant blue evening gown that concealed her injured arm. Her silver hair was styled differently, but there was no mistaking her face. Beside her stood another woman he recognised from her team on Serris.

'How the hell did she get here so quickly?' he muttered.

Zaphir followed his gaze, her body tensing against his. 'Is that...?'

'Yes it is. And one of her team.' Bache's mind raced.

'They're supposed to be back on Serris helping Tyrett,' he whispered.

'Are we being monitored wherever we go, or do they think something's wrong?' Zaphir said, her voice barely audible.

Before Bache could respond, Shrell's eyes met his across the room. There was no surprise in her gaze…only the barest nod of recognition before she deliberately turned away, engaging her companion in conversation.

'They must think we need backup here to risk this,' Bache muttered. 'Let's see if we can get Shrell's attention without being too obvious. I need to know what she's doing here.'

Before they could make a move, Xaam reappeared at their side, his presence so sudden that Bache nearly spilled his drink.

'Mr and Mrs Spindaker, I'd be honoured if you'd join me for a private toast,' Xaam said, wearing that same predatory smile from before. 'I have a special vintage I save for my most…distinguished guests.'

Bache exchanged a quick glance with Zaphir. This could be a trap or the opening they needed.

'We'd be delighted,' Bache replied, hiding his concern and adjusting his cufflinks casually while scanning for Shrell's location. She seemed to have disappeared from view.

Xaam led them through the crowd towards a discreet door at the rear of the pavilion. As they passed a large potted palm, Bache felt something slip into his pocket…so smoothly he almost missed it. From the corner of his eye, he caught a glimpse of Shrell's companion moving away, her face a mask of casual indifference.

Two security personnel flanked the private door, stepping aside at Xaam's approach. The corridor beyond was dimly lit, panelled in rich dark wood that absorbed the light. Xaam's shoes clicked against the polished floor as he led them deeper into the private wing.

'My personal collection is quite extensive...'

Xaam was halfway through his sentence when the lights flickered and went out. Bache tensed, his hand instinctively reaching for Zaphir in the darkness. Something flashed through the air, momentarily illuminating the corridor and ending in a thud and a grunt. He yanked Zaphir down to the floor, covering her body with his own as two more stun shots flashed overhead. Glasses smashed. Two more thuds and clatters as unconscious bodies dropped, one over Bache's legs.

'Stay down,' he whispered against Zaphir's ear. He could hear the music in the reception and hoped it was enough to cover this noise.

Even with his eyes closed, the afterimage of the laser shots burned against his retinas. Shouting erupted around them, followed by several grunts and the weight across his legs lifted away. A hand gripped his shoulder. firm but not threatening.

'It's me,' Commander Shrell's voice came low near his ear. 'We need to move now and fast.'

Bache blinked rapidly, his vision gradually returning to reveal Xaam's unconscious form being lifted by two of Shrell's operatives. The security guards lay crumpled against the wall, taken down with surgical precision.

'This wasn't the plan,' Bache hissed, helping Zaphir to her feet.

'Operational plans change,' Shrell replied tersely. 'We intercepted communications. Xaam was about to have you both detained. Move.'

He hurried down a service corridor, the unconscious Xaam being dragged between Shrell's operatives like a sack of vegetables.

Bache kept Zaphir close, one arm protectively around her shoulders as they followed Shrell's team through a maze of passages towards the rear of the mansion. The unconscious Xaam bounced between his captors, his silver-streaked head lolling with each hurried step.

'Where are we taking him?' Bache whispered to Shrell, who moved with remarkable agility despite her injured arm.

'Transport's waiting on the north side,' she replied tersely. 'Less security at the back, more cover for the ship behind the tree line.'

'When the hell did you have time to plan this?' he asked, trying to catch his breath as they ran.

A distant alarm began to wail behind them. Bache gritted his teeth. Someone had discovered the unconscious guards and Xaam missing.

'Go, go,' Shrell ordered, her voice raised and urgent.

They burst through a service door into the night air. The humidity hit Bache full on as they sprinted across a carefully manicured lawn towards a stand of dense palms. Bache's flat formal shoes slipped on the damp grass, and he nearly lost his footing. Zaphir's hand steadied him, her grip firm despite the tremor he could feel in her fingers.

A large black vessel de-cloaked in a small clearing beyond the trees, its matte finish absorbing the moonlight rather than reflecting it. A boarding ramp was already lowered, and two more of Shrell's operatives stood, weapons aimed over their heads to warn off any potential pursuit.

Bache sprinted up the ramp after Zaphir, his lungs burning. He threw a glance over his shoulder as the resort's security officers emerged through the tree line, their weapons raised. A volley of stun bolts crackled through the night air, dissipating harmlessly against the ship's shields.

'Get strapped in,' Shrell barked, following the team carrying Xaam's unconscious form.

The ship's interior was military grade – all function, no comfort. Bache guided Zaphir to a pair of jump seats along the side bulkhead and helped fasten her restraints before securing his own. The deck plates vibrated beneath his feet as the engines spooled up to full power and the ship lifted.

'What the hell was that?' he demanded as Shrell dropped into the seat across from him. 'You were supposed to be on Serris.'

'You can thank me later,' she replied, her face taught with pain as the ship screamed skyward. Her injured arm was clearly bothering her more than she let on. 'We intercepted evidence indicating your cover was blown before you even landed.'

The ship banked hard, pressing Bache against his restraints. Through the small viewport, he caught a glimpse of the resort receding rapidly below them, its lights twinkling against the darkness and the flashes of weapons fire flashing upwards from the grounds – Xaam's security contingent shooting upwards, probably more in frustration than anything else.

'How did they know who we were?' Zaphir asked, her knuckles white as she gripped the edge of her seat.

'Your cover was blown before you even arrived,' Shrell admitted. 'We don't know how, but luckily for you our ship is faster than your civilian transport and we were able to get here just before you.'

Bache glanced across at Xaam, unconscious and strapped to a gurney.

'What are you going to do with him?' he asked, nodding at the prisoner.

Shrell rubbed her shoulder and grimaced.

'Best you don't know,' she said. 'Plausible deniability and all that.'

'I almost feel sorry for him,' said Zaphir.

Bache looked at her out of the corner of his eye.

'Almost,' she repeated.

9

Special Operations Vessel, unknown location

THE SHIP JUMPED. The familiar sensation, though it felt different than he'd expected from a small tactical vessel.

'Where are we headed?' he asked.

'Secure location,' Shrell replied, her expression giving nothing away. She tapped a command into her wrist unit, and the ship's interior lighting dimmed to a soft blue.

Bache glanced at Zaphir, who raised an eyebrow in silent communication. Something wasn't quite right about this vessel. He unfastened his restraints and stood, steadying himself against the bulkhead. The vibrations beneath his feet carried a distinctive resonance he thought he recognised – the unique harmonic signature of an older Xephoni drive. Only destroyers in the GDA fleet had used that configuration.

'This isn't really a tactical insertion vessel is it?' he

said, running his hand along a panel seam. The construction was unmistakable, even beneath the cosmetic modifications. 'It's a Raptor-class destroyer. Decommissioned, I'm guessing, then converted.'

Shrell's eyes narrowed slightly. 'You recognise your father's distinctive designs, don't you? Even when modified.'

'Yes, my father designed the Raptor-class power distribution system,' Bache confirmed, suddenly understanding.

'Is there anything he didn't have a hand in?' Shrell muttered, rolling her eyes.

***

Bache and Zaphir had been given a small cabin with bunkbeds. Totally spartan, like the rest of the ship, but comfortable all the same.

'I think I preferred the honeymoon villa,' Zaphir had said when they'd entered. Two days later, the destroyer's engines powered down to a low hum as they approached what looked like an asteroid field. Bache stared at the cabin's view screen, as it showed they were approaching a large asteroid or moonlet. A seemingly solid section of rock face slid aside to reveal a cavernous opening. The ship glided inside, its landing struts extending with a mechanical whine below.

Zaphir followed Bache as they made their way up to the main reception room behind the bridge. He found Shrell sitting at one of the tables tapping away on her tablet.

'Where the hell is this?" he asked, looking down at Shrell and waving at the holomap above her.

'Somewhere safe,' was all she said, her expression unreadable.

Bache studied her face for any hint of what she was thinking. The commander had been evasive since they'd left Panemorfi, spending most of her time interrogating Xaam in a sealed compartment somewhere in the rear of the ship. Bache reasoned the noise of the drives back there would almost certainly mask the screams of any spirited questioning.

Zaphir appeared at his side as they disembarked, her fingers brushing against his. 'Do you recognise any of these ships?' she whispered.

The hangar was massive, carved directly from the moon's interior. Several other vessels were docked in orderly rows, all unmarked, all military. Bache counted at least three more converted destroyers and what appeared to be a former GDA frigate. This was no small operation.

He shook his head.

'This isn't a GDA facility,' he said, not expressing it as a question.

Shrell's mouth tightened slightly. 'Let's get our guest delivered, then we'll talk.'

'All former GDA vessels though,' he murmured back. 'But I'll bet this facility isn't on any GDA star chart,' he said, scanning the hangar again.

A day later, Bache still had no idea where they were. The hollowed-out moon – if that's what it truly was – contained a fully operational base with a crew of at least fifty. None wore official uniforms or insignia, though they moved with the smooth efficiency of military personnel. Each time he'd asked Shrell for their location, she'd deflected with practised ease.

'You'll be briefed when necessary, Chief Engineer,' was all she would say before changing the subject.

Bache stood in the observation gallery overlooking the main hangar bay, watching the constant activity below. Three more vessels had arrived since yesterday, all former GDA craft with their identifiers stripped and replaced with what appeared to be a stylised flame insignia he had never seen before.

'Quite the operation, isn't it?' Zaphir said, joining him at the viewport. She kept her voice low, though Bache had swept their cabin for listening devices twice and found nothing.

'Too big for an unsanctioned mission,' he replied, eyes tracking a weapons shipment being offloaded from a newly arrived transport. 'And definitely not standard GDA procedure.'

Something cold settled in Bache's stomach as he watched Shrell cross the hangar floor below, stopping to confer with a tall woman whose bearing screamed military. They exchanged tablets, their faces grim as they reviewed whatever information was displayed.

'We really need to know where we are,' he muttered.

Bache's thoughts were interrupted by the clatter of tools from the far side of the hangar. He narrowed his eyes, spotting a group of technicians working on one of the modified destroyers. Something about their movements caught his attention – they lacked the military precision of Shrell's other personnel.

'I'm going to have a look around,' he murmured to Zaphir. 'See if I can find out anything about where we are.'

She nodded, her eyes still tracking Shrell across the hangar floor. 'I'll watch her. Be careful.'

He descended the metal staircase to the main hangar level, keeping his movements casual. He'd changed into the standard grey coveralls provided by Shrell's people... perfect camouflage among the base's technical personnel. The antigrav hoists hummed overhead as they transported cargo between levels, masking the sound of his footsteps on the metal grating.

Approaching the destroyer under repair, he circled wide to appear as though he was simply passing by. The exposed drive housing confirmed his earlier assessment – Xephoni configuration, older model, but with substantial modifications. His father's work, unmistakably, but altered in ways that made Bache's engineering instincts twitch with unease.

One of the technicians looked up as Bache paused near the hull breach they were repairing. The girl's eyes widened in recognition.

'Chief Engineer Loftt?' she whispered, glancing furtively left and right. 'What the ancients are you doing here?'

Bache froze, heart pounding in his chest. He glanced around quickly, making sure no one else had heard.

'Keep your voice down,' he whispered, stepping closer to the technician and pretending to examine the drive housing. 'How do you know who I am?'

The technician wiped grimy hands on her coveralls and

leaned in, using the exposed panel as cover for their conversation. 'I worked on the *K2* during the refit after the Berge incident. Engineering bay fourteen. You probably don't remember me…I was just part of a civilian engineering support crew.'

Bache studied the girl's face, searching for any sign of deception. The technician was older than him, maybe early to mid-thirties, with dark circles under her eyes and callused hands that spoke of genuine engineering work.

'What's your name?' Bache asked, keeping his voice low.

'Stevns. Ash Stevns.' The technician glanced nervously over her shoulder. 'Look, I don't have much time. The supervisor makes rounds every fifteen minutes.'

'What is this place, Ash?' Bache asked, adjusting a connection that didn't need adjusting.

'They call it Pyros Base.' Ash's voice dropped even lower. 'Most of us were transferred here after being told our ships were decommissioned. The reality? We're building something new. Something big. I've heard stuff about Commander Shrell too.'

A chill ran down Bache's spine.

'What kind of stuff?'

'This destroyer…' Ash gestured subtly at the vessel they stood beside, '…it's her personal project and being fitted with experimental weapons systems. Something not in any GDA registry. She calls it Project Cleansing.'

Bache racked his brain, but couldn't recall a project by that name. 'Cleansing you say?'

A shadow fell across them.

Ash's eyes widened suddenly, and she stiffened.

'Careful,' she whispered, her fingers tightening on the wrench in her hand. 'Incoming.'

Bache turned to see a thin man in dark coveralls approaching. The man's gaze flicked between them, suspicious and calculating.

'You two have a problem with that drive coupling?' The newcomer's voice was quiet but carried an unmistakable warning.

'Just showing him the modified Xephoni configuration,' Ash replied, her voice steadier than her trembling hands.

The thin man stepped closer, positioning himself so his back was to the nearest security camera. 'They're listening everywhere,' he muttered, barely moving his lips. 'Especially around the ships. Don't talk about Cleansing here if you want to keep breathing.'

Bache maintained his casual posture, though the hairs on the back of his neck stood up.

'Appreciate the heads-up,' he said.

'Maintenance bay six, third shift rotation,' the man continued, pretending to examine the drive housing. 'Less monitoring. Find me there if you need to talk.' He raised his voice to normal levels. 'That coupling looks fine to me. Stop wasting time and finish the port stabiliser calibrations.'

The thin man walked away without looking back, disappearing into the organised chaos of the hangar.

Ash released a shaky breath. 'That's Jorven. He's been here longer than most of us.' She glanced around nervously. 'He's right though. We should shut up.'

10

Pyros Base, unknown location

'MAINTENANCE BAY SIX, THIRD SHIFT,' Bache whispered to Zaphir later that evening as they sat in their sparse quarters. He kept his voice low, though he'd checked the room again for listening devices. 'That's where we'll find Jorven.'

Zaphir nodded, her dark eyes serious in the dim light. 'You think he knows more about this Project Cleansing thing?'

'I'm hoping so. And I want to know what Shrell's really up to and who the hell is financing this whole affair.' Bache checked his watch. 'Third shift starts in twenty minutes. We should move now while most of the base is in the mess hall.'

The corridors were eerily quiet as they made their way through the facility. Bache had memorised as much of the layout as he could during his "casual" explorations over the past day. The maintenance sections were located on the lower levels, accessible via a series of narrow utility passages that branched off from the main corridors like capillaries from an artery.

'I believe it's this way,' he murmured, guiding Zaphir around a corner. The lighting dimmed and fixtures became less frequent as they descended, transitioning from the bright white of the main levels to a dull amber that cast longer shadows across the metal walls.

Maintenance bay six was marked by a simple numeric designation stencilled on a heavy steel door. Bache pressed his palm against the entry panel, relieved when it flashed green. Standard GDA override codes still worked, at least for basic systems.

The door shuddered open reluctantly, seemingly in need of some maintenance itself.

Inside maintenance bay six, the air hung heavy with the sharp tang of solvent and machine oil. Bache hesitated at the threshold, letting his eyes adjust to the dimmer lighting. The bay was larger than he'd expected, a cavernous space filled with partially disassembled equipment, stacks of replacement parts, and diagnostic stations.

'Jorven?' Bache called softly, stepping further into the room. His voice echoed slightly against the metal walls.

A shuffling sound came from behind a rack of power couplings. The thin man from earlier emerged, wiping his hands on a rag. His eyes darted nervously to the door behind them.

'You actually came,' he said, sounding surprised. 'Shut that door.'

Zaphir reached back and tapped the control panel. The heavy door juddered closed with a pneumatic hiss. Bache felt a momentary sense of unease at being sealed in with a stranger, but his curiosity outweighed his caution.

'You wanted to tell us more,' Bache said, keeping his voice low. 'About Project…'

Jorven flinched and held his hand up to stop Bache before he said more. He glanced up at the ceiling. 'Not here, not directly under that,' he mouthed almost silently and pointing at a censor of some kind. He motioned them deeper into the bay, weaving between workbenches until they reached a small alcove surrounded by stacked equipment crates. The space was tight, forcing the three of them to stand close together.

'The sensors in this section are looped,' Jorven said, his voice barely above a whisper. 'We've got maybe fifteen minutes before someone notices.'

Bache glanced at Zaphir, her face half-shadowed in the dim light of the maintenance bay. Her eyes were alert, focused entirely on Jorven.

'Tell us about this Cleansing project,' Bache said, keeping his voice low. 'What's Shrell planning?'

Jorven's thin face tightened with anxiety. 'It's not just a weapons system. It's planetary-scale. They've been testing components for months.' He pulled a small data chip from his pocket. 'This contains partial schematics. I've been collecting bits and pieces, trying to understand what they're building.'

Bache reached for the chip, but Jorven hesitated.

'You need to know…this goes much higher than Shrell. She's just a small cog. The funding, the orders…

they're coming from someone with serious political connections.'

'Flast?' Zaphir asked.

Jorven shook his head. 'I don't know names, just that there's a shadow council. They call themselves the Originators.'

They heard the maintenance bay door suddenly judder open. Bache instinctively pulled back deeper into the hidden alcove. Jorven's face pinched. He grabbed a nearby container of spooler lubricant and shoving the data chip into Bache's palm, then stepped around them.

'I'm sick of that fucking sticky door,' he announced in a loud voice and disappeared around the corner.

Bache bent down and peered through a small gap in some shelving. It was Shrell, with four armed guards. She seemed a little surprised to see Jorven strolling towards her with a can of oil, but the bewilderment soon faded and her usual stern demeanour returned.

'Loftt…I know you're in here,' she barked.

'Abso-bloody-lutely,' Bache called back, sticking his head around the corner with a big grin on his face. 'Have you seen the kit in this room? There's engineering spares in here that've been discontinued for years. I'd love some of this on the *K2* if you want to get rid of any of it?'

He emerged from the alcove and pointed up to a large crate on one of the higher shelves.

'Look…that's a brand new Krell Dunst spooler assembly still in its box, I've had to machine new bits for those for ever…and you've got new ones sitting in a store.'

The look on Shrell's face was of complete disbelief.

'Who gave you permission to come down here?' she asked.

'Permission?' he queried. 'I'm a chief engineer. I outrank almost everyone here, including you actually.'

One of the guards with her scoffed and she turned and glared at the man.

The guard shifted nervously, but Bache kept his grin firmly in place. He could feel the data chip pressing against his palm, and he casually slipped it into his pocket while everyone's attention was on the uncomfortable guard.

'Chief engineer or not,' Shrell growled, turning back to him with narrowed eyes. 'This is a restricted area. You need proper clearance.'

Bache chuckled and shrugged, feigning ignorance. 'When did you mention that? All the doors are unlocked… I just walked in.' He gestured towards Jorven. 'Found this helpful fellow who was showing me around. Some of these parts could really help with maintenance on the *K2* when we get back.'

Zaphir stepped out from behind the shelving, her expression carefully neutral. 'The supply inventory on this base is impressive, Commander. I've never seen such a stockpile outside a major GDA facility. This is wonderful.'

Shrell puffed out her cheeks, her eyes darting between them. Her injured arm was still in its sling but her good hand fidgeted near her sidearm. The tension in the room thickened like congealing oil.

'What exactly were you looking for down here?' she hissed, her voice dangerously quiet.

'Just familiarising ourselves with the facility,' Bache

replied, keeping his tone casual despite the rapid drumming of his heart. 'Since you've ignored us and been busy chatting up your handsome guest, we thought we'd make ourselves useful.'

Jorven had moved around behind Shrell and busied himself with the door mechanism, but Bache noticed how the man's hands trembled slightly as he oiled the hinges over and over again, desperately trying to be invisible.

'This isn't a fucking leisure cruise,' Shrell barked, pulling a face as she jerked her injured arm. 'You're here because we need information from Xaam about his connection to Flast's operation, not to poke around in maintenance bloody bays.'

'Yeah, whatever,' Bache shrugged, as he pushed past Shrell and the guards. 'Just remember who you're talking to in future... Come on, Mye. Let's go and get some dinner.'

11

Pyros Base, unknown location

SHRELL MOTIONED TO THE GUARDS. 'Escort them back to their quarters.'

'Commander, with respect…' Bache began.

'That wasn't a request, Chief Engineer,' she cut him off. 'You're confined to quarters until further notice and I'll have that weapon back too.'

He handed it to her while two guards flanked them, weapons not drawn but clearly ready. Bache exchanged a quick glance with Zaphir, a silent agreement passing between them. Now wasn't the time to resist. The data chip felt heavy in his pocket as they were escorted back through the corridors.

Once sealed in their quarters, Zaphir waited until the guards' footsteps faded before speaking.

'That went well,' she whispered.

Bache pulled out the data chip, turning it over in his fingers. 'Let's see what's on this before Shrell decides to search us.'

They spent half the night reviewing the fragmented data Jorven had collected. Project Cleansing appeared to be some kind of massive-scale weapon system, capable of targeting specific genetic markers across entire populations. The implications made Bache's blood run cold.

'This is genocide technology,' Zaphir whispered, her face illuminated by the glow of the tablet. 'They could wipe out an entire planetary species with this.'

Bache rubbed his temples. 'We need to get this information to President Xutan.'

'Can we trust him?' Zaphir countered. 'Remember, Shrell works for him.'

'Or does she? It was Shrell that told us that. It doesn't mean it's true.'

Zaphir nodded and stared into space for a moment.

'How the ancients do we send a message anyway, now we're locked up in here?' she asked.

'Get some sleep, we'll worry about that in the morning.'

Bache woke to the sound of a distant alarm. It was the one that sounded as the main hangar door opened. His neck ached from falling asleep in the uncomfortable chair, tablet still clutched in his hand. The data chip with Project Cleansing's information lay on the small table beside him. He grabbed it and stuffed it in an inside pocket.

'Zaphir,' he whispered, glancing at her sleeping form on the lower bunk. She stirred immediately, eyes snapping open with the alertness of someone accustomed to danger.

'What time is it?' she asked, her voice husky with sleep.

'Just after 0600 hours.'

He glanced at his tablet as it pinged an alert and a message scrolled across the screen. His eyebrows shot up. The chip had detected a familiar ship signature in the hangar – his GDA ship from Serris Adelaine. The one they'd left behind when Shrell's team had extracted them.

Bache moved to the door, pressing his ear against the cool metal. The corridor beyond seemed silent. 'I believe our ship from Serris has just arrived here.'

He studied the door's locking mechanism – standard GDA issue, despite this being a non-GDA facility. Reaching into his pocket, he felt for his multitool. Within seconds, he had the cover panel off, exposing the internal electrics.

'You're going to short it out?' Zaphir asked, appearing at his shoulder.

'Better than that.' Through his tablet, he activated his dermal chip and pressed his wrist against the exposed circuitry. The lock system accepted the override code with a soft click. 'Unlocked. Not disabled. They won't detect that until after we're gone.'

Bache eased the door open a crack. The corridor was empty, the distant alarms still wailing faintly. He slipped out, Zaphir close behind.

They moved quickly through the narrow maintenance passageways, avoiding the main corridors where Shrell's personnel would be most concentrated. Bache led the way, navigating the unfamiliar facility with the aid of his tablet's rudimentary map he'd been building over the past days.

'This way, I think,' he whispered to Zaphir, pulling open a low door to a narrow service tunnel that should lead them to a high service gantry overlooking the main hangar.

The metal grating beneath their feet rattled slightly with each step, forcing them to move more slowly than Bache would have liked. His heart was in his mouth as they reached a narrow hatch at the end of the service tunnel. He pressed his ear against it, listening for any movement beyond.

'Seems clear,' he mouthed to Zaphir, then carefully turned the manual release wheel.

The hatch opened onto a dimly lit catwalk suspended high above the hangar floor. Bache crawled out first, staying low to avoid being spotted from below. Zaphir followed, closing the hatch silently behind them. They crept forward on hands and knees until they reached a section of the catwalk partially obscured by conduit piping and ventilation ducts.

Bache nervously peered down through the grating. From this vantage point, he had a clear view of their char-tered civilian vessel – the same one that had brought them to Serris and Panemorfi. It sat in a far corner of the hangar, dwarfed by the surrounding vessels.

But what really made his heart rate leap was the sight of Shrell's operatives carrying what appeared to be two cylindrical containers into the ship.

'Those look like thermobaric demolition charges,' he

whispered, squinting to get a better view. The distinctive red markings on the casings were unmistakable. 'Military grade.'

Zaphir pressed against him, her body tense as she watched over his shoulder. 'She's planning on killing us, isn't she?'

'It's the only explanation,' admitted Bache.

'What do we do now?'

'We do exactly what she's expecting.'

They waited about four minutes for Shrell's two saboteurs to file out after hiding the charges on the ship. Bache's muscles ached from holding still on the catwalk, but he'd used the few minutes to work out where he would've hidden them.

'Now,' he whispered to Zaphir, easing himself up into a crouch.

They descended via a maintenance ladder at the far end of the catwalk, Bache leading the way. Every sound seemed amplified in the cavernous space – the soft tap of their boots against metal, their controlled breathing, the distant wheeze of the base's environmental systems.

The ship sat looking deceptively normal. Bache approached cautiously, scanning for any sign of guards or surveillance. Nothing. Shrell certainly had confidence in her trap.

'I'll check in the drive bay first,' Bache murmured as they reached the vessel. 'That's where I'd put them if I wanted to ensure complete destruction.'

They approached the starboard airlock that faced the wall. Bache keyed in the entry code, and the airlock cycled open with a soft hiss. The familiar interior and smell of a new vehicle greeted them, though it felt like a lifetime since they were last here.

'Watch the hangar,' he told Zaphir. 'If anyone enters, let me know straight away.'

She nodded, taking position near the airlock as Bache made his way to the engineering section at the rear of the vessel. He knew Shrell's men had only been on the ship about four minutes, so they wouldn't have had time to remove panels or anything.

Sure enough, the charges were taped to the back of one of the main drive housings, well out of sight. Gently peeling them off, he returned to the airlock and getting a nod from Zaphir, dropped down onto the hangar floor again.

Bache approached the nearest ship and crept along the destroyer's hull, the charges heavy in his hands. His pulse drummed in his ears as he scanned for any movement in the hangar. The massive vessel loomed over him, its matte-black surface absorbing the dim light. He recognised the modified Xephoni configuration immediately, likely being outfitted for Project Cleansing.

He spotted what he was looking for – an open antigrav service hatch, its cover panel propped against the hull. The maintenance crew had left it exposed during their work cycle. Perfect.

He glanced back at Zaphir. Her eyes constantly sweeping the hangar for any sign of trouble, she gave him a quick nod and he slipped beneath the destroyer's massive bulk, the cold metal of the deck plates seeping through his thin coveralls. The antigrav service hatch gaped open like a wound in the vessel's underbelly, revealing the complex array of conduits and regulators within. Bache's fingers traced the familiar configuration, once his father's design, but now barely recognisable.

'Have some of this,' he muttered to himself as he carefully wedged the first charge deep within the housing. He positioned it where the explosion would cascade through the primary antigrav spoolers, ensuring catastrophic failure. The second charge he placed at the junction where the power conduits met the regulatory systems and behind the bulkhead where he knew the ship's armoury was located, so as to induce a few secondary detonations.

A sound of footsteps caught his attention. Bache froze, his heart missing a beat as he peered out from beneath the destroyer's bulk expecting to find weapons pointing at him. Two figures darted between storage containers, moving with the furtive caution of people who didn't want to be seen.

'Shit,' he muttered, easing himself out from under the ship. He recognised them immediately…Ash Stevns and Jorven, the technicians from earlier. They were heading directly towards his and Zaphir's ship.

Bache signalled to Zaphir, who had already spotted them. She moved quickly to intercept. Bache circled around the other side, cutting off their retreat path.

'What are you doing here?' Bache hissed as he stepped out from behind a cargo loader, blocking their path.

Ash jumped, her hand flying to her mouth to stifle a yelp. Jorven's thin face was pale with fear, his eyes darting around the hangar.

'We have to leave with you,' Jorven whispered urgently, glancing over his shoulder. 'They know I downloaded the data. We're both dead if we stay. We know too much about the project.'

Bache sighed and glanced at Zaphir, who had positioned herself behind them.

'This isn't a bloody passenger shuttle,' Bache hissed, but then thought about the explosives that would probably kill these two if they left them.

'Get in quickly,' said Zaphir, giving Bache an apologetic shrug. 'They helped us and will most certainly die if we don't,' she whispered to him, nodding at the destroyer he had just left.

'I know,' he said. 'I was about to make the same call, I'm glad we're on the same page. Come on, let's go.'

12

———

Pyros Base, unknown location

'Zaphir do the honours,' he said, jabbing a thumb at the pilot's seat. He grabbed his tablet and pressed his wrist against it, the dermal chip connecting instantly. The hangar security protocols appeared before him, complex but familiar enough after his days of observation. His fingers flew across the screen, bypassing firewalls and override systems.

'What the hell is that?' Ash whispered, her face pale with fear.

'Getting us the hell out of here,' Bache muttered, not looking up from his work.

'The hangar door's closed,' she said, peering out the front screen.

The low hum of the ship's systems coming online vibrated through the deck plates beneath their feet.

'Ah…there you are,' said Bache as the atmosphere barrier flickered on.

'There's no way they'll just let us fly out,' Jorven said, his thin voice trembling. 'Just jump away.'

'There is a reason for us to do that,' Bache said, his lips curved into a tight smile as the final firewall collapsed. The massive hangar doors began to grind open, the distant sound of alarms wailing through the cavernous space. 'There you go.'

He moved over and slid into the co-pilot's seat beside Zaphir. Her hands were already dancing over the icons, the ship's systems responding and engines spooling up.

'Antigravs at seventy percent,' she reported, not looking up. 'Shields charged.'

'We've got company,' shouted Jorven from behind and pointing out the side window. 'It's Shrell.'

Bache looked out the front screen, watching as Commander Shrell strolled into the hangar, her injured arm still in its sling. What made his breath catch was her expression…a cold, calculating smile. She raised her good hand in what appeared to be a friendly wave.

'Why isn't she trying to stop us?' said Ash, her voice trembling behind him. 'And why the ancients is she waving?'

'Because she wants us to leave,' Bache muttered, a chill running down his spine. 'She's counting on it, because she planted explosives on the ship.'

'What?' Jorven exclaimed. 'She's going to blow us up?'

The ship lifted, turned and shot forward through the now open hangar doors. Bache changed the main cockpit screen to the rear facing camera, they watched Shrell and her henchman's figures grow smaller, that unsettling smile still visible until she became too small.

'She thinks she's going to blow us up,' said Bache. 'I found the explosives and placed them on one of the destroyers.'

'What?' said Ash, her face suddenly losing all its colour. 'Which one?'

'The nearest one,' Bache replied, turning to regard Ash with a questioning gaze.

'Oh fuck… Its magazine is full of tycelerin warheads.'

Bache's eyes widened.

'Shit, Zaphir, get us out of here fast,' and he turned back to watch the screen and the small moon shrinking behind them. It hung against the void, deceptively silent and still.

'Can we jump anywhere yet?' Bache asked, urgently.

'Where to?' Zaphir asked, her voice steady despite the tension evident in Bache's voice.

'Any fucking where,' he shouted.

'Oh, err…five seconds,' she said, suddenly realising he was serious.

Behind them a bright flash emanated from inside the hangar, leading to the mother of all detonations only a fraction of a second later. They all shielded their eyes as the moon vaporised, suddenly becoming infinitely brighter than the star of the system they were currently in.

'Zaphir, hit it…hit it,' shouted Bache. 'Shock wave.'

The wave came at them so fast it was as if they were travelling backwards.

'Jumping,' called Zaphir.

Bache shut his eyes as the wave front slammed at them. He felt a slight nudge through his seat and then nothing.

'Are we dead?' he heard Ash ask.

Bache opened his eyes. The ship's systems hummed around them, seemingly intact and operating. They'd escaped. The jump had occurred as the shock wave hit.

'No...we're alive,' he said, slumping back in his seat with relief. He glanced at the holomap to confirm their position. 'Well done, Zaphir, you did it.'

She exhaled slowly beside him, her knuckles white where she'd grabbed the seat arms.

'That was a lot closer than I would've liked,' she mumbled.

Ash and Jorven were huddled behind them, both pale-faced and trembling. Jorven looked like he might be sick.

'I can't believe it,' Ash whispered. 'The entire base... everyone there...gone.'

Bache felt a pang of guilt, but quickly pushed it aside. Those people had been building a weapon of mass genocide. Shrell had tried to kill them. Still, the scale of destruction weighed heavily on him.

'The tycelerin warheads amplified the explosion beyond what I anticipated,' he said, running a hand through his hair. 'I only expected to damage one of the destroyers. We need to see what's left.'

Zaphir nodded, taking a deep breath and already plotting a return jump. 'Shields at maximum...coordinates set. Jumping back in three...two...one...'

When the holomap reset, it showed only an expanding debris field. Where Pyros Base had once been, there was nothing. Huge chunks of rock were beginning to impact the planet a hundred thousand kilometres away.

'Please tell me that rock wasn't populated?' Bache asked, leaning forward again and pointing their array at the planet to do the scan himself. 'Thank the ancients for that,' he added, after confirming it really was what it seemed, a barren lifeless rock.

Bache stared at the debris field, his mouth dry. The enormity of what had just happened crashed over him. Dozens of people…possibly innocent technicians like Ash and Jorven, had just been vaporised in an instant. Because of his actions.

'Shit,' he whispered, his voice barely audible over the hum of the ship's systems.

'You couldn't have known about the warheads,' Zaphir said quietly beside him. Her face was drawn, eyes fixed on the expanding cloud of rock. 'This is on Shrell, not you.'

But the weight of responsibility pressed down on his chest all the same. He forced himself to breathe deeply, to focus on what needed to happen next.

'We need to contact President Xutan directly,' he said, straightening in his seat. 'No intermediaries, no channels that could be intercepted. The data chip Jorven gave us proves there's a secret council inside the GDA developing genocidal weapons. Shrell was part of that…do either of you know who she reported to?'

Ash straightened in her seat suddenly, a contemplative expression quickly replaced the frightened one.

'Hang on,' she said, pulling out her tablet. 'Shrell had a visitor a few weeks ago. I noticed she was quite subservient to whoever he was.'

'You didn't recognise him, or get a name?' Zaphir asked.

'No…but I think I got a picture. I always get a shot of my finished work, just in case…you know? I'd finished replacing an aft array pivot on one of the old destroyers, just as they walked through the hangar.'

She tapped away on her battered tablet for a moment, before she found what she was looking for.

'There,' she said, turning the screen around and handing it to Bache.

Bache took the unit and could see two figures in the background of the picture. He zoomed the image in and caught his breath as he recognised the man with Shrell. Zaphir's eyes widened as he showed her.

'You know who that is?' Jorven asked.

'It's Admiral Hollander, chair of the Naval Finance Committee,' said Zaphir, shaking her head.

'He was my father's captain long before I joined the navy,' said Bache.

Jorven sat forward, his thin face peering over at the picture. 'D'you think he could be one of the Originators… the shadow council I mentioned?'

'They have operatives everywhere. If they realise we escaped with evidence…' Ash added nervously.

'They'll think we're dead when they get this news,' Bache pointed out. 'So long as Shrell had reported us being here. For now, we have the advantage of being ghosts.'

13

Civilian transport, approaching Hadset, Jarris Vee system

'Where d'you want dropping, Jorven?' Bache said, turning to face their unexpected passengers. After the destruction of Pyros Base, they'd been jumping through a series of remote systems to ensure they weren't being followed.

The ship hummed quietly around them as they approached the small agricultural world of Hadset, Jorven's home planet. On the holomap, Bache could see its blue-green surface growing larger, scattered landmasses breaking up the vast oceans.

'My family comes from here,' Jorven said, pointing to a northern area of one of the largest landmasses. His thin face showing relief for the first time since they'd left the base. 'They think I've been working on a classified GDA project. They'll be glad to see me.'

Ash remained silent, her eyes fixed on the approaching planet. She'd barely spoken since they'd escaped the explosion, spending most of her time analysing the data salvaged from Jorven's chip.

'What about you, Ash?' Zaphir asked, glancing at her. 'Would you be wanting to get off here?'

Ash looked up from her tablet, her expression suddenly resolute. 'I don't have anywhere to go. Not really.' She tucked a strand of hair behind her ear. 'I've been thinking…I want to stay with you two.'

Bache raised an eyebrow. 'That's not exactly the safest option. We're heading straight into the mouth of the beast.'

'That's precisely why I want to stay,' Ash replied, her voice stronger now. 'I spent three years working bloody hard on starship systems for that lot and would've probably been murdered at the end of it. It's not as though they paid that well either. I just want to find out who was doing all this and why.'

'Only if you're sure,' said Bache, getting a glance from Zaphir. 'You're a civilian contractor and we can't be held responsible for your safety.'

'I understand,' said Ash, looking up to watch as the planet became very large through the front screen.

They descended through Hadset's upper atmosphere, eventually breaking through heavy cloud to reveal sprawling farmland below. Jorven guided Zaphir down to his drop point, landing in a secluded clearing surrounded by tall purple-tinged grasses.

'This is close enough,' he said, gathering his few belongings. 'My settlement's about three kilometres that way.' He pointed towards a distant cluster of buildings on a small hilltop. 'I can walk from here. Better if they don't see me getting off the ship.'

Bache followed him to the airlock, feeling the weight of responsibility for the man's safety. 'Are you certain you don't want us to take you all the way?'

'No,' Jorven said firmly. 'This is my home. I know how to disappear for a while here.' He extended his hand to Bache. 'Thank you for saving my life and I hope you get the bastards.'

Zaphir opened the airlock and waved as he went to step down.

'Shit,' she shouted, lifting the ship and turning fast, causing Jorven to fall back inside.

'What the hell?' Bache exclaimed, almost sliding out of his seat.

The ground where the vessel had been sat only a split second before erupted. Grasses, small shrubs and soil crashed over the ship, sliding off their shields and dropping back below. In the distance the hilltop settlement exploded in a series of detonations.

'NO,' screamed Jorven, witnessing the destruction of his home through the mud-covered front screen.

'Jump,' Bache called, as an ugly matte-black ship decloaked only a few hundred metres above the destroyed village.

Only a split second after the airlock resealed, they emerged back in space and Zaphir immediately began plotting an embedded jump, so they couldn't be chased.

'Who the fuck was that?' Zaphir shouted as she took the ship on a random course, waiting for the jump icon to glow. When it did she mashed it and once again they were in a completely different place.

'Do another one, quickly,' said Bache. 'And keep doing them until I tell you to stop. They're tracking the ship somehow.'

He pressed a few icons on his tablet and began waving it around the cockpit. Finding nothing there, he went from room to room, until finally he found what he was looking for. A loud pinging noise confirmed something was emitting a low frequency pulse and it was coming from under a bed in one of the cabins.

'Found it,' he hollered, crouching down and finding a small grey tube wedged under the mattress. He threw it in the nearest airlock and as fast as he could, cycled the doors. The tube flashed away as the outer door cracked open. 'Jump now,' he called through to Zaphir.

The lights dimmed as she did just that. Bache scanned the remainder of the ship before finally slumping back into his seat.

Ash had his arm around Jorven, who was in a right state.

'Those murdering fuckers,' he raged between sobs. 'Four hundred innocent people lived on that hill.'

Bache sat in silence and stared at the floor.

'They must've had a cloaked guard ship permanently nearby,' said Zaphir.

'Where do we go now?' asked Ash, her eyes darting between Bache and Zaphir.

'My family…' Jorven's raised voice broke as he staggered to his feet, face contorted in grief. 'My mother was there. My sisters, their children.' His thin frame shook violently. 'We need to go back. We need to kill them all.'

He lunged for the ship's controls, but Bache caught him by the shoulders and struggled to hold him back.

'They're not tracking us now,' Bache shouted, tightening his grip as Jorven thrashed against him. 'Going back is complete suicide.'

'I don't care,' Jorven screamed, his face flushed with rage. Spittle flew from his mouth as he fought against Bache's restraint. 'They murdered everyone…four hundred people…children.'

He broke free and slammed his fist against the bulkhead with a sickening crack. Blood smeared across the metal as he pulled back for another strike.

'Jorven, stop now,' Ash shouted, as he moved between him and the wall, her hands raised. 'This won't bring them back.'

'Get out of my way.' He tried to shove past her, his eyes wild. 'We have a ship. We have weapons. We can make them pay.'

'We don't have weapons, this is a leased civilian vessel,' Bache said, calmly. While he circled around, ready to restrain him again if necessary. The raw grief in Jorven's face was almost unbearable to witness.

'That ship that attacked your settlement,' Bache said, keeping his voice steady despite the adrenaline surging through his body. 'It was one of those converted destroyers that you will've worked on.'

'No fucking way,' Jorven spat. 'I knew the crews to those ships, ate with them, drank with them. There's no way they would've knowingly done that.'

'I think "knowingly" is the operative word here, Jorven,' said Ash. 'I've been inside those ships, seen the missile operators' stations…they wouldn't have had a clue what the target actually was, they're just given a target coordinate and a fire order. And anyway, they probably felt the same way as you after witnessing Pyros Base vaporising. They won't have known it was their own weapons that did it.'

Jorven finally sat down again, his face flushed with anger.

'If I ever find out who gave that order…I'm going to tear their fucking limbs off and feed them to a pack of starving sabre dogs.'

'Don't worry,' said Bache. 'We won't stop you doing that.'

'In the meantime, we need a destination,' said Zaphir.

'And transport with more teeth,' said Bache.

He stared at the tablet in his hand, an idea forming. The dermal chip implant in his wrist had been his ace in the hole more times than he could count. While standard communications might be monitored, there were still ways to get a message out without detection.

'I know how to reach the president,' Bache said, fingers already moving across the tablet's surface. 'And I know where to get a ship that can actually put up a fight.'

'How? Where?' Zaphir quizzed, leaning over his shoulder to peer at his tablet.

Bache accessed his encrypted communication protocol, a system that operated through data bursts hidden underneath routine communication bursts. 'Remember Clunk?'

Zaphir's eyebrows shot up. 'The pilot who helped you

take down those Gata battleships? The one who flies like he's got a death wish?'

'The very same.' Bache's lips curved into a tight smile as he coded the message. 'After our adventure three years ago, on my recommendation, he was promoted to skipper a small patrol vessel. The *Valediction* if my memory serves me right. Small but nasty little thing…based on the Klatt-designed hunter-killers…and equipped with the latest stealth technology too.'

'And you trust him?' Ash asked, her voice tense.

'With my life,' Bache replied without hesitation. 'He owes me and he's stationed at the Pargoots Outpost, monitoring for smuggling activities near the Klatt border. It's only about eight jumps from here.'

Zaphir raised her eyebrows.

'Want me to go there?'

'Uh-huh,' grunted Bache. 'I'll send an encrypted message.'

14

Civilian transport, en route to the Pargoots Outpost

BACHE'S FINGERS flew over the tablet, composing a message that would make sense only to Clunk. A reference to their shared past, to the battle at Berge, and a request for assistance that wouldn't flag any monitoring systems. He also sent a short coded message to President Xutan, using an old private code that he had acquired a few years ago and hoped was still active. If it was, it would only appear on Xutan's private tablet.

He spent the next hour altering the ship's recognition codes, methodically working through each security protocol. He knew changing the transponder signature wasn't enough…they needed to modify the drive harmonic patterns too. Anyone looking for them would be scanning for the specific energy signature of their civilian transport.

'Hand me that calibrator,' he said to Ash, who had proven surprisingly adept at technical modifications.

She passed it over, watching intently as he adjusted the final settings.

'Will this really fool their sensors?' she asked.

'It should,' Bache replied, wiping a bead of sweat from his eyebrow. 'I'm reconfiguring our emissions profile too, to match a standard Daxicorp personnel hauler. There are loads of them in this sector. We'll be just another ship making a routine personnel drop-off.'

Zaphir called their progress from the pilot's seat.

'Seven jumps completed. One more to Pargoots.'

Jorven had retreated to one of the cabins, his grief too raw for company. Bache didn't blame him. The destruction of his home settlement weighed heavily on all of them, but of course especially Jorven.

'Ready for the final jump if you are,' Zaphir announced.

The familiar sensation of displacement washed over them as the ship popped into the emergence zone of the bustling Pargoots system. The outpost hung against the backdrop of a massive swirling gas giant, its six docking arms extending like the legs of some massive space spider.

'Incoming transmission,' Zaphir said, turning to Bache, her finger hovering over the communications panel.

'Daxicorp Security Control to unexpected personnel vessel,' a stern voice crackled through the comm system. 'Halt your approach to Pargoots Outpost. Prepare to be boarded for inspection.'

Bache's stomach dropped. He exchanged a panicked glance with Zaphir.

'What the hell?' he muttered, scanning the sensor readings. 'Is nothing simple these days?'

A small sleek black vessel had detached from one of the outpost's legs and was accelerating towards them.

'Daxicorp Security has no jurisdiction here,' Zaphir whispered, her hand still hovering over the communications panel. 'This is a GDA outpost.'

Bache's mind raced. 'They shouldn't, but Daxicorp has corporate agreements with most frontier outposts for contraband interdiction. Stall them.'

She nodded and opened the channel. 'This is personnel hauler *Indigo Seven* responding to Daxicorp Security. We're on a scheduled delivery run. What seems to be the problem?'

Ash appeared at Bache's shoulder, concern written across her face. 'If they board us, they'll know this isn't a personnel hauler. We've got no one who's supposed to be delivered here.'

'I know,' Bache hissed, already moving towards the ship's central corridor. 'Jorven...we need you, now.'

The security vessel grew larger on their holomap, its hull sporting the distinctive red and black insignia of the Daxicorp consortium.

Jorven appeared in the doorway, his eyes red-rimmed but alert. 'What's happening?'

'Unexpected inspection,' Bache replied tersely. 'It could be random...but somehow I doubt it. Everyone remember your cover stories. We're a standard small personnel hauler making a delivery run.'

'Delivering who?' Jorven asked.

'Who and why is what I'm trying to determine,' Bache replied. 'Has either of you been here before?'

Both Ash and Jorven shook their heads.

'You need to think of something quick,' said Zaphir, as the Daxicorp vessel matched their velocity and manoeuvred alongside with deft precision.

Another voice Bache recognised immediately came through on a different channel.

'Is that you, Berge boy? Have you got my new technician on board?'

'Certainly have, Clunky. Can you let these guys know I'm supposed to be here?' Bache replied with a sly grin, recognising the subterfuge and instantly playing along.

A very aggressive-looking GDA hunter-killer uncloaked right next to the Daxicorp ship. It had all its plethora of weapons pods extended and certainly oozed an ambiance of piss off.

'Daxicorp security vessel…this is Captain L'Clers of the GDA hunter-killer *Valediction*. I booked this personnel arrival with a member of your team last night when I met him in the Swamp Pig. If he had too many pints of Regg'taa Euphoria and forgot to log it in…then it's certainly not the fault of the delivery crew is it?'

There was an awkward pause for a few moments, before the security vessel messaged again.

'Personnel hauler *Indigo Seven*, you are clear to dock on leg G, docking point fourteen. Security out.'

The small black ship dropped away, disappearing around the other side of the station.

Bache chuckled to himself and knew he certainly owed Clunk a beer for that.

'They never seem to hire any cleaners in here,' Clunk remarked as he met them at the door and guided them through the Swamp Pig's crowded interior. The floor stuck to Bache's boots with each step, the accumulated grime of what smelled like decades' worth of spilled drinks, dropped food, and who knows what else.

The bar was exactly what its name suggested – a dingy establishment reeking of body odour and poor life choices. Bache wrinkled his nose as they stepped through the crowd. The bar occupied a cramped corner of Pargoots's commercial sector, its dim lighting barely illuminating the assortment of off-duty crew members, smugglers, and station workers hunched over their drinks.

Clunk led them to a booth in the far corner, partially hidden from the main floor by a cracked partition. He'd grown a beard since Bache had last seen him, and his uniform had the comfortable, lived-in look of someone who'd made this outpost his home.

'So,' Clunk said after they'd settled in and a server had brought a round of drinks, 'you want to tell me what the hell is going on? Your message mentioned the word Berge, which usually signals trouble.'

Bache took a long swig from his glass, the synthetic whiskey burning a path down his throat. He needed it after the past few days. 'It's complicated.'

'It always fucking is with you,' Clunk replied with a grin, before turning his attention to Zaphir. 'And Specialist Mye,' Clunk said, nodding at her with a knowing smirk. 'Still keeping this idiot alive, I see.'

Zaphir's lips quirked upward. 'Someone has to.'

Clunk's eyes shifted to Ash and Jorven, sitting on the end seats.

'And who are these fine people? Your new crew?'

'More like unexpected passengers,' Bache said, quietly and checking around to make sure they weren't overheard. 'They're Ash and Jorven, former Pyros Base technicians.'

'Pyros what?' Clunk questioned, raising his eyebrows. 'Sounds like an outer planet strip club.'

'It was a secret weapons facility,' Bache said, keeping his voice low. 'Or it was until I accidentally vaporised it.'

Clunk choked on his drink, spraying liquid across the table.

'And here I thought I'd had an exciting three years,' Clunk muttered, wiping his mouth with the back of his hand. 'You're telling me there's a shadow council within the GDA, your father was framed, and you just blew up an entire secret base?'

Bache nodded grimly. 'And someone's trying very hard to make sure we don't tell anyone about it.'

Clunk leaned back, his weathered face thoughtful as he processed everything they'd shared. The noise of the bar provided perfect cover for their conversation…no one could hear them over the din of drunken spacers and the blaring music from huge old speakers.

'We need to get this information directly to President Xutan,' Bache continued, lowering his voice further. 'But we can't trust the normal channels. We don't know how deep this goes. That's why we need your ship. The *Valediction* has stealth capabilities, weapons, and most importantly, it's not being tracked.'

'My ship also has secure communications,' Clunk offered. 'But even those could be compromised if what you're saying about Admiral Hollander is true. Bloody hell…the Finance Committee chair? That's…that's…'

'Insane, I know,' said Zaphir.

Jorven leaned forward, his grief-hollowed eyes intense.

'These people murdered four hundred civilians today. My entire family. They're developing weapons to target specific genetic markers…genocide technology.'

Clunk's eyebrows shot up.

'Fuck the ancients…really?' he muttered, downing the remainder of his drink in one swallow. 'That's so illegal, and of course you've got the proof I hope?'

Bache tapped his pocket where the data chip rested. 'Enough to implicate Admiral Hollander at the very least.'

Clunk drummed his fingers against the sticky tabletop and stared across the room for a moment.

'The first step would be getting to Kentro without detection,' he said.

15

The Swamp Pig bar, Pargoots Station

A SUDDEN CLATTER of boots interrupted their drinking. Four armed Daxicorp security officers strode into the bar, their weapons visible in holsters, eyes scanning the crowd with predatory intent.

'Uh-oh…time to go, people,' Bache said, sliding out of the booth. 'Now.'

Clunk nodded and led them through the back into a narrow service corridor that reeked of spoiled food and industrial cleaners. He opened a hatch in the wall that emerged into a maintenance shaft, the dim emergency lighting casting long shadows as they hurried up the ladders to the docking levels.

'The *Valediction* is three levels up,' Clunk whispered. 'Maintenance tube will get us there without going through the main corridors.'

They climbed in silence, the only sound their laboured breathing and the occasional distant clang and rumble from the station. Bache's mind raced through scenarios, calculating their odds. If Daxicorp was compromised, the entire station could be watching for them.

When they reached the right level the *Valediction*'s docking bay was only forty metres away. Clunk punched in his access code with confident efficiency. He cycled them through the airlock with a soft hiss as the pressure equalised, revealing the sleek interior of the hunter-killer vessel.

'Welcome aboard,' Clunk said with a flourish. 'She's not the *K2*, but she'll get us where we need to go.'

Bache stood on the bridge of the *Valediction*, watching as Clunk's small crew prepared for departure. The hunter-killer was everything Bache remembered from the specifications – sleek, deadly, and built for both stealth and combat. Its bridge was compact but efficient, every system optimised for rapid response and maximum firepower.

'Let's get outta here,' Bache said, settling into one of the auxiliary seats on the *Valediction*'s compact bridge. The ship hummed around them, its systems coming online with well-drilled smoothness as Clunk's capable crew prepared for departure.

Clunk swivelled in the captain's chair, his beard doing little to hide the grin spreading across his face. 'I'll have us out of here in two minutes. My people know what they're doing.'

Bache watched as the crew worked with calm precision, their movements economical and focused. The *Vale-*

diction might be small compared to the *K2*, but its systems were cutting-edge and its crew clearly well trained.

'Undocking sequence initiated,' called a young navigator from the helm station. 'All umbilicals disengaged.'

'Stealth systems online, Captain,' another crew member reported. 'Signature dampeners at maximum efficiency.'

Bache felt the slight vibration as the ship detached from Pargoots Outpost. Looking up at the holomap above, he watched as the massive structure began to recede.

'Where to, Chief?' Clunk asked, his fingers dancing across his control panel.

Bache exchanged a glance with Zaphir. The data they carried was too explosive, the conspiracy too far-reaching to trust anyone but those they knew without question.

'The *K2*,' Bache said decisively. 'We need to talk to Captain Whipper. He'll help us navigate this mess and give us a fair hearing.'

Zaphir strapped herself in next to him, her expression serious. 'Are you sure Captain Whipper will help us? This goes far beyond standard GDA protocols.'

'If anyone will believe us, it's him,' Bache replied. 'He's one of the GDA's most experienced officers and has faced Flast's conspiracies before. He's never been one to blindly follow orders when something doesn't add up either.'

'Mr Whippy's a cranky old bastard,' said Clunk. 'But he's got a moral compass that always points in the right direction.'

'To the *K2* it is,' Clunk announced, punching in coordinates. 'We can be there in nine jumps if we push it.'

Bache heard the familiar surge of the powerful engines as the *Valediction* pulled away from Pargoots Station. The vessel's lightweight design made it far more responsive than the civilian transport they'd been in earlier. Despite everything, he felt a small measure of relief at being aboard a proper warship again.

'I've got multiple security vessels powering up,' the tactical officer called out. 'Looks like they're coming after us.'

Clunk snorted. 'Too late, suckers…and as if those little buzz boxes could do anything to us.' He engaged the cloaking system with a dramatic flourish. 'Jump when ready, Lieutenant.'

The navigator nodded, and seconds later the familiar disorientation of jump travel washed over them. Bache looked up as the lights dimmed and the holomap stars blurred and reformed into an entirely different pattern.

'First embedded jump complete, Captain,' the navigator reported. 'Resetting coordinates and charging.'

Ash and Jorven had been given a small cabin to rest in, though Bache doubted Jorven would find any peace after what had happened to his settlement. Zaphir remained beside him on the bridge, her face tense as she studied the ship's systems.

'The crew seems…competent,' she whispered.

'Clunk might be unorthodox, but he knows how to pick good people,' Bache replied, watching as the captain moved efficiently around his bridge.

Zaphir leaned closer to Bache.

'D'you think we should send a message ahead to Whipper?'

'Too risky,' Bache murmured. 'If Hollander's monitoring communications to and from GDA vessels, we'd be painting a target on our backs.'

Eleven hours later, the *Valediction* completed its ninth jump into the Davineer system, also skirting the border of Klatt space. The navigator had emerged them very close to a massive blue gas giant to hide their signature.

The tactical officer's urgent voice cut through the bridge atmosphere. 'Captain, proximity alert…scans detecting a vessel at the edge of our range. Stealth configuration…almost didn't catch it.'

Bache, who'd been dozing, jolted upright in his seat and scanned the tactical display. A faint signature flickered at the periphery of their sensor range, hiding in an asteroid belt and barely distinguishable from the background radiation.

'Show me,' Clunk ordered, his earlier jovial demeanour instantly replaced by the focused intensity Bache remembered from their Berge campaign.

The tactical display magnified, revealing the partial outline of a vessel's shield deflecting the smaller rocks in the asteroid field. Its drive signature was masked, but not completely hidden from the hunter-killer's sophisticated detection systems.

'I think that's another of those old Raptor class destroyers,' Bache said, leaning forward to study the readings. 'With that level of shielding it's definitely military, but I bet its identifiers are scrubbed.'

Zaphir's shoulder pressed against his as she joined him at the tactical station. 'Might be the same one as before. How did they find us? We've been jumping with embedded signatures.'

'They didn't follow us,' Bache muttered, the implications chilling him to the bone. 'They were already here, waiting and watching.'

Clunk's expression darkened. 'Which means they knew we were heading for the *K2*.'

'I don't imagine they knew we were coming here,' said Bache. 'It would've been a fair guess though. They've probably got ships watching Dasos and perhaps Deelatayne too.'

'Why Deelatayne?' Clunk asked.

'It's my home planet and I have a lot of friends there.'

The navigator's voice wavered slightly. 'Captain, we're approaching rendezvous coordinates. The *K2* is logged to be arriving in this system sometime today.'

Bache received a worried glance from Zaphir.

'You don't think they're planning on attacking the *K2* do you?' she said.

'I can't see that being anything other than a suicide mission,' said Clunk. It's a Katadromiko for ancients' sake.'

'Unless they have something we don't know about,' said Bache, glancing over at their two guests.

'We were propulsion engineers,' said Ash. 'The weapons guys kept themselves to themselves and were highly secretive.'

'Actually, now you come to mention it,' Jorven piped

up, 'I did overhear part of a conversation from two of them when they didn't know I was there…'

He paused as everyone on the bridge turned to face him.

'Oh…err…yeah, well they said something about a trigithian blade emitter, at least I think it was called that.'

'It's a trolithin blade emitter,' Bache corrected him. 'It was a system they were working on probably ten years ago. It proved too difficult to control and considered just as much risk to the host vessel as to the target. The project was cancelled and mothballed.'

'What was it supposed to do?' Clunk asked.

'It was designed to produce multiple blades of pure energy that would cut a targeted ship into slices, straight through its shields.'

'Shit,' said Clunk. 'If they've got one of those then the *K2* is in serious trouble.'

16

Hunter-killer *Valediction*, stationary in the Davineer
system

BACHE LEANED FORWARD, studying the tactical display
with narrowed eyes. A plan began to form in his mind…
risky, but potentially a very good one. He turned to the
navigator, who was intently monitoring their position relative to the lurking destroyer.

'Lieutenant, what do you think about jumping us
directly into that asteroid field? We could position
ourselves right behind the destroyer.'

The navigator's eyebrows shot up. 'Behind it, sir? In the
asteroids?' He studied his calculations for a moment puffing
out his cheeks. 'It's risky, but…yes. I could get us within fifty
metres of its aft section if we time it right. Their sensors would
be focused outward, in the other direction, waiting for the *K2*.'

'So it's possible, yes?' Bache pressed.

The young officer studied his calculations for a moment. 'Theoretically, yes, if I get it right. If I don't...' He left the implications hanging.

Clunk swivelled in his chair, a slow grin spreading across his face as he caught on to Bache's plan. 'Oh, I see where you're going with this. Nasty. I like it.'

'What exactly are you planning?' Zaphir asked, her voice low enough that only Bache could hear.

'We pop up from behind the destroyer, unleash everything we've got at the *K2*, and jump away before they can identify us.'

Zaphir's eyes opened wide. 'Attack our own ship? Have you lost your mind?'

'Not to destroy it, or even damage it for that matter,' Bache clarified, lowering his voice.

'You mean, just get their attention to reveal the hidden ship and make it look like the cloaked destroyer has lethal intentions,' Zaphir realised. 'We'll be gone and the destroyer will be immediately engaged.'

'Exactly,' Bache said. 'They'd never expect us to fire on our own ship.'

The navigator ran his fingers through his hair.

'I can get us there, but the timing would need to be perfect. We'd need to know the moment of the *K2*'s arrival, so I can jump us in fractionally before.'

'Surely we can hack into the GDA arrival registry,' Ash said suddenly, looking up from her tablet. She'd been quiet since boarding the *Valediction*, but now her eyes sparked with intensity. 'All vessels have to log their expected arrival times for traffic control, especially the big ones.'

Bache turned to her, surprised. 'GDA ships use encrypted channels for those logs.'

'Yes, but…' Ash's fingers were already flying across her tablet. 'When I was at Pyros Base, we regularly intercepted GDA communications. I still have some of those protocols stored in my personal device.' She glanced up, a hint of defiance in her expression. 'What? You think I didn't make backups of everything I thought might be useful?'

Clunk leaned forward in his captain's chair.

'Can you really access the arrival registry?'

'Not directly,' Ash admitted. 'But I can piggyback on the system alerts that go out to all vessels in a system when a Katadromiko class ship is inbound on a peaceful mission. Those alerts aren't as heavily encrypted since they need to reach civilian vessels too.'

Bache exchanged a glance with Zaphir.

'That could work,' he said. 'Why didn't I think of that?'

'How quickly can you set it up?' Clunk asked.

'Give me ten minutes,' Ash replied, already connecting her tablet to one of the ship's auxiliary input ports. 'I'll need to reconfigure some of my old protocols to match the current navy's frequency bands.'

'I've got it,' Ash announced a few minutes later, her eyes reflecting the blue glow of her tablet as she glanced over.

'*K2* is scheduled to arrive in exactly four minutes, twenty-three seconds.'

Bache felt his pulse quicken. 'That's cutting it close.'

'Navigator,' Clunk barked, spinning in his chair. 'Can you get us into position in time?'

The young officer's hands flew over his console.

'Yes, sir. Jump coordinates locked. Charging now.'

'Make sure you have the escape jump back here available immediately,' Clunk ordered.

'Yes, sir.'

Bache moved to the tactical station, peering over the shoulder of the weapons operator and familiarising himself with the *Valediction*'s defence systems. The hunter-killer class packed impressive firepower for its size – six medium-range lasers and four missile tubes. Perfect for what they needed.

'Weapons online,' Clunk requested. 'Prepare to target the *K2*'s shields.'

Zaphir appeared at his shoulder.

'You're sure this will work?'

'It has to,' Bache muttered. 'We just need to make it look convincing without causing actual damage.'

'Two minutes to *K2* arrival,' Ash called out.

Clunk's voice cut through the tension. 'All personnel, secure for combat jump. This is going to be tight.'

The bridge crew strapped in, faces tense with concentration. Jorven had retreated to a corner seat, his grief momentarily overshadowed by the imminent action.

'Jump in thirty seconds,' the navigator announced.

'Shields at maximum,' Clunk ordered. 'Weapons systems hot.'

The weapons officer's hands flew across his console. 'Weapons ready, Captain.'

Bache held his breath. If his timing was off by even seconds, the plan would fail catastrophically. The destroyer would detect them, or worse, the *K2* would detect them instead of the destroyer as a threat.

'Emergence locked in,' called the navigator, his fingers hovering over the jump controls. '*K2* arrival in five… four…three…'

Bache gripped the arms of his seat as the *Valediction* jumped. The momentary disorientation passed quickly, replaced by the jarring proximity alarm as they emerged mere metres from the destroyer's aft section. On the holomap, Bache could see the larger vessel's displacement against the backdrop of tumbling asteroids, completely unaware of their presence.

'*K2* emerging,' called the tactical officer.

The massive form of the *Katadromiko 2* materialised in the distance, its slab-like bulk instantly recognisable to Bache. His chest tightened at the sight of his ship.

'Fire!' Clunk shouted.

The *Valediction*'s weapons systems erupted, sending a spectacular display of laser fire and a full rack of missiles towards the *K2*. Deliberately calibrated to skim the huge ship's shields, the beams crackled harmlessly around the massive vessel's hull, illuminating its shields in forked lightning flashes of blue and purple as the missiles exploded against the impenetrable barrier.

'Jump away now,' Clunk ordered.

Again the bridge lighting dimmed as the small ship returned to its hiding place adjacent to the blue gas giant.

'Preparing emergency jump,' said the navigator.

Everyone else turned to stare at the holomap as it reset and panned in on the two larger ships. The *K2* had turned abruptly and returned a barrage of fire at the hidden destroyer. It didn't stay hidden for long as its shields fluoresced a deep red. They must've been caught severely off guard, as they failed to jump away and their shields were quickly overwhelmed by the sheer weight of fire. As they collapsed, the well-trained gunners took out the destroyer's array and engine nacelles rendering the vessel completely helpless.

'They're definitely finished,' Bache said, watching the disabled destroyer drift helplessly on the holomap. A grim satisfaction settled in his chest as he witnessed the *K2*'s precision strikes. 'Perfect timing. Let's make contact before they decide to finish the job.'

Clunk nodded and gestured to his communications officer. 'Open a secure channel to the *K2*.'

Bache stepped forward, straightening his posture instinctively as the comms system connected. The holomap flickered to reveal Captain Whipper's scowling face. His expression darkened further when he recognised Bache.

'Loftt? What in the name of the seven fucking moons of Jagnorite are you doing?' Whipper's voice thundered through the bridge speakers. 'You just fired on my fucking ship…don't you think that might be a particularly suicidal way to say good morning?'

'Sir, we needed to reveal the destroyer that was lying in wait for you,' Bache explained quickly. 'We believe it was equipped with a trolithin blade emitter. They were planning to ambush you.'

Whipper's scowl didn't soften, but something shifted in his eyes. 'And your brilliant solution was to fire on us?'

'It worked, didn't it?' Clunk chimed in, moving into view beside Bache.

'Captain Handis bloody L'Clers,' Whipper acknowledged with a roll of his eyes. 'I might've known you'd be involved in this stupidity. I want the pair of you in my office within the hour. You can park that little boy's ship in hangar fifty-three and if we detect just one weapons system activated, you won't be alive to claim your pensions…do I make myself clear?'

'Yes, sir,' they both said in unison.

17

Captain's bridge office, *Katadromiko 2*, stationary in the
Davineer system

AN HOUR LATER, Bache stood at rigid attention in Captain Whipper's office aboard the *K2*, trying not to fidget under the intense scrutiny of his commanding officer. Clunk stood beside him, somehow managing to look both casual and almost respectful at the same time.

'So let me get this straight,' Whipper said, leaning forward in his chair, his eyes boring into Bache's. 'A shadow council within the GDA is developing genocidal weapons. They've framed your father. They've blown up a civilian settlement. And now they're trying to assassinate all of us by slicing my ship into pieces with experimental weaponry we abandoned a decade ago.' He paused, sitting back again. 'And you discovered all of this shit while on a farming investigation?'

'Err, yes, sir,' Bache replied. 'I know it sounds a bit far-fetched.'

'No shit, Chief,' the captain replied, crossing his arms across his wide chest.

'Commander Shrell claimed to be working for President Xutan, but we have evidence linking her to Admiral Hollander instead,' Clunk said, piping up for the first time.

Bache handed over the data chip containing Jorven's files. Whipper inserted it into his personal tablet, his expression darkening as he scrolled through the schematics for Project Cleansing.

'This, I must admit, is…disturbing,' Whipper muttered. 'But what about this trolithin blade emitter? That's quite an accusation.'

'Jorven overheard weapons technicians discussing it at Pyros Base before we escaped. Given they just tried to ambush a *Katadromiko* with a single destroyer, I think it warrants investigation.'

Whipper's comm unit chimed, and he tapped it with an irritated flick of his finger.

'Sir, preliminary boarding report from Commander Riccs,' said a voice. 'You're going to want to hear this.'

'Go ahead,' Whipper said, his eyes not leaving Bache's face.

'We've secured the vessel, sir. Crew is in custody. And…' The voice paused. 'We've confirmed the presence of an experimental weapons system. Initial analysis matches the specifications of a fully operational trolithin blade emitter, sir. It was powered up and locked on the *K2*'s coordinates. Had they activated it before we disabled them…' The major's voice trailed off.

Bache felt his stomach tighten. The confirmation of the weapon's presence hit harder than he'd expected. They'd been only seconds from disaster.

'Transmitting visuals now,' Riccs continued.

Whipper's tablet lit up with footage from the marine's helmet cam. The image showed a massive array of crystalline emitters arranged in a circular pattern, pulsing with an eerie blue-green light. Even through the video feed, Bache could see the distinctive configuration that marked it as a trolithin blade system. He'd been right, but the confirmation still hit him like a physical blow.

'Holy shit,' Whipper whispered, his face paling slightly. 'Continue securing the vessel, Commander. I want every piece of that technology documented and every crew member interrogated, as a priority.'

'Yes, sir.'

Whipper ended the communication and sat back heavily in his chair. For a moment, the only sound in the office was the faint wheeze of the ship's systems.

'Looks like your wild accusations just got a whole lot more credible, Loftt,' Whipper said, his voice uncharacteristically quiet. 'A functioning blade emitter. If they'd activated that thing onto my ship...' He shook his head. 'The *K2* would have been sliced into ribbons.'

'They were waiting for you to arrive, sir,' said Bache. 'We had to do something and I take full responsibility for the decision to fire on you. Captain L'Clers was sceptical about doing that but I insisted.'

Bache caught Clunk turning his head slightly in his peripheral vision, which didn't go un-noticed by Whipper either.

'Of course he was,' Whipper replied, the corner of his mouth twitching up slightly on one side. He rose from his chair and strode around, circling his personal holomap. 'This is bigger than I thought. We need to take this directly to the president.'

Bache nodded, relief washing through him.

'We've been trying to reach him, sir. But with Hollander potentially monitoring communications, it's proving difficult to…'

'I know,' Whipper cut him off, turning back to face them. 'Which is why we're going to Kentro. In person.'

Clunk's eyebrows shot up.

'The whole *K2*? Won't that be a bit…obvious?' he blurted.

'That's precisely the point,' Whipper said, a grim smile playing at the corners of his mouth. 'They'll be expecting us to skulk around, trying to avoid detection. Instead, we're going to march right up to the Presidential Palace with a Katadromiko cruiser and bang on the door with forty-seven thousand witnesses.'

Bache felt a surge of hope. It made sense…no one would attempt to attack them openly in the heart of the GDA.

What about Jorven and Ash?' Bache asked. 'They've lost everything helping us.'

'They'll come with us,' Whipper said decisively. 'Their testimony will be crucial. And speaking of testimony…' He activated his comm unit. 'Commander Riccs, I need you to bring the destroyer's commanding officer to my office. Immediately.'

Bache exchanged a glance with Clunk.

'Sir,' Bache continued, 'I believe our priority should be identifying all the members of this shadow council. Admiral Hollander is clearly involved, but he can't be working alone.'

Clunk cleared his throat. 'The captured destroyer might give us some answers. Ship logs, communication records…'

'Already on it,' Whipper interrupted. 'Riccs is the best at what he does. If there's anything to find, he'll find it.'

Twenty minutes later, Bache stood in the corner of Captain Whipper's office watching as Commander Riccs marched in with a woman in a torn and stained uniform, her hands secured behind her back. Despite her dishevelled appearance, she carried herself with the rigid bearing of someone accustomed to command. Her eyes scanned the room quickly, calculating, before settling on Captain Whipper with undisguised contempt.

'Captain Yara Kast of the destroyer *Killeet*,' Riccs announced, shoving her roughly in front of Whipper's desk. 'We found her attempting to wipe the ship's logs when we boarded, sir.'

Whipper's expression remained neutral as he studied the woman.

'Thank you, Commander. What else did you find?'

Riccs placed a data tablet on the desk.

'The ship was officially decommissioned three years ago, supposedly stripped for parts and sent to the scrapyard. But obviously that never happened. We found communications logs, encrypted, but my specialists soon cracked them. Orders came directly from Admiral Hollander's private channel.'

Bache felt a surge of vindication that made his heart race. This was the proof they needed.

'There's more, sir,' Riccs continued, his voice hardening. 'We found a detailed schematic of the *K2*. Every weakness, every potential vulnerability mapped out. They knew exactly where to target the blade emitter for maximum effect.'

'Inside information, eh,' Whipper muttered. 'It seems Hollander's been a very busy traitor…isn't that right, Miss Kast?'

'It's Captain and I demand to be treated as a prisoner of war under GDA regulations,' she hissed through clenched teeth.

'Is that so,' said Whipper. 'Two things – firstly, I have absolutely no information regarding us being in a state of war with anyone, and secondly, you're a civilian pretending to be a navy captain in, it seems, a stolen vessel containing highly illegal weaponry.'

Whipper rose slowly from behind his desk, his expression darkening.

'We're private security.'

'Private security? That's the best you can conjure up is it?' he snapped, picking up his tablet and flipped it around to show footage of the trolithin blade emitter. 'Most private security ships don't carry prototype weapons capable of slicing a GDA warship into confetti.'

Kast laughed, a bitter sound that echoed through the office. 'You have no idea what's really happening, do you?

This isn't just about Admiral Hollander or some shadow council.' She glanced at Bache, her eyes narrowing. 'Your father's designs were always the key. But not because of what they could do…because of what they could hide.'

Bache felt his mouth go dry.

'What are you talking about?'

'The Xephoni drive configuration.' Kast's voice dropped to almost a whisper. 'It creates the perfect resonance frequency to mask the presence of Nkris technology integrated within GDA systems.'

The room went utterly silent. Bache felt as if the floor had tilted beneath him.

'The grey Nkris?' Whipper's voice was dangerously quiet. 'You're claiming there's alien tech built into our ships' systems?'

'Not claiming. Stating fact.' Kast's eyes gleamed with a strange pride. 'They've been here for decades, integrating their technology piece by piece. Why do you think the Theos keep their distance from the GDA? They can detect it. We've been preparing humanity for the ultimate evolution.'

Bache's mind raced, connecting pieces he'd never considered before. The strange modifications to his father's designs. The unexplained efficiency increases. The peculiar power fluctuations in the *K2*'s systems that had always been dismissed as normal variance.

'You're insane,' muttered Whipper. His expression hardened. 'And what exactly does all this accomplish?'

'Genetic purity,' Kast replied, her eyes gleaming with an unsettling fervour. 'The reclamation of humanity's rightful place in the galaxy. The Gata, the Klatt, all the

other species that have been limiting human expansion…
they'll be gone. One deployment, billions of non-humans
eliminated, and their worlds ready for human settlement.'

Bache felt his blood turn to ice. This wasn't just about
corruption or power…it was about systematic genocide on
a galactic scale.

'You're talking about eliminating entire civilisations,'
Bache whispered, his voice tight with horror.

Kast turned to him and grinned.

'Exactly…how beautiful will that be?'

18

Captain's bridge office, *Katadromiko 2*, stationary in the
Davineer system

KAST SAT UPRIGHT AWKWARDLY, her restraints cutting into
her wrists and seemingly without any remorse for what the
secretive council she served were attempting to achieve.

'I follow orders, Captain. Just as you do.'

'Not orders to murder forty-seven thousand of my own
people, I don't,' Whipper growled in return.

Bache noticed Riccs's tablet flashing with an incoming
message. The marine commander glanced at it, his expression shifting subtly before he cleared his throat.

'Captain, we've just intercepted a transmission heading
for the prisoner's ship that you might want to read.' Riccs
handed the tablet to Whipper. 'It appears to be an
itinerary.'

Whipper studied the screen, his eyebrows raising slightly.

'Well, well. Look at this, Chief.' He turned the tablet so Bache could see.

Bache leaned forward, scanning the document. His eyes widened as he recognised the GDA insignia at the top of what appeared to be a schedule of events.

'The Annual Mining Finance Symposium on Krix'ir?' He read further down the list of attendees and felt his pulse quicken. 'Admiral Hollander is listed as the keynote speaker.'

'Three days from now,' Whipper confirmed, a calculating look crossing his face. 'They're requesting the destroyer to be present as security for Hollander.'

Kast's face tightened almost imperceptibly, but Whipper hadn't missed it.

'Chief Engineer, how quickly can you have that destroyer operational again?'

Bache understood where the captain was coming from.

'In time to get there,' he said, already planning what he would need to repair. 'Shouldn't be a problem, we have the spares necessary in stock on this ship.'

The hardness in Kast's gaze faltered slightly as she met Whipper's stare.

'You have no idea what you're dealing with,' she managed.

Bache stepped forward. 'Then enlighten us.'

She turned to him, the coldness and bravado returning.

'I answer to powers beyond your comprehension, Chief Engineer. The GDA is rotting from the inside out. We're simply accelerating the inevitable.'

Whipper slammed his palm on the desk.

'Commander Riccs, I've heard enough of this crap…. Take her to the high-security brig. I want round-the-clock surveillance, she goes nowhere, talks to no one, is that clear?'

'Yes, Captain.'

Riccs grabbed Kast by the shoulders, spun her around and with a push in the back, marched her off to the main security centre deep in the bowels of the ship.

When she was gone, Bache turned back to the captain.

'Krix'ir, Captain,' he said. 'What's the travel time from here?'

Whipper sat back at his desk and pulled up a navigation screen.

'Around thirty hours if we pull out all the stops,' he said. 'You'd better get busy, Loftt.

Twenty-seven hours and forty-three minutes later, Bache leaned back from the destroyer's drive control panels, wiping sweat from his forehead with his sleeve. His muscles ached from crawling through access tunnels and contorting his body into small maintenance spaces designed for a contortionist. The engineering bay stank of ozone, burnt insulation, and the acrid tang of cooling solder.

'That's it,' he called to Ash, who was just finishing the final connections on the targeting systems. 'Main drive is back online.'

She gave him a thumbs-up from her position halfway

inside an open panel. 'Targeting systems are green across the board. We should be able to maintain a convincing Kast impression when we arrive.'

Bache checked his tablet one more time, scrolling through the diagnostic readouts. He'd managed to repair the destroyer's main propulsion systems and get the array back online, though the ship's offensive capabilities remained deliberately limited. Captain Whipper had been clear – they needed the vessel operational enough to approach Krix'ir without raising suspicion, but not so functional that it posed a threat if something went wrong.

'Clunk,' Bache said into his comm unit. 'How's the bridge coming?'

'All systems in the green,' came the reply. 'Just finished installing the remote override protocols you designed. If anyone tries anything stupid, we can shut this thing down from the *K2* in a heartbeat.'

The captured destroyer, despite its illegal modifications, was fundamentally sound. Bache had focused on repairing the propulsion systems and critical life support, deliberately leaving the trolithin blade emitter disconnected. The weapon remained in place – they needed the evidence – but he'd personally removed the power couplings and locked them in a secure container.

Captain Whipper's voice sounded through the comm system.

'Status report, Chief?'

'She's ready to fly, sir,' Bache replied, sliding into the co-pilot's seat beside Clunk. 'We can depart for Krix'ir immediately.'

'Good work. The *K2* will jump in five minutes.

Remain in distant formation. We will be cloaked for the foreseeable future as we technically no longer exist.'

'Understood, *Killeet* out,' Bache replied, giving the navigator and pilot a nod. 'When you're ready gentlemen, you may proceed.'

The stars vanished and reformed on the holomap as the destroyer emerged from its final jump. Bache's fingers flew across the console, cycling through the post-jump diagnostics. The status indicators blinked green, a minor miracle considering the patchwork repairs he'd performed yesterday.

'We've arrived,' Clunk announced, the pilot easing the ship into a standard planetary approach. 'Krix'ir control is hailing us.'

Bache's back still ached from crawling through access tunnels, and his hands were covered in small burns from splicing power conduits.

'Right on schedule,' he said, suppressing a yawn. 'Put them on.'

A stern-faced traffic controller appeared on the screen. 'Destroyer *Killeet*, this is Krix'ir Orbital Control. Transmit your authorisation codes.'

Clunk looked to Bache, who nodded and activated the forged credentials they'd prepared. The controller studied something off-screen, then returned with a curt nod.

'Confirmed, *Killeet*. Proceed to low orbit on this trajectory,' the navigation computer chimed. 'Admiral Hollander's shuttle is scheduled to arrive in forty minutes. You're cutting it close.'

'Understood, Control. Had a minor drive coupling issue. Nothing serious,' Clunk replied smoothly.

Bache watched the screen go dark as the comm link terminated. He glanced at Clunk's pilot, who was already manipulating the controls with practised ease, guiding the destroyer into the designated orbital path.

'The *K2* is maintaining position on the far side of Krix'ir's second moon,' Clunk reported, his voice low. 'Cloaked and running silent.'

Bache nodded, checking the scanners for any sign of unusual activity around the planet. Krix'ir glowed beneath them, its surface a patchwork of industrial complexes and mining operations that had stripped away much of the world's natural beauty. The Annual Mining Finance Symposium was being held in the planet's capital Goss'in-ray, a sprawling metropolis that sat in the middle of the northern continent.

'Any sign of other GDA vessels?' Bache asked, scanning the orbital traffic patterns on the holomap.

'Nothing obviously military,' Clunk replied, his fingers dancing across the control panel. 'Just the usual mining freighters, corporate shuttles, and maintenance vessels.'

Ash appeared in the doorway of the bridge, her face smudged with grease but her eyes alert. 'Targeting systems are holding stable,' she reported. 'We have use of the ship's lasers but nothing else.'

'Nice, good work,' Bache said. He tapped his comm unit on and off four times. The agreed signal to the *K2* that everything was going to plan. Tapping it twice meant trouble.

Bache received the expected four beeps of confirmation from the *K2*. Everything was proceeding as planned, but tension still knotted his shoulders. He couldn't help but feel they were walking into something bigger than they'd anticipated.

'Incoming vessel,' Clunk announced, pointing to a blinking light on the scanner. 'Looks like an armed diplomatic shuttle.'

Bache leaned forward, studying the approaching craft. White, sleek and polished, it bore the distinctive markings of a GDA official transport. 'That's him all right. Bang on schedule.'

Ash had slipped into one of the auxiliary stations, her fingers flying across the controls with fluent efficiency. 'I've configured our transponder to match exactly what they'd expect from *Killeet*. If they scan us, everything will look normal.'

The small craft glided into orbit, its attitude jets flaring as it adjusted course towards the planet's surface. Bache watched its descent path with narrowed eyes.

'Incoming transmission from the admiral's shuttle,' Clunk said, raising an eyebrow at Bache.

'Put it through,' Bache replied, straightening his posture. 'Audio only.'

The bridge speakers crackled to life.

'Destroyer *Killeet*, this is the admiral's transport. We're commencing planetary approach. Confirm your escort formation.'

Clunk cleared his throat and adopted the clipped,

formal tone they'd heard in Captain Kast's voice recordings. 'Confirmed. *Killeet* will maintain escort position through atmospheric entry and on to Goss'inray.'

There was a brief pause before the shuttle responded. 'Acknowledged, *Killeet*.'

The destroyer followed and descended through Krix'ir's upper atmosphere, its heat shield beginning to glow. Below, the sprawling industrial landscape of the mining planet spread out in all directions…refineries belching plumes of steam, massive excavation pits scarring the surface, and the dust-covered buildings of Goss'inray rising at the centre of it all.

19

Destroyer *Killeet*, upper atmosphere, Krix'ir, Krix'ir
system

THE BRIDGE suddenly bucked beneath Bache's feet, throwing him hard against the console. Alarms blared as the ship shuddered violently, the metal groaning around them like a wounded animal.

'What the hell was that?' Clunk shouted, as the pilot fought to keep the ship at the correct angle of attack.

Bache's fingers flew across the diagnostic panel, muscle memory taking over as his mind flashed through the possible reasons. What he saw shocked him.

'We're taking fire. From two massive energy weapons on the planet's surface,' he shouted across to Clunk.

The destroyer lurched again, its shields flaring brilliant blue on the holomap. Even though the flashes were blinding, Bache caught glimpses of powerful laser bolts cutting through Krix'ir's atmosphere, striking with surgical precision.

'Those aren't standard planetary defences,' Ash yelled over the cacophony of alarms. 'Krix'ir doesn't have any. Those are mobile military-grade weapons.'

Bache stared down at the rapidly failing shield indicators, cold realisation washing over him.

'This was a trap. They knew we were coming.'

The ship bucked violently to starboard as one of the beams sliced through their port stabilisers. Sparks erupted from a nearby console, showering Clunk who swore colourfully as he batted at his smouldering sleeve.

'We're losing attitude control,' the pilot shouted, wrestling with the unresponsive helm. 'Can't maintain the correct angle.'

Bache punched the comms. '*K2*, this is Loftt. We're under attack from planet-based weapons. Our shields are failing, request immediate assistance. *K2*, I repeat, we're under attack…'

Bache's message was cut short as another blast rocked the ship, throwing him hard against the bulkhead. Blood trickled down his temple as pain exploded through his skull.

Warning klaxons screamed across the bridge. On the failing holomap, he watched as their shields finally collapsed in a cascade of blue-white energy.

'Shields are down,' Ash shouted, her voice barely audible over the din of failing systems. 'Hull breach on deck two.'

The destroyer pitched violently to port. Bache clawed his way back to the console, his fingers slipping on the controls as the artificial gravity fluctuated. The deck plates vibrated beneath his boots – a death rattle he recognised all too well.

'Main engines are down, antigravs are down,' he shouted, reading the flashing red indicators. 'We've got seconds before this ship breaks up.'

Clunk slammed his palm on the emergency evacuation alert. 'Abandon ship, everyone to the lifeboats, now.'

The next blast tore through the starboard nacelle. The ship spun wildly, throwing Ash across the bridge. Bache lunged and caught her before she slammed into the navigation console. The acrid smell of burning circuitry filled the air as smoke began to pour through the ventilation system.

'Can you walk?' he shouted in her ear.

She nodded, blood streaming from a gash on her forehead.

Clunk pointed to the bridge lifeboat hatch.

'Everyone in right now,' he ordered.

They all stumbled in that direction, the artificial gravity phasing in and out, with wall and ceiling panels dropping around them. Bache batted a light fitting away as it fell on him and Ash. Jorven reached the lifeboat first and uncovering the deployment button, he slapped it hard.

The two small airlock doors slid aside and they began piling in.

The floor pitched violently beneath Bache as the destroyer entered a flat spin. He stumbled, crashing to his knees as the artificial gravity suddenly peaked high and then failed completely. The grinding shriek of tearing metal filled his ears.

'Bache,' Clunk yelled as the ship twisted again.

The sudden movement sent Bache sliding across the deck towards the open space where a wall panel had torn away. He clawed desperately at the smooth metal floor, fingernails breaking as he sought purchase. His body lifted in the failing gravity, the void of Krix'ir's atmosphere beckoning beyond the jagged hole.

Clunk lunged forward from the lifeboat doorway, his upper body hanging precariously out while Jorven grabbed his belt from behind. The destroyer shuddered again, metal screaming as it tore apart around them.

'Grab my hand,' Clunk shouted, stretching his arm towards Bache.

Bache kicked wildly, trying to propel himself back towards the lifeboat, but the ship's erratic spinning worked against him. He felt his foot catch on something solid… Clunk's outstretched hand. The captain's fingers clamped around his ankle with surprising strength.

'I've got you,' Clunk yelled, his face contorted with effort.

Bache glanced over his shoulder and saw Ash tumbling towards the same breach, her eyes wide with terror. He twisted his body and managed to snag her wrist as she flew past.

'Hold on,' he shouted, feeling the strain in his shoulder as he gripped her.

Clunk heaved backward, dragging Bache by the ankle while Bache maintained his hold on Ash.

'Pull,' Clunk roared to Jorven, who yanked backward with everything he had.

The ship lurched violently, metal screaming around them as the hull tore itself apart. Bache felt the agonising strain in his shoulder as Ash's full weight dangled from his grip. Her face was pale with terror, eyes locked on his as her free hand desperately sought anything to grab onto.

'Don't drop me,' she screamed over the howling wind rushing through the breach.

Clunk and Jorven heaved again, pulling Bache inch by excruciating inch towards the lifeboat. Bache's ribs scraped painfully along the deck plating, but he maintained his death grip on Ash, refusing to release her even as his muscles burned with the effort.

With one final mighty pull, Clunk dragged Bache far enough that Jorven could grab his collar. Together they hauled him through the lifeboat doorway, Ash still dangling from his grip.

'Get her in,' Bache gasped, his arm feeling like it might tear from its socket.

Jorven lunged forward once more, grabbing Ash's free arm. Together, they pulled her into the lifeboat just as another explosion rocked the dying ship.

Clunk mashed the door close toggle and hit the launch button hard, even though they weren't strapped in.

'Brace, brace,' Clunk shouted, only a millisecond before the lifeboat's explosive bolts blasted them away from the wreck.

Bache heard the crack of the head shield deploying almost immediately and the building scream of the anti-grav motor winding up.

The lifeboat shuddered wildly through Krix'ir's atmosphere, its stabilisers fighting against the turbulence. Bache clung desperately to a handhold as the small vessel juddered and bucked, threatening to tear itself apart. He rubbed his shoulder that screamed in agony from where he'd nearly dislocated it holding onto Ash.

The lifeboat pitched sideways, throwing them against each other and the seats. Through one of the small viewports, Bache watched as the ground rushed up to meet them – a patchwork of mining scars and industrial waste. The altimeter spun downward at a sickening rate, as the noise from the antigrav grew to fever pitch.

'Thirty seconds,' Clunk shouted over the roar. 'This could be a hard one…brace for impact.'

Bache just managed to get his back tight against a seat when the lifeboat slammed into the planet's surface. The impact drove the breath from his lungs and sent pain lancing through his already battered body. Metal screeched against rock as they skidded across the barren landscape before finally grinding to a halt.

For several seconds, no one moved. The sudden silence felt almost unnatural after the cacophony of their descent. Smoke curled from a damaged console, filling the cabin with an acrid stench.

'I'm getting sick of this shit,' Bache croaked, tasting blood in his mouth. He did a quick assessment of his injuries. Nothing seemed broken, though his entire body felt like one massive bruise.

Ash groaned nearby, pushing herself up from where she'd been thrown. A nasty gash on her forehead had painted half her face with blood, but her eyes seemed clear.

'Are we down?' she whispered, wincing as she turned to peer around.

Bache dragged himself to his feet, fighting a wave of dizziness. His shoulder throbbed mercilessly, but he forced himself to help Ash get up and together with the others, they managed to force open the circular airlock.

20

Unknown location, Krix'ir, Krix'ir system

THE SALTY, fishy air of Krix'ir hit Bache's lungs as the airlock door swung open with a protesting groan. His shoulder throbbed in time with his pulse, and he blinked dust from his eyes as he squinted at their surroundings. The majority of the surface of Krix'ir was a long-dried-up ocean bed.

They had crash-landed on the outskirts of what appeared to be a small mining settlement – old prefabricated structures hunched against the barren landscape like ancient weathered garden sheds.

'I can't believe we made it,' Ash whispered beside him, her voice hoarse.

Relief washed through Bache as he helped her down from the lifeboat. Jorven followed, his face streaked with grime and blood, while Clunk, the pilot and the navigator brought up the rear, limping but still managing grim smiles.

'Any landing you can walk away from,' Clunk muttered, surveying the crumpled nose of their lifeboat. 'Though I'd prefer not to do that again anytime soon.'

Bache took a shaky breath. They were alive. Somehow, against impossible odds, they had survived. He opened his mouth to suggest they seek help in the settlement when a familiar high-pitched whine cut through the air.

His blood ran cold as he looked up. A sleek white vessel descended towards them, its polished hull reflecting the harsh sunlight. It bore no markings, but Bache recognised the custom configuration immediately – Admiral Hollander's personal transport.

'It flared and landed facing them in a cloud of the grey dust that covered everything.

'Do we run?' Jorven asked.

'Where to?' Clunk answered, waving an arm at their barren surroundings.

The whine of the shuttle's engines died as a dozen soldiers in black combat armour jumped down from the vessel, forming a tight circle around them with weapons raised. Their faceplates reflected Bache's battered appearance back at him as they closed ranks, leaving no avenue for escape.

Bache's hand instinctively moved towards his side where his weapon should have been, finding only empty air. His shoulder throbbed with renewed intensity as the adrenaline that had carried him through the crash began to fade.

The shuttle's side airlock slid open with a pneumatic

hiss. Admiral Hollander emerged, resplendent in his dress whites despite the dusty surroundings. His silver hair caught the harsh sunlight as he descended the ramp with measured steps, a smile playing at the corners of his mouth that struggled to reach his cold eyes.

'Chief Engineer Loftt,' Hollander called out, his voice carrying easily across the distance between them. 'I must say, you've proven remarkably difficult to eliminate. First at Pyros Base, Hadset, then Pargoots, and now here.' He brushed an imaginary speck of dust from his immaculate sleeve. 'But persistence has always been one of your more annoying qualities. When those lovely new defence batteries opened fire, I gave you about a five percent chance of making it to the surface alive. But let's just say, your quite surprising luck and stratospheric rise through the ranks stops now, as it seems you've become surplus to requirements.'

Bache's mind raced, cataloguing their limited options. Six injured people against twelve armed soldiers and whatever personnel remained on the shuttle. The odds were catastrophically bad.

Bache's shoulder throbbed as he straightened to his full height.

'You knew we were coming.'

'Of course I knew.' Hollander laughed, the sound devoid of any real humour. 'Did you really think these old destroyers wouldn't have fail-safes in place? The moment you accessed the ship's systems, I was alerted.' He gestured to the armed soldiers who had formed a perfect circle around them. 'I must say, your little charade was quite entertaining to watch unfold and you gave me the perfect opportunity to dispose of the evidence of the *K2*'s demise.'

Bache felt Clunk tense beside him, ready to launch into some ill-advised heroics. He placed a restraining hand on his friend's arm, wincing as he forgot about his injured shoulder again.

'Ah, now there's the thing, Hollander,' Bache said, shaking his head, trying to keep his voice steady despite the fury building in his chest.

'It's Admiral to you, you insolent shit,' Hollander screamed, the half-smile and his calm persona vanishing in a split second.

'Oh dear, they were right…you really are mentally deranged,' said Bache, taking a big chance.

'You ordered the murder of four hundred innocent people on Hadset,' Jorven joined in, snarling at the man, his body tensing with anger. 'Some of them were my fucking family.'

Bache stuck out an arm to stop Jorven doing anything stupid.

Hollander went red in the face and was about to say something when Bache beat him to it.

'Mr Hollander, you are under arrest for the murder of civilians on Hadset, the destruction of two vessels, one GDA civilian research ship and one Klatt military vessel and of course, the attempted murder of the forty-seven thousand crew of the *Katadromiko 2*.'

'What d'you mean, attempted?' he spat.

Bache ignored the question and continued.

'You are relieved of your rank, you will order you men

to stand down and await here for removal by a GDA security team. Is that quite clear?'

Hollander was opening and closing his hands into fists. Bache didn't think he could go any redder…but he did.

'Kill them,' he hissed. 'Kill them all.' Hollander and his crimson face of thunder turned and marched back towards his ship.

He didn't turn when the crackle of twelve laser bolts thudding through flesh broke the silence. He'd almost reached his shuttle when a voice called out again and he froze on the spot.

'You will also be charged with treason, plotting multiple counts of genocide and producing and operating an illegal weapon system.'

Hollander turned slowly, and his complexion went from bright red to white in a split second. All twelve of his security detail lay on the ground in various levels of dismemberment.

'I don't think I've ever seen a better example of low orbital marksmanship than that. How about you, Hollander?' said Bache, strolling over nonchalantly with his hands in his pockets.

Hollander's cocksure bravado had deserted him. His eyes flicked to his ship.

'I wouldn't if I were you,' said Clunk, following closely behind Bache.

Jorven suddenly arrived with one of the dead soldiers' weapons in his hands.

'You fucking murdering arse wipe, this is for my village and my family…'

Bache slapped the barrel upwards as he fired. The bolt

of white-hot energy sizzled through Hollander's perfectly coiffed hair and rebounding off his shuttle's front shields, causing his pilot to duck down out of sight.

Hollander backpedalled frantically towards his shuttle, his face contorting with rage and fear. 'You've made the biggest mistake of your miserable...'

As Bache took the weapon out of Jorven's hands, the thunderous roar of engines cut Hollander off mid-sentence. A massive shadow swept over them as a GDA marine gunship appeared seemingly from nowhere, descending through the dusty air with startling speed. Its matte-black hull blocked out the sun as it hovered directly above Hollander's shuttle, weapon systems tracking and locking onto the smaller vessel.

The marine gunship's side doors slid open before it had even come to a full stop. Two dozen marines in full combat gear rappelled down on lines, hitting the ground in perfect formation. They fanned out with military precision, weapons raised and ready.

'Admiral Hollander,' boomed an amplified voice from the gunship. 'By order of President Xutan, you are under arrest for treason against the GDA.'

Bache's mouth curled into a grin as he recognised the voice. Commander Riccs. He glanced at Clunk and laughed despite the pain in his shoulder.

Hollander's face twisted with disbelief. 'This is outrageous. I am the chairman of the Naval Finance Committee. You have no authority...'

'Secure the prisoner,' Riccs ordered, his voice cold and efficient.

Four marines moved forward, restraining Hollander

despite his flailing resistance. He screamed and thrashed as they secured his wrists behind his back, his pristine white uniform now stained with Krix'ir's omnipresent grey dust.

'I DEMAND TO SPEAK TO XUTAN,' he screamed, spittle flying from his mouth. 'YOU HAVE NO IDEA WHO YOU'RE DEALING WITH.'

Riccs's amplified voice cut through Hollander's tirade. 'Take him to the gunship. Secure and sedate him if necessary.'

As the marines dragged the still-protesting admiral away, Bache turned his attention to Hollander's shuttle. It sat gleaming in the dull grey landscape, its pristine white hull already gathering dust from Krixir's perpetually dry atmosphere.

'That's our ticket back to the *K2*,' he said, nodding towards the vessel. 'We must secure it. It'll have navigation records, communication logs…evidence that could lead us to the rest of his network.'

Clunk followed his gaze. 'Fancy ride. Bet it has actual food on board too and perhaps a nice bottle of wine.'

Bache's stomach rumbled at the mention of food. He couldn't remember when they'd last eaten properly.

'Let's find out.'

They approached the shuttle cautiously, aware that Hollander's pilot was still inside.

'GDA Security,' Bache called out, raising his borrowed weapon. 'Exit the vessel with your hands visible.'

A moment later, the side airlock hissed open again and a nervous-looking young man in a flight uniform stepped out, hands trembling above his head.

'Don't shoot, I'm just the pilot,' he stammered. 'I had no idea what the admiral was involved in, I swear.'

Riccs approached them from the gunship, his eyes quickly assessing their battered condition. 'You all look like shit.'

'Feels worse than it looks,' Bache grinned, then winced as he tried to rotate his injured shoulder. 'How did you find us so quickly?'

'One of the *K2*'s arrays tracked your lifeboat's emergency beacon,' Riccs replied. 'Mr Whippy's on his way with a medical team. He figured you might need some treatment after your little atmospheric adventure.'

Bache watched as the marines finally bundled Hollander onto the gunship, the man's furious protests growing increasingly desperate. He exchanged a glance with Clunk, both of them sharing a moment of pure relief. After everything they'd been through, seeing Hollander in restraints felt like validation.

21

VIP Shuttle, unknown location, Krix'ir, Krix'ir system

Riccs tapped his wrist unit. 'The captain will be here in approximately twenty minutes. Try not to get into any more trouble until then, he's a bit pissed.'

Bache nodded, wincing as pain flared through his shoulder again.

'No promises,' he quipped.

As Riccs returned to the gunship, Bache turned towards the shuttle. The sleek vessel beckoned with the promise of comfort after their harrowing escape. He exchanged a meaningful look with Clunk and waved for the others to follow.

'Might as well check out the ex-admiral's accommodations while we wait,' Bache said, heading up the ramp with the other five following close behind.

The interior of the shuttle was opulent beyond anything

Bache had expected. Plush cream leather seats lined the walls, and polished wood panelling gleamed under soft recessed lighting. The air smelled clean and faintly perfumed – a stark contrast to outside and the acrid smoke and dust that clung to their clothes and skin.

'Well, well,' Clunk whistled, running his hand along a marble-topped bar stocked with crystal decanters. 'The Naval Finance Committee clearly pays better than I thought.'

Bache's stomach growled loudly as he spotted a refrigerated compartment behind the bar. He pulled it open to reveal platters of carefully arranged delicacies – thinly sliced meats, exotic fruits, and small pastries that looked fresh enough to have been prepared that morning.

'Anyone hungry? Hollander was planning to eat well after watching us die,' Bache muttered, grabbing a plate and loading it with food. His body ached everywhere, his shoulder throbbed mercilessly, but his hunger overrode the pain.

Ash appeared behind him, her face still streaked with dried blood. 'Is that…real meat?' she asked, eyes widening at the spread.

'Help yourself,' Bache said, passing her a plate. 'Seems only fair we enjoy the hospitality of our would-be executioner.'

Jorven joined them, his earlier rage temporarily subdued. He found a bottle of Chaixion wine, the deep purple liquid catching the light as he held it up. 'Vintage 11231,' he said. 'That's six years old…was that a good year?'

'I don't care,' said Clunk. 'That stuffs a month's wages a bottle…crack it open.'

Bache was halfway through a particularly delicate pastry when the floor beneath them shuddered slightly. Through the viewport, he watched as a GDA shuttle settled onto the dusty surface with considerably less grace than he would have expected from navy pilots. The shuttle's landing struts compressed unevenly, causing the vessel to tilt slightly to one side.

'That'll be the captain,' Clunk said, hastily wiping crumbs from his beard. 'Better look busy.'

Bache swallowed his mouthful and made a half-hearted attempt to straighten his battered uniform. His shoulder protested every movement, and he could feel dried blood caking the side of his face, but the food and wine had done wonders for his spirits.

The shuttle's side airlock cycled open, and Captain Whipper emerged, his face set in a thunderous scowl. Behind him trailed a medical team carrying equipment cases. The captain's eyes swept the scene – the downed soldiers, the crashed lifeboat, and finally settled on Hollander's shuttle where Bache and the others stood framed in the doorway.

Whipper strode towards them, each footfall kicking up small clouds of grey dust. 'Do any of you have the slightest idea how much fucking paperwork you've generated?' he bellowed as he approached. 'You destroyed the destroyer, that was a huge lump of bloody evidence you've just fucked up.'

'Sir, we were just…'

'Save it, Loftt,' Whipper hissed, nostrils flaring as he

pushed his way onto the ship. 'You're supposed to be my chief engineer, not some reckless cadet playing at espionage. You nearly got yourself and five others killed and now you're drinking on duty,' he added, noticing the wine glasses.

Clunk cleared his throat.

'Technically, sir, we're all currently off duty due to injuries sustained in the line of…'

'Shut it, L'Clers,' Whipper growled, but his eyes had already drifted to the open bottle on the marble counter. He stepped closer, squinting at the label.

'Is that…Chaixion 11231?' he asked. his tone mellowing suddenly. He turned to Bache. 'Where's my bloody glass then?'

Whipper drained his glass of the Chaixion in one impressive gulp and set it down on the marble counter. His scowl had softened slightly, but his eyes remained sharp as he surveyed the battered crew.

Riccs appeared in the doorway, his imposing frame nearly filling it.

'Captain, my team has located the weapons. They're mobile units, sir. Apparently only installed a few hours before we arrived.'

'Hollander's order?' Whipper asked.

'Confirmed, sir. Transport logs show they were rushed here overnight from a private military storage facility. The installation crew is still on site and were in the process of removing them again.'

Bache raised an eyebrow.

'So he planned the exact time for us to arrive,' Bache

muttered. 'He's been tracking our progress the whole time.'

'And conveniently scheduled his symposium speech to coincide with our destruction,' Whipper added. 'Perfect alibi. I was giving a speech when that secret supposedly scrapped destroyer attacked.'

'It was the perfect way to get rid of the evidence of the *K2* attack and put the blame on me. The only thing he didn't know was the *K2* hadn't been destroyed,' said Bache.

The *K2* seemed almost eerily quiet as Bache made his way through the familiar corridors. His shoulder still throbbed despite the medical team's best efforts, and exhaustion weighed on him like a physical presence. But curiosity drove him forward.

'You're going to want to see this,' Captain Whipper had told him just moments ago, his expression uncharacteristically troubled. 'Both of them are singing like birds, but their stories don't align.'

Bache stepped into the observation room adjacent to the high-security interrogation chamber. Through the one-way glass, he could see Hollander slumped in a chair, his pristine white uniform now rumpled and stained. The admiral's face was haggard, his earlier bluster completely deflated.

Commander Riccs stood beside Bache, arms crossed over his broad chest.

'He cracked up faster than I expected,' Riccs said, his

voice low. 'Started rambling about "the voices" almost immediately.'

'Voices?' Bache asked, leaning closer to the window.

'Claims the Nkris have been communicating with him for years. Says they promised him control of the entire sector once their "cleansing" was complete.'

Bache watched as Hollander suddenly sat upright, eyes darting around the room as if tracking invisible presences. The admiral's lips moved in silent conversation with entities only he could perceive.

'Could he be conversing with an outside party?' Bache asked.

'These rooms are completely electronically sealed,' Riccs replied.

'So Hollander's got imaginary friends. What about Kast?'

'Kast seems to be more forthcoming,' Riccs said, nodding towards the adjacent interrogation room where the former destroyer captain sat opposite Commander Shrell.

Unlike Hollander, Kast was maintaining her composure, answering questions with measured precision. Her calm demeanour made the content of her revelations all the more disturbing.

'The Originators have been planning this for decades,' Kast's voice came through the speakers, clear and unwavering. 'The genetic targeting system isn't just aimed at Gatas or Klatt. It's designed to be modifiable for any species...including specific human genetic markers.'

Bache felt his blood run cold. He exchanged a look with Riccs. He had suspected something like this, but hearing it stated so plainly sent a chill down his spine.

'They're planning to purge selected human populations too?' he asked, his voice barely above a whisper.

'The "undesirables", as she puts it,' Riccs confirmed grimly. 'Anyone with genetic markers they've deemed inferior. It would have been a two-phase operation. First, eliminate all non-human species from contested systems, then begin the "human purification" phase.'

Bache stared at the woman in the interrogation room, trying to reconcile her calm demeanour with the monstrous plan she was describing. His shoulder throbbed with renewed intensity as tension built in his muscles.

'Does she know who the other Originators are?'

'She's given us three names so far. Two high-ranking naval officers and a cabinet minister. President Xutan has already ordered their quiet detention.' Riccs's normally impassive face showed a flicker of disgust. 'But she insists there are others she's never met…people who communicated only through encrypted channels.'

The door to the observation room slid open, and Captain Whipper entered, his expression grim.

'The president wants to speak with you,' he said to Bache. 'Immediately.'

Bache nodded, straightening despite his fatigue. 'What about my father? Have there been any developments?'

'That's what he wants to talk to you about. Use my office.'

22

Captain's office, *Katadromiko 2*, orbiting Krix'ir, Krix'ir system

BACHE MADE his way to the captain's bridge office, each step reminding him of the battering his body had taken. The bridge seemed bigger than usual, his muscles protesting with every movement. By the time he reached the door, his shirt was sticking to his back with sweat.

The office door slid open with a soft hiss. He stepped inside, immediately noting the familiar smell of Whipper's preferred Serisian coffee – bitter and slightly metallic. The captain's personal terminal sat ready on the desk, its screen glowing with the GDA seal.

He lowered himself gingerly into the chair, wincing as his shoulder throbbed in protest. He tapped the secure comm icon and found the interactive message, his fingers leaving smudges on the glossy surface. After a moment, the screen flickered and President Xutan's weathered face appeared, lines of exhaustion etched deeply around his eyes.

'Chief Engineer Loftt,' Xutan said, his voice carrying that distinctive gravelly quality that countless public addresses had made familiar throughout GDA space. 'It seems you have a talent for uncovering conspiracies.'

'Not by choice, Mr President,' Bache replied, trying to straighten his posture despite the pain. 'I'd much prefer a quiet life maintaining starship drives.'

A ghost of a smile crossed Xutan's face.

'Nevertheless, you've done the GDA an immeasurable service. The scope of this plot – it's beyond anything we could have imagined. Your "job" seems to regularly include uncovering galaxy-wide conspiracies and preventing mass genocide. Perhaps we should adjust your job description accordingly.'

Bache felt heat rise in his face. 'Sir, about my father…'

Xutan's expression softened. 'He was released from custody. All charges have been dropped, effective immediately.'

He paused, his expression darkening again.

'That's why I wanted to speak with you directly. The security detail I sent to Deelatayne found his residence empty. There were signs of a struggle.'

The words hit Bache like a physical blow. He gripped the seat arms, his knuckles turning white and his shoulder screaming in protest.

'Your father is a huge asset to the GDA, as well as a

personal friend. Which is why I've authorised Captain Whipper to utilise his ship and its resources to find him.'

Bache listened, but was unable to say anything as the president continued.

'The captain, quite rightly, has misgivings about you being included in the investigation, not only because of your closeness to your father, but he feels you might, because of the situation, take unnecessary risks and jeopardise not only your own safety, but that of the ship and crew.'

'That will not be the case, Mr President,' Bache managed.

'That's what I thought,' said Xutan. 'I was on your side. Therefore, the captain and I have agreed to a compromise. Commander Riccs will lead the investigation, you and Specialist Mye will report to him and every decision any of you make has to go through Captain Whipper first…is that clear, Chief Engineer?'

'Crystal, Mr President and just one other thing.'

Bache could sense Whipper glowering at him.

'Did you authorise a Commander Shrell to provide military backup for us on Serris Adelaine?'

'No, Chief Engineer…she wasn't sent by me.'

Two hours later the *K2* was on its way to Deelatayne. Bache stood staring at the mini-holomap in his quarters, watching the stars as the massive ship moved at full power through normal space, preparing for its next jump. His shoulder throbbed despite the medical team's best efforts, a constant reminder of how close they'd all come to death.

He reached up to the holomap, pretending to touch each star in turn. His father was out there somewhere. The thought of him being taken – most likely by the same people who'd orchestrated the entire conspiracy – made his stomach clench.

'Chief engineer to the bridge,' the comm system announced, breaking his daydream.

He made his way through the familiar corridors, nodding to crew members as he passed. The ship felt different somehow. News of the conspiracy and the ship's close call had spread quickly, and he could sense the anxiousness in the air, the sideways glances, the hushed conversations that stopped when he approached.

The bridge doors slid open with a soft hiss. Captain Whipper stood at the central holomap, his face illuminated by its blue glow as he studied what appeared to be a tactical overlay of the Deelatayne system. Commander Riccs loomed beside him, arms folded across his broad chest. Zaphir was there too, standing slightly apart, her dark eyes meeting Bache's as he entered.

'Ah, Loftt,' Whipper said without looking up. 'Good timing. We've just received an update from the Deelatayne planetary police.'

'What did they find?' Bache asked, his throat tightening as he approached the holomap. The blue glow illuminated the faces of everyone gathered around it, casting harsh shadows that made them all look more severe.

'Quite a lot I'm afraid,' Whipper replied, his mouth set

in a grim line. 'They've secured your father's house and conducted a preliminary forensic sweep. Blood traces confirmed – human, male, O-negative. Analysis confirms it's your father's, but the quantity suggests injury rather than…' he trailed off, glancing at Bache.

'Rather than something worse,' Bache finished for him, his voice quiet.

Zaphir moved to stand beside Bache, close enough that he could feel her presence without her actually touching him. The subtle support steadied him. Bache sighed and pursed his lips.

Riccs nodded, turned back to the console and tapped an icon, a series of images appeared in the air above them. Bache recognised his father's living space immediately – the cluttered workbench where he'd tinkered with projects since Bache was a child, the old-fashioned physical books lining the walls, the worn chair by the window where he'd spend hours tapping away on his tablet.

'Signs of a struggle here and there,' Riccs said, high-lighting sections of the room. Overturned furniture, scattered papers, and the dark stain on the floor that made Bache's stomach lurch.

'There's a bit more,' Whipper continued, manipulating the holomap to zoom in on a residential district of Deelatayne's capital. 'The police found this.'

The image shifted to show a small metallic object, roughly cylindrical and no larger than a thumb.

'What am I looking at?' Bache asked, leaning forward.

'It's a Nkris communication device,' Riccs said. 'Or at least, that's what our preliminary analysis suggests.

Similar technology was found in Hollander's personal quarters.'

Bache's mind raced. 'The Nkris are actually involved? I thought Hollander was just delusional.'

'That's what we all thought,' said Riccs. 'And finally, there's this. Security footage from a neighbouring residence caught this.'

The image shifted to grainy surveillance footage. Three figures in unmarked combat gear half dragging, half carrying a fourth person between them. Even with the poor quality, Bache recognised his father's lanky frame immediately.

'Timestamp?' he asked.

'Two days ago,' Whipper said. 'Right after the president ordered his release.'

Bache's jaw tightened as he stared at the frozen image of his father being dragged away.

'They knew,' he muttered. 'They knew we were getting close, so they took him as insurance.'

Riccs nodded grimly.

'That's our assessment as well. Whoever's behind this, they're well-connected enough to know about your father's release almost immediately.'

Bache swallowed hard, his eyes fixed on the grainy image of his father. The knowledge that Tirexion had been fighting back eased the knot in his chest slightly. His father was nothing if not resourceful.

'Have we identified the abductors?' Bache asked, his voice steadier than he felt.

Riccs shook his head.

'Faces obscured, no identifying marks on their gear.

Professional job. But…' he manipulated the image, zooming in on a small detail at the edge of the frame, '… their transport had a partial registration visible. Deelatayne authorities traced it to a rental agency near the spaceport.'

'Let me guess,' Bache said, 'rented with falsified credentials.'

'Surprisingly, no,' Whipper cut in. 'That's where it gets interesting. The vehicle was checked out by an employee of Daxicorp.'

Bache's eyebrows shot up. 'Daxicorp again? The same corporation that tried to intercept us at Pargoots?'

'The very same,' Whipper confirmed. 'And there's a little more. The Daxicorp employee who rented the vehicle was found dead in his apartment yesterday. Apparent suicide, though Deelatayne authorities are treating it as suspicious.'

'Bloody right they should,' said Bache, rubbing his chin in thought. 'Do we have any leads on where they might have taken him?' he continued, forcing his voice to remain steady despite the fear churning in his gut.

'Nothing concrete yet,' Whipper replied. 'But we've identified the vehicle they used to transport him.' He tapped another control, and the holomap shifted to show a sleek black shuttle lifting off from a secluded landing pad on the outskirts of the city. 'It's registered to a shell corporation that we've linked to one of the companies Hollander used to funnel funds to Pyros Base.'

'The shuttle's drive signature?' Bache asked, his engineering mind automatically seeking the most reliable tracking method.

'Masked,' Riccs answered. 'But not perfectly. Our

analysts are working on isolating the unique harmonic pattern. Every drive has one, no matter how well disguised.'

Zaphir stepped closer to the holomap.

'What about his contacts?'

'My father had some associates on the Theo home world,' Bache replied, his mind racing through possibilities. 'Scientists mostly. People who shared his scepticism about certain GDA technologies.'

'The Theos?' Whipper's eyebrows shot up. 'They keep themselves to themselves. Getting information from them is nearly impossible.'

'Not for my father,' Bache insisted. 'He maintained relationships with them for decades. After the *K2* incident, he became even more convinced certain GDA technologies had been compromised.'

Riccs leaned forward. 'You believe your father might have reached out to them about the Nkris infiltration?'

'I think it's a definite possibility,' Bache said. 'If he suspected what was happening, he would have sought allies outside the GDA command structure.'

Whipper stroked his chin thoughtfully.

'The Theos have always been wary of Nkris technology. They refused to incorporate any of it into their systems, even when the benefits seemed obvious.'

'Maybe they knew something we didn't,' Zaphir suggested.

Bache nodded, feeling a glimmer of hope for the first time since hearing of his father's abduction. 'There was one Theo scientist in particular – Sarhaan Pell. He and my father corresponded regularly. If anyone would know where my father might have gone for help, it would be her.'

'It sounds like a visit to Paradeisos after Deelatayne is a good bet,' said Whipper, crossing his arms and reclining back in the big chair. 'Get some rest, all of you…busy day tomorrow.'

23

Chief engineer's cabin, *Katadromiko 2*, orbiting
Deelatayne, Tyraan system

BACHE WOKE BEFORE HIS ALARM, the pain in his shoulder a dull throb that medication had reduced but not eliminated. Sleep had been fitful at best, his dreams filled with fragmented images of his father being dragged away. He dressed quickly and headed for the shuttle bay where Commander Riccs would be waiting.

The massive marine was already there when Bache arrived, checking equipment with methodical precision. Riccs acknowledged him with a curt nod, his expression betraying nothing of his thoughts.

'Ready to go, Chief Engineer?'

'As I'll ever be,' Bache replied, trying to keep his voice steady despite the anxiety churning in his gut. The thought of seeing his old home after the attack made his stomach tighten.

The shuttle's interior was stark and utilitarian, designed for efficiency rather than comfort. As they boarded, Bache noticed the small security team already strapped in – four marines in light combat gear, their expressions professionally neutral. Riccs had clearly selected them personally.

'The local authorities have secured the area,' Riccs said as they strapped in, the shuttle's engines already spooling up. 'But I'm not taking chances,' he added, jabbing a thumb at the other four.

Bache nodded, grateful for the commander's thoroughness. The descent through Deelatayne's atmosphere was a little bumpy as always, the shuttle's pilot navigating the early morning thermals with a reassuring nonchalance. Through the screen, Bache watched as the capital city of Tyraan came into view, its random higgledy-piggledy layout in contrast to most other cities on the planet.

His old home was right out on the western fringe, bordering the huge expanse of the Jaan desert and he directed the pilot to the correct remote residence.

'Your father liked his privacy,' said Riccs, as the ship settled in a dust cloud facing absolutely nothing.

'He didn't like being disturbed after my mother was killed,' Bache said, releasing his belts and moving towards the airlock.

Riccs sat where he was for a moment, seemingly taking that bit of information on board.

Bache felt a strange sense of gratitude that Riccs didn't push for more details about his mother. The commander seemed to understand some wounds were best left undisturbed.

'Let's move,' Riccs ordered, standing and gesturing to his team. 'Standard search formation. Keep comms open.'

The marines filed out first, weapons ready but not raised, scanning the perimeter with seasoned efficiency. Bache followed, the familiar dry heat of Deelatayne's climate hitting him like a physical wall as he stepped from the shuttle. The air smelt of dust and the faint tang of the resilient native vegetation that somehow managed to survive even here at the edge of the desert.

His father's house stood exactly as it had for decades, a low, sprawling structure of local stone designed to remain cool even in the harshest summer heat. Its simple lines blended with the landscape, making it seem like a natural extension of the desert itself rather than an imposition upon it.

But now a yellow security beam glowed, circling the house, marking it as a crime scene.

Bache swallowed hard, his throat suddenly dry. It wasn't just the heat. This place had been his refuge during his school and academy years, a sanctuary where he and his father had spent countless hours discussing engineering principles or simply sitting in companionable silence watching desert sunsets.

'Your childhood home?' Riccs asked, coming alongside him.

'No,' Bache replied, his voice rougher than he intended. 'My father bought this after she died.'

'I understand,' Riccs replied, his voice softening slightly. 'Let's go in.'

The local police officer deactivated the perimeter beam with a quick scan of his credentials. Bache hesitated at the threshold, steeling himself before stepping inside.

The door creaked as Riccs pushed it open, revealing the interior Bache had known so well. Now it felt like a stranger's home. Furniture overturned, data pads shattered, and his father's prized collection of physical books scattered across the floor, their spines broken as if someone had deliberately destroyed them in anger rather than during a struggle.

'Looks like they were searching for something specific,' Riccs observed, carefully stepping around a broken chair. 'This wasn't just a kidnapping. They wanted information.'

Bache's gaze fixed on the dark stain on the floor – his father's blood. He swallowed hard, trying to maintain his professional demeanour even as his stomach churned.

His father's meticulous organisation had been violated, possessions scattered across the floor in chaotic disarray. The familiar scent of machine oil and his father's preferred Klattian tea was now tainted with the metallic tang of dried blood.

'Damage marks on the walls and overturned furniture indicate he was conscious and fought back,' Riccs said.

Bache nodded, unable to speak for a moment. He moved to his father's workbench, fingers hovering over the scattered tools and components. Everything had been rifled through, drawers yanked open, contents dumped unceremoniously.

'You're right…they were definitely looking for something,' he said finally, his voice steadier than he felt. 'My father was organised to the point of obsession. He could find any component or data chip blindfolded.'

Riccs gestured to his team, who spread out through the house, examining each room with methodical precision. Bache's attention was drawn back to the workbench. Unlike the rest of the house, this area seemed to have received special attention from the intruders. The console had been completely disassembled, components scattered across the floor, some of them crushed underfoot.

'If nothing else, they were thorough,' Bache muttered, kneeling to examine the wreckage. His fingers brushed over the shattered remains of his father's personal tablet. The memory core had been physically removed, not just wiped. 'Whatever they were looking for, they didn't want to leave any trace of it behind.'

He moved to the bookshelf where his father had kept his most treasured possessions. The physical books – increasingly rare in an age of digital information – had been pulled down and many lay with broken spines. But something caught Bache's eye. One shelf remained relatively undisturbed, as if the searchers had overlooked it or considered it unimportant.

'Commander,' Bache called, his voice low. 'This doesn't make sense.'

Riccs moved to his side, his massive frame casting a shadow over the bookcase.

'In what way?'

Bache reached for a small piece of wood tucked between two ancient engineering texts. It was simple, unadorned, easily overlooked...and appeared to be a simple shelf divider, exactly as it was probably intended.

'This shouldn't be here,' Bache said, turning the box over in his hands. He ran his fingers along its edge, feeling for the hidden catch his father had shown him years ago. There was a soft click, and the divider sprang open a fraction of an inch.

Inside lay a single data chip, unlike any standard GDA issue. Its casing glinted with an iridescent sheen that seemed to shift colours as Bache tilted it in the light.

'It's Theo,' he said.

Riccs leaned closer, his expression betraying nothing.

'You're sure?'

'Positive. As I said before, my father had contacts among their scientific community, but even he shouldn't have had access to their proprietary data storage.' Bache carefully lifted the chip, feeling its surprising weight. 'They must definitely have given this to him for a reason.'

'Could it contain information about what he was working on?' Riccs asked.

'Almost certainly.' Bache thought about the possibilities. 'But we can't access it conventionally. Theo chips are biometrically locked to their intended user.'

Riccs grunted, his expression thoughtful.

'So we need your father to unlock it?'

'Or a Theo with the right access codes. This confirms we need to speak with Sarhaan Pell on Paradeisos.'

He slipped it into his pocket, not quite ready to hand it over even to Riccs. The commander seemed to understand, giving him a slight nod before turning to examine the rest of the shelf.

'Sir, over here,' one of the marines called from the hallway. 'You need to see this.'

They followed the voice to his father's bedroom. The marine stood by the bed, pointing to what appeared to be a perfectly ordinary section of wall. 'Thermal scan shows a small rectangular void behind this wall.'

Riccs ran his hand over the surface.

'No visible seam.'

'There wouldn't be,' said Bache, pushing past the marine.

He knelt down and pressed his palm against the smooth section of wall. He felt for the hidden pressure point his father had shown him years ago, applying gentle pressure in a pattern – three short taps followed by two longer ones. The wall responded with a soft click, and a small panel slid open.

'How did you know to do that?' Riccs asked.

'My father showed me when I was twelve. Said I should always know where the emergency supplies were kept.' Bache reached into the revealed compartment and withdrew a small metallic case.

He opened it carefully. Inside lay a second data chip – this one standard GDA issue – along with a small hand-written note on actual paper. His father's neat, precise handwriting brought a lump to his throat.

"Bache…if you're reading this, I've either trusted you with this information or something has happened to me. Hopefully you have the Theo chip too and you know who you have to speak to about that. Daxicorp isn't what it seems. It's a cover for Project Cleansing. Trust no one in the GDA except Xutan and Whipper.'

Bache handed the note to Riccs, who read it quickly, his expression darkening.

'Your father knew they would come for him,' Riccs said, folding the note carefully and returning it to Bache.

'He always planned for contingencies.' Bache tucked both chips securely in a breast pocket. 'We need to get back to the *K2*,' he said.

24

———————

Captain's office, *Katadromiko 2*, orbiting Deelatayne,
Tyraan system

ONCE BACK ON THE *K2*, Bache found himself in the secure
operations room with Whipper and Riccs. His father's
GDA chip sat in a reader at the centre of the holotable, its
small indicator light pulsing with a steady green rhythm.

'Let's see what your old man was hiding,' Whipper
muttered, initiating the data extraction protocol.

The holotable illuminated, casting eerie blue shadows
across their faces as schematics began to form in the air
above them. Bache recognised the familiar outlines of a
standard Xephoni drive configuration – his father's
specialty – but something about it looked wrong.

'Wait, that's not right,' Bache said, leaning closer and
pointing out several conduit pathways. 'These standard
power conduits have been strangely modified, with addi-

tional pathways that are not necessary on the standard design. These don't seem to form any function.'

Riccs circled the table, his massive frame blocking part of the projection as he studied it from different angles. 'So, what *are* we looking at, Chief?'

'It's a modification to the standard Xephoni drive,' Bache replied, zooming in on one particular section. 'But these additional pathways…they don't serve any propulsion function I'm familiar with.'

'Could it be a weapons system?' Whipper suggested, his eyes narrowing as he studied the schematic.

Bache shook his head.

'No, the power requirements would be all wrong.' He manipulated the projection, rotating the display and studying the patterns from a different angle. 'It's almost like…wait a minute.'

He noticed something he'd missed before. When viewed from a certain perspective, the additional pathways formed a distinct pattern – one that reminded him of a device he remembered seeing in his father's notebook.

'I think these modifications create a resonance frequency,' Bache said, his voice dropping to almost a whisper. 'Dad always said the Xephoni drive had unusual harmonic properties. These alterations would amplify specific frequencies.'

'What would be the purpose?' Riccs asked, leaning forward to study the display more closely.

'Communication,' Bache replied, the realisation hitting him like a physical blow. 'But not with conventional systems.' He pointed to a section that seemed particularly intricate. 'These modifications would generate subspace frequencies outside our normal detection range.'

Whipper's expression darkened.

'You're saying these drive modifications create a covert communication system?'

'Not just any communication system,' Bache said, the pieces falling into place. 'One that would potentially communicate with Nkris technology without being detected by standard GDA monitoring systems.'

'Bloody hell,' Whipper muttered, straightening up. 'How many ships in the fleet have this version of the drive?'

Bache's stomach tightened as he scanned through the data. 'According to this, the modified design was implemented in all Katadromiko class vessels constructed in the last five years, plus seventeen destroyers and over a hundred smaller patrol craft.'

Whipper cursed under his breath, his face hardening as he absorbed the information.

'And the *K2*? Does it have this modification?'

Bache scrolled through the data, heart hammering in his chest. 'According to this…no. The *K2*'s drive was one of the original Xephoni configurations. It predates these modifications.'

Bache ran his hands through his hair, trying to process the implications. His father had discovered this and had been working on it in secret. No wonder they'd taken him.

'There's more data here,' he said, scrolling through the files. 'My father was developing a countermeasure…a way to detect and neutralise the communications without alerting whoever might be monitoring them.'

Riccs leaned over the display, his massive frame casting shadows across the holographic schematics.

'Was he successful?'

'Partially. He created a detection algorithm that could identify the subspace frequencies without triggering alerts.' Bache expanded another section of the schematic. 'But the neutralisation component was still experimental. He needed Theo technology to truly complete it.'

'Which explains the Theo chip,' Whipper muttered. 'It's what they were looking for.'

'And the reason they took him,' Bache added, his voice tight. 'He knew too much, and he was close to developing a countermeasure.'

The captain's comm unit chimed. He tapped it with an irritated flick of his finger.

'Captain, we've completed our analysis of the shuttle's drive signature,' came the voice of one of the *K2*'s array officers. 'We've identified a unique harmonic.'

'Do we know where it went?'

'We believe we have the trajectory,' the officer replied. 'They seem to have taken a series of jumps through the outer systems, but the harmonic pattern is just distinctive enough that we think they went to one of the private mining facilities in the Auriga Sector. Arriving approximately twenty-six hours ago.'

Bache leaned forward, immediately recognising the significance.

'The Auriga Sector? That's close to Klatt territory.'

'It gets better,' the officer continued. 'One of the facilities is registered to a subsidiary of Daxicorp called Nexus Extraction. According to public records, it's a low-yield thorium operation, but looking at their local power usage, it far exceeds what would be needed for that kind of operation.'

Whipper's jaw tightened.

'How far?'

'Eight jumps, sir. We can be there in under sixteen hours at maximum speed.'

'Don't forget we need to go to Paradeisos, Captain,' said Bache.

'I haven't,' Whipper said. 'We need to follow your father first. They're only a day ahead, they think this ship is destroyed and they don't know we have Hollander.'

'Set a course for Auriga,' Whipper ordered. 'And keep this information contained. Bridge crew and senior officers only.'

'Yes, sir.'

Bache felt a surge of hope mixed with dread. They had a location, but what would they find when they got there? His father could still be alive, or they could be heading into an elaborate trap.

'Remote enough to avoid scrutiny,' he said. 'But with enough traffic that another vessel wouldn't attract much attention. And close enough to non-GDA space to make a quick exit if needed,' Bache added, the tension making his shoulder ache again. His father was out there, possibly injured, definitely in danger. The thought made him feel quite nauseous.

Whipper nodded grimly.

'Right…no more speculation, let's wait until we get there.'

25

Chief engineer's cabin, *Katadromiko 2*, en route to Auriga

THE *K2* BARRELLED its way through space, its massive engines hurling the vessel up to its maximum speed. Bache sat in his quarters, staring at the Theo data chip in his palm. The iridescent casing caught the light, shifting from deep blue to violet as he turned it. His father had risked everything to hide this chip. Whatever information it contained must be critical.

A soft chime at his door broke his concentration.

'Come in,' he called, slipping the chip into his pocket.

Zaphir entered, her face drawn with concern.

'How's the arm?'

'Better,' he lied. It still throbbed with every heartbeat, but he'd grown accustomed to ignoring it. 'Any updates?'

She sat across from him, her dark eyes searching his

face. 'We'll reach Auriga in four hours. Riccs has assembled a strike team. Twenty marines and one of the new gunships.'

Bache nodded, trying to ignore the knot in his stomach. His father had been in the hands of these people for days now. The bloodstain on the floor of his home flashed in his memory.

'You should get some rest,' Zaphir said softly. 'You look exhausted.'

'I can't,' he admitted. 'Every time I close my eyes, I see him being dragged away.'

'We'll find him,' she said, her concern warming him and he closed his eyes.

He was dragged out of a deep sleep by an immediate attendance call from the bridge. Zaphir was gone and he realised he'd been asleep for nearly four hours. Splashing some cold water on his face, he quickly boarded a tube carriage for the bridge deck.

The room was bustling with activity when Bache arrived. The command crew hunched over their stations with an intensity that made the air feel thick with tension. Captain Whipper stood at the central holomap, his broad frame silhouetted against the pulsing blue glow as he studied what appeared to be a mining facility schematic.

'Ah, Chief Engineer,' Whipper said without looking up. 'Nice of you to join us.'

'Sorry, sir. I was...' Bache trailed off, not wanting to admit he'd fallen asleep.

'Doesn't matter. Come take a look at this.'

Bache stepped up to the holomap, the familiar ache in his shoulder flaring as he leaned forward. The display showed a sprawling industrial complex carved into the side of an asteroid. Multiple docking bays dotted the exterior, with a labyrinthine network of tunnels and chambers spreading throughout the rocky mass.

'Nexus Extraction's main facility,' Whipper explained, gesturing to the schematic. 'Supposedly mining thorium, but our scans show minimal activity of that nature.'

'Then, what are they actually doing in there?' Bache asked, studying the complex layout.

'That's what we're going to find out. Look here.' Whipper zoomed in on a section near the centre of the asteroid. 'High energy readings concentrated in this area. Far more than needed for any standard mining operations.'

Bache studied the station's layout, committing the key details to memory. The structure was bulky and industrial, all sharp angles and functional design with none of the aesthetic considerations that went into civilian stations. Four large docking arms extended from the central hub, one of them currently occupied by what appeared to be a mid-sized freighter.

'Any sign of the shuttle that took my father?' he asked, his voice tight.

'No,' Riccs answered from behind them. 'But there are shielded areas we can't see into. It may be hidden in one of those.'

Bache's pulse quickened as he noted the reinforcements around the central chamber. Triple-reinforced walls, security checkpoints at every access point.

'Whatever they're protecting in there, they don't want anyone getting near it,' Bache observed, studying the layout more carefully. 'Those security measures are military grade. Far beyond what you'd need for a mining operation.'

Commander Riccs joined them, his massive frame casting a shadow across the captain's raised dais.

'My team are ready, Captain. We've identified three potential insertion points.' He highlighted sections of the exterior. 'This maintenance airlock here has the least security coverage. We can deploy up to it in stealth mode and be inside before they know we're coming.'

Whipper nodded grimly.

'Good. We'll position the *K2* on the far side of the asteroid field to avoid any unwanted collisions. Your team will take the gunship in. Chief Engineer Loftt will accompany you.'

Bache's heart leapt at those words. Despite his injury, he couldn't imagine sitting on the *K2* while others went to rescue his father.

'Thank you, Captain,' he said, trying to keep his voice steady.

'Don't thank me yet,' Whipper replied, his eyes hard. 'You're going because you know your father's work better than anyone. If there's Nkris tech in there, I need someone who can recognise it. But you follow Riccs's orders to the letter. Is that understood?'

'Yes, sir.'

'Departure in thirty minutes. Dismissed.'

Bache suited up in the marines' ready room, wincing as

he slipped his injured arm through the sleeve of the light combat suit. The armour wasn't as heavy as the full battle rigs the marines wore, but it could deflect a standard laser blast if needed. His shoulder protested with each movement as he fastened the various clasps and seals.

'Need help with that?' Zaphir asked, appearing beside him. She was already fully geared up, her dark hair pulled back tightly, making her facial features look sharper in the harsh lighting.

'I'm fine,' he muttered, fumbling with a particularly stubborn fastener. Pride kept him from admitting how much his shoulder still hurt, but his fingers weren't cooperating.

Zaphir ignored his protest and stepped forward, efficiently securing the remaining fastenings.

'You should have let the medical team finish the bone fusion treatment,' she said quietly, her fingers working deftly.

'There wasn't time.' The thought of his father enduring who knew what while he lay in a medical bay was unbearable. 'Thanks,' he added, testing the mobility of the suit with a roll of his shoulders. Pain flared again, but it was manageable.

The ready room buzzed with activity as Riccs's marines performed final equipment checks. The atmosphere was tense but controlled, each member of the strike team moving with well-oiled efficiency. These weren't the standard security personnel who patrolled the *K2*'s corridors, these were Riccs's elite squad, veterans who had seen real combat.

Riccs himself stood at the front of the room, his massive frame appearing even larger in the black combat armour. His face was set in the stern expression Bache had come to recognise as his pre-mission focus.

'Listen up,' Riccs called, his voice cutting through the murmured conversations. 'This is not a standard extraction. We're dealing with an unknown number of hostiles with potentially advanced weapons. Our primary objective is to locate and secure Tirexion Loftt. Secondary objective is to gather intelligence on whatever operation they're running in that facility.'

He activated a holomap showing the mining station's layout.

'We'll insert here, at the maintenance airlock on the station's underside. Team Alpha will secure our exit point. Teams Beta and Gamma will move towards the central chamber where energy readings are highest. Chief Engineer Loftt and Specialist Mye will accompany me with Team Beta.'

Bache nodded. The facility's winding corridors and multiple access points would make navigation challenging, but also provided multiple escape routes if needed.

'Rules of engagement,' Riccs continued, his voice hardening. 'We expect resistance, but remember this is a GDA operation on GDA territory. Stun settings only unless you encounter lethal force. We need prisoners for interrogation.'

The marines nodded in unison.

'Questions?' Riccs asked.

When none came, he tapped his wrist unit.

'Bridge, this is Riccs. Ready for departure.'

The gunship lifted from the hangar floor with barely a shudder. On the small holomap above them, Bache watched as the gunship left the massive cruiser and the pilot negotiated his way carefully through the asteroid field.

26

———

Marine gunship, approaching a mining facility, Auriga
system

THE GUNSHIP MOVED SILENTLY, its stealth systems masking
its approach to the mining facility. Bache leaned forward
in his seat, eyes fixed on the tactical display. His muscles
tensed as they closed in on the target.

'Two minutes to insertion point,' the pilot announced,
his voice calm and measured. 'No signs of detection.'

Bache's gaze shifted to Riccs, who sat motionless
across from him, checking his weapon with methodical
precision. The commander's face betrayed nothing, but
Bache had worked with him long enough to recognise the
focused intensity in his eyes. This wasn't just another
mission for any of them.

'Remember,' Riccs said, addressing the strike team,
'our priority is locating Tirexion Loftt and securing any

evidence of Nkris technology. Maintain comm discipline and stay with your assigned teams.'

The gunship slowed as it approached the maintenance airlock, manoeuvring between jagged asteroid fragments with surprising agility for its size. Through the viewport, Bache could see the mining facility growing larger, a sprawling industrial complex grafted onto the side of a massive asteroid. Its dull metal surface was pockmarked with airlocks and docking ports, utilitarian and imposing against the blackness of space.

'Docking sequence initiated,' the pilot reported. 'Matching rotation.'

Bache felt the subtle shift through his seat as the gunship's artificial gravity adjusted to synchronise with the station's rotation. His shoulder throbbed with a fresh wave of pain, and he shifted in his seat, trying to find a more comfortable position. The combat suit felt heavier than it should, the fabric catching on his half-healed wounds.

'You good?' Zaphir asked quietly beside him.

'I'm fine,' he muttered, not meeting her eyes. The lie came easily, but he knew she wasn't fooled. Still, she didn't press the issue.

A soft thud reverberated through the hull as they made contact with the airlock. Red warning lights bathed the cabin in crimson as the atmosphere equalised between the two vessels.

'Seals confirmed,' the pilot announced. 'We're locked on.'

Riccs stood, towering over the seated marines.

'Team Alpha, secure the perimeter. Beta and Gamma, prep for entry.' He turned to Bache and Zaphir. 'Stay behind me at all times. If we encounter resistance, find cover and stay there. Clear?'

'Clear,' Bache replied, his mouth suddenly dry.

The airlock cycled open with a soft hiss, revealing a dimly lit maintenance tunnel beyond. Team Alpha moved swiftly through, weapons raised, checking corners and shadows with controlled efficiency. Bache followed with Team Beta, his own weapon drawn but held low. The corridor smelled of machine oil and recycled air, the metal flooring vibrating subtly beneath his boots.

Three intersections and two security doors later, they encountered their first resistance. Two guards in Daxicorp uniforms stepped from a side corridor, their expressions shifting from boredom to alarm as they spotted the strike team.

'Hey, you can't be…'

Riccs's weapon discharged with a soft whump, the stun bolt catching the first guard square in the chest. The second guard scrambled for his sidearm, but one of the marines dropped him before his fingers closed around the weapon.

'Secure them,' Riccs ordered, gesturing to two marines who quickly moved to bind the unconscious guards.

Bache glanced at the fallen men, noting the standard issue uniforms but with an unfamiliar insignia on their shoulders – a stylised black helix wrapped around what appeared to be a star.

'That's not a Daxicorp logo,' he whispered to Riccs, pointing to the emblem.

The commander nodded grimly. 'Bag one of those patches. The intelligence guys will want to see it.'

They continued deeper into the facility, the corridors growing wider as they approached the central chambers. The industrial aesthetic remained consistent – exposed pipes running along ceilings, harsh lighting casting sharp shadows, and occasional warning signs indicating high-energy areas ahead.

Bache's arm throbbed with each step, but the adrenaline coursing through him dulled the worst of it. His mind raced with possibilities of what they might find. Was his father still alive? What were they doing to him

They reached a junction where the corridor split in three directions. Riccs consulted his tactical display, then signalled Team Gamma to take the left path while Beta would continue straight ahead.

'Energy readings are strongest down this way,' he said, pointing forward. 'If they're holding your father, it's likely near whatever they're powering.'

Bache nodded, his throat tight. The closer they got to the central chamber, the more his anxiety built. His fingers tightened around his weapon, the grip slick with sweat beneath his gloves.

They reached the reinforced door, and Bache immediately recognised the security panel beside it as a standard military unit...far beyond what a mining operation would use.

'Can you bypass it?' Riccs asked, positioning his marines to cover both approaches to their position.

Bache nodded, already pulling his tablet from his belt pouch. He pried off the panel cover, revealing a complex array of circuits beneath. He connected the tablet to the access port with a thin cable. His fingers worked quickly despite the pain in his shoulder, bridging connections and rerouting power.

'Hurry,' Zaphir urged, her eyes fixed on the corridor behind them.

The panel beeped, and the massive door began to slide open with a hydraulic hiss. Riccs moved through first, weapon raised, with Team Beta fanning out behind him.

The chamber beyond stole Bache's breath. It was vast, easily thirty metres across, its ceiling lost in shadow overhead. But it wasn't the size that shocked him…it was what the chamber contained.

In the centre stood a massive crystalline structure, pulsing with an eerie green light that cast shifting shadows across the walls. The apparatus towered nearly to the ceiling, its surface etched with intricate patterns that seemed to move when viewed from the corner of the eye. Surrounding it were dozens of workstations, each occupied by technicians in white lab coats who hadn't yet registered the intruders.

'Holy ancients,' Bache whispered, recognising the technology immediately. 'That's Nkris design.'

The structure resembled nothing in standard GDA technology. Its crystalline components were arranged in geometric patterns that defied conventional engineering principles. The pulsing light emanating from it made Bache's skin crawl with an instinctive revulsion.

'What is it?' Riccs asked, his voice low as he signalled his team to secure the perimeter.

'Some kind of resonance amplifier,' Bache replied, his eyes tracing the familiar yet alien configuration. 'Similar to what we found in the modified Xephoni drives, but…

massive. This could broadcast to every modified ship in the galaxy.'

A technician finally noticed them and shouted an alarm. Chaos erupted as lab workers scattered, diving beneath workstations or fleeing towards emergency exits. Riccs's team moved with smooth efficiency, stunning those who resisted and securing the others.

Bache scanned the room frantically, searching for any sign of his father. His heart hammered against his ribs as his eyes darted from face to face. Then he spotted a sealed chamber at the far end of the room, its walls transparent. Inside, slumped in a chair and surrounded by monitoring equipment, sat a thin figure with familiar features.

'There he is,' Bache shouted, already moving before Riccs could stop him. 'That's him.'

Pain lanced through his shoulder as he sprinted across the chamber, dodging between workstations and stunned technicians. His boots echoed on the metal flooring, each impact sending jolts of agony up his arm, but he pushed on through it, focused only on reaching the transparent enclosure.

Tirexion Loftt sat strapped to what looked like a medical chair, his head lolling forward. Something was attached to his temples, and intravenous lines ran from his arms to machines humming beside him. His normally vibrant face was ashen, cheekbones prominent against skin that seemed stretched too tight.

Bache skidded to a halt at the sealed door, frantically searching for the release mechanism. 'Dad,' he shouted, pounding on the transparent material. 'Dad, can you hear me?'

His father's head lifted slightly, eyes unfocused and glazed. There was no recognition in his gaze, just a vacant stare that chilled Bache to the bone.

'Stand back,' Zaphir ordered, arriving beside him with a heavy chair.

She proceeded to hurl it at the enclosure's door, but it just flexed the transparent door and bounced back at their feet.

'Shit,' said Zaphir, as Riccs went past them both and melted the door's hinges with his laser rifle.

Bache dived inside as the door fell with a crash, dropping to his knees beside his father's chair. Tirexion Loftt's head was down on the console, his eyes closed, face pale and drawn. A nasty gash on his temple had been poorly bandaged, the dressing stained with dried blood.

'Dad,' Bache said again, softer this time, reaching out to touch his father's shoulder. 'Dad, it's me.'

Tirexion's eyes fluttered open, unfocused at first, then widening with recognition.

'Bache?' he whispered, his voice cracked and weak. 'How…? They said the *K2* was destroyed.'

'They lied,' Bache replied, relief flooding through him as he saw the brightness in his father's eyes. 'We're here to get you out.'

'Unplug him and let's go,' shouted Riccs, as the sound of laser weapon fire emanated from the corridor.

27

Daxicorp mining facility, Auriga system

BACHE SCANNED THE MONITORING EQUIPMENT, his fingers trembling as he traced the tubes and wires leading to his father's frail body. He'd worked with enough complex systems to recognise the pattern…they were extracting information, not just restraining him. With each tube he disconnected, his father's breathing grew stronger, more regular.

'They're…using me,' Tirexion whispered, his voice strengthening as Bache freed him from the final neural connector. 'The resonance patterns…they're trying to perfect the communication frequency.'

'We know…save your strength,' Bache said, his throat tightening as he worked at the restraints. The straps fell away, and his father slumped forward into his arms. Despite the pain shooting through his injured shoulder,

Bache held him tight, feeling the alarming lightness of his father's frame.

The sound of weapons fire intensified in the corridor.

'We need to move now,' Riccs commanded, his frame filling the doorway. 'Team Gamma reports resistance at the north junction. Our exit window can't stay open forever.'

Bache helped his father to his feet, supporting him as his legs threatened to give way. Tirexion's skin felt paper-thin beneath his touch, and Bache could feel each rib as he wrapped an arm around his father's waist.

'Can you walk?' he asked.

Tirexion nodded weakly.

'Just...give me a second.' He straightened slightly, determination hardening his gaze. 'We can't leave that device intact. It's the primary node...if they activate it fully, they can control every modified drive in the fleet.'

Riccs glanced at the crystalline structure dominating the centre of the cavern.

'I've already ordered explosive charges placed around its base. We'll detonate once we're clear.'

'No,' Tirexion shook his head, the movement clearly causing him pain. 'Won't work. The crystal matrix will simply reconfigure. It's self-healing.'

Bache's mind raced through possibilities.

'What about an overload? If we reverse the power flow through the main conduits...'

His father's eyes lit with recognition.

'Yes. The primary junction control.' He pointed with a shaking hand to a control panel on the far side of the room. 'Redirect the flow there, and the feedback will shatter the resonance pattern.'

Zaphir was already moving. 'I'll do it. Cover me.'

Bache watched her dart across the chamber, dodging between workstations as Riccs provided covering fire. The pain in his shoulder flared as he shifted to better support his father's weight, but he pushed it aside, focusing on the mission.

'We need to get clear before the overload,' Tirexion warned, his breathing laboured. 'The energy release will be…substantial.'

Zaphir reached the control panel and began working, her fingers flying over the interface. Bache could see the concentration on her face even from across the room.

'The Theo chip,' Tirexion said. 'They wanted to know what was on it.' His hand clutched weakly at Bache's arm. 'You found it? The hidden compartment in my home?'

'Both chips,' Bache confirmed. 'But I haven't been able to access the Theo one yet.'

Relief washed over Tirexion's haggard features. 'Good. It contains the countermeasure. It's the only way to completely neutralise the Nkris influence in our systems.' His voice grew stronger as he continued. 'We need to get it to Sarhaan Pell on Paradeisos. She has the equipment to implement it across the fleet.'

'Done,' Zaphir called from across the room. 'Power flow reversed.'

A high-pitched whine filled the chamber as the crystalline structure's glow intensified. The green light pulsed faster, shifting to a sickly yellow that cast harsh shadows across the walls. Technicians who hadn't already fled were now scrambling for the exits.

'We need to move,' Riccs commanded, his voice cutting through the rising cacophony. 'Now.'

Bache supported his father as they moved towards the exit, each step a struggle against the pain and fatigue. The crystalline structure was now vibrating visibly, sending tremors through the deck plates beneath their feet. Small fractures appeared along its surface, spiderwebbing outward as the power surged beyond its design parameters.

'How long?' Bache asked, glancing back at the deteriorating structure.

'Minutes at most,' Tirexion replied, his breath coming in ragged gasps. 'The resonance cascade will accelerate exponentially once the core destabilises.'

They reached the corridor where the rest of Riccs's team waited, securing their retreat path. The sounds of fighting echoed from further down the passageway, where Team Gamma were engaging hostile forces.

'This way,' Riccs ordered, guiding them towards the maintenance tunnel that led back to their insertion point.

The facility's emergency alarms had blared to life, bathing the corridors in pulsing red light. Beneath their feet, the deck vibrated with increasing intensity as the overloading crystal structure approached critical failure.

Bache's shoulder screamed with every step, but he forced himself forward, half carrying his father through the winding corridors. Tirexion stumbled occasionally, his weakened legs struggling to keep pace.

'Almost there,' Bache encouraged, feeling his father's weight grow heavier against him.

They rounded a corner to find four guards blocking their path, weapons raised. Before Bache could react,

Riccs and his marines opened fire, the corridor filling with the sharp crack of laser rifles. Two guards went down immediately, while the others ducked for cover.

'Go left,' Riccs commanded, laying down suppressing fire as he directed them towards an adjacent corridor.

The alternate route was longer but hopefully undefended, and they pushed forward with renewed urgency. Behind them, the facility's tremors intensified, metal groaning as structural supports began to fail.

'The cascade is accelerating,' Tirexion gasped, his face pale with exertion. 'The entire facility will be compromised when it fails.'

They reached the maintenance airlock, where the rest of Team Alpha waited, securing their extraction point.

Bache kept his grip on his father as the team moved towards the gunship. The tremors intensified, metal groaning and dust falling from overhead conduits. His shoulder burned with agony, but he focused only on getting his father to safety.

'The gunship's prepped for immediate departure,' one of the marines reported, cycling the airlock open.

They rushed through into the safety of the gunship, Bache carefully lowering his father onto one of the padded seats. Tirexion's breathing was laboured, his face ashen, but his eyes remained alert.

'Get us out of here,' Riccs ordered as the last marine boarded. 'Away from this station, now.'

The pilot didn't hesitate. Bache felt the jolt as the gunship detached from the station, the engine tone rising to a roar. On the holomap, he watched the mining facility recede, its exterior now showing visible signs of structural failure. Fissures appeared along its surface, venting atmosphere in white plumes.

'We need to put more distance between us and that station,' Tirexion said, his voice stronger than before. 'When the crystal fully collapses, it'll be like a thousand nuclear warheads detonating.'

Bache gripped a handhold as the gunship accelerated, weaving between asteroid fragments with alarming speed. His father slumped against him, exhaustion finally claiming him, but his breathing remained steady.

'Medical kit,' Bache called, and Zaphir immediately retrieved one from a wall compartment.

As he applied a healing patch to the gash on his father's temple, the mining facility disappeared from view, hidden behind a particularly large asteroid. Seconds later, a blinding flash illuminated the holomap, followed a few seconds after by a shock wave that rocked the gunship violently. Bache braced himself against the bulkhead, shielding his father from being thrown. He heard the pilot swear as all the rocks around them were hurled about and the ship's shields took several impacts.

'That's the end of their resonance amplifier,' Zaphir said, steadying herself against a seat.

Riccs approached, filling the narrow aisle.

'*K2* reports they've detected the explosion. They're moving to rendezvous with us in the clear zone beyond the asteroid field.' He glanced at Tirexion. 'How's he doing?'

'He needs proper medical attention,' Bache replied, checking his father's pulse. 'But he's relatively stable.'

Tirexion's eyes fluttered open, fixing on Bache with surprising intensity.

'The Theo chip,' he whispered. 'We need to get it to Paradeisos as quickly as possible. Before they can rebuild.'

'We will,' Bache assured him, squeezing his hand gently. 'Rest now.'

The eighteen-minute journey back to the *K2* passed in tense silence. Bache remained at his father's side, monitoring his condition while occasionally glancing at the holomap display showing their progress through the asteroid field. When they finally buzzed through the atmosphere barrier into the *K2*'s hangar bay, a medical team was already waiting, hovering reassuringly with stretchers and equipment.

Bache watched as they carefully transferred his father onto a stretcher. Tirexion's eyes fluttered open at the movement, his gaunt face turning towards Bache.

'Don't let them separate us,' he whispered, his bony fingers gripping Bache's wrist with surprising strength. 'They might still have infiltrators on this ship.'

'I won't,' Bache promised, walking alongside the stretcher as the medical team moved swiftly towards the lifts. 'I wouldn't have thought so, as they meant to destroy it,' he reasoned.

The ship's familiar corridors blurred past, his focus narrowing to his father's pale face and laboured breathing.

Captain Whipper intercepted them at the medical bay entrance, his expression grave as he surveyed Tirexion's condition.

'Get him stabilised,' Whipper ordered the medical team before turning to Bache. 'My office, as soon as he's settled.'

Bache nodded, not taking his eyes off his father as they

wheeled him into the treatment area. The chief medical officer, Dr Renn, was already waiting, her sleeves rolled up and her sharp eyes assessing Tirexion's condition with cool efficiency. After a couple of minutes assessing the patient, she spoke.

'Severe dehydration, malnutrition, evidence of neural tampering,' she muttered, scanning his father with a hand-held diagnostic device. 'Multiple injection sites…they've been keeping him drugged.'

Bache's stomach clenched.

'Will he fully recover?'

'Given time and proper treatment, I don't see why not.' Dr Renn's tone softened slightly. 'Your father is resilient, Chief Engineer. But he needs rest and constant monitoring.'

'I'm staying with him,' Bache said, not a request but a statement.

Dr Renn nodded.

'For now, that's fine. But Captain Whipper…'

'Can wait a while,' Bache interrupted, pulling up a chair beside his father's bed as the medical team worked around him, attaching monitors and starting fluid replacement.

His father's eyes opened again, clearer now as the medical treatments began taking effect.

'The chip,' he whispered, his voice barely audible over the medical equipment's soft beeping. 'Did you bring it?'

Bache patted his pocket. 'Safe and sound. We'll get it to Paradeisos.'

Tirexion relaxed slightly, his head sinking deeper into the pillow.

'They wanted to know how to neutralise it. That's why they took me.' His voice grew stronger, more urgent. 'The Nkris have been infiltrating our technology for decades, Bache. The modified drives are just the beginning. They're preparing for something…something big.'

'Save your strength,' Bache urged, but his father shook his head.

'No time. Listen.' Tirexion's fingers tightened around Bache's wrist. 'The resonance crystal you destroyed was just one node. There are another two.'

'Oh crap,' muttered Bache.

28

The bridge, *Katadromiko 2*, en route to Paradeisos

TWO WEEKS LATER, the *K2* arrived in orbit around Paradeisos. Bache stared down at the planet from one of the observation decks, its distinctive blue-green oceans and golden landmasses glinting in the light of the binary stars. The Theo home-world was renowned for its beauty, but also for its isolation and secrecy. Few outsiders were ever granted permission to visit, and even fewer were welcomed into the mysterious domed cities that dotted its surface.

'It's beautiful isn't it?' his father said, joining him at the viewport. Tirexion still moved slowly, but the haunted look had faded from his eyes, and some colour had returned to his face. The medical team had worked wonders, though Dr Renn insisted he was still far from fully recovered.

'I've never been here before,' Bache admitted, studying the planet's surface where the distinctive shimmer of dome shields could be seen even from orbit. 'Have you?'

'Once, many years ago. Before you were born.' Tirexion's voice carried a hint of nostalgia. 'The Theos were more open then, before they grew concerned about the GDA and its security measures. They do have their own problems. There's a population of aggressive humans living underground called the Timoria. They attack the Theos at every opportunity, but being pacifists they don't retaliate.'

'Why are they underground?'

'A nuclear war hundreds of years ago left the surface too polluted and the Timoria blame the Theos for causing it. That's why the cities are domed.'

'Hmm,' Bache grunted, fingering the iridescent chip in his pocket. 'Do you think Sarhaan Pell will help us?'

'If we can find her.' His father's expression grew serious. 'The Theos don't exactly maintain public directories.'

The door to the observation deck slid open, and Captain Whipper strode in, his uniform crisp despite the early hour.

'Gentlemen,' he said, nodding to them both. 'We've received clearance to send a shuttle to the surface. The Theos have granted us landing permission at Oasis Seven only.'

'Just like that?' Bache asked, surprised by the lack of resistance.

Whipper's mouth quirked in what might have been amusement.

'Apparently your father's name carries some weight down there. When I mentioned Tirexion Loftt was aboard and seeking to speak with Sarhaan Pell, their response time improved dramatically.'

Tirexion smiled faintly.

'Sarhaan and I collaborated on several projects in the past. She's one of the few Theos who maintained connections with the outside galaxy and the GDA.'

'Well, whatever the reason, we have our window,' Whipper said. 'Shuttle leaves in thirty minutes. Commander Riccs will accompany you two, along with Specialist Mye.'

'Thank you, Captain,' Tirexion said.

After Whipper left, Bache turned to his father.

'You never mentioned you had friends among the Theos before.'

'There are many things I haven't told you, son,' Tirexion replied, his eyes distant. 'Some for your protection, some because I thought there would be time later.' He shook his head. 'I should have prepared you better for all of this.'

The shuttle descended through Paradeisos's atmosphere, buffeted by turbulence that made Bache grip his seat. His father sat across from him, looking frail despite his insistence that he was well enough for the journey. Through the front screen, Bache watched as they passed through wisps of cloud and the domed cities came into view…massive transparent hemispheres scattered across the golden land-scape like dewdrops on velvet.

'There,' Tirexion said, pointing to one of the smaller domes. 'That's Oasis Seven. Sarhaan's research facility is located in that dome.'

As they approached the landing pad, Bache noticed how empty the city appeared. The gleaming structures within the dome stood pristine and beautiful, but the streets between them were deserted, devoid of the bustling activity he'd expected from a major research centre.

'Where is everyone?' Zaphir asked, echoing his thoughts.

Tirexion's expression darkened.

'Underground,' he said, gruffly.

She turned to him and raised her eyebrows.

'Long story,' Tirexion added, and turned to stare out the front screen.

Zaphir opened her mouth to reply just as the shuttle touched down with a gentle thud. Commander Riccs stood immediately, his frame filling the narrow aisle as he concealed his sidearm.

'Remember…' he said, his deep voice booming in the small cabin, '…the Theos are pacifists. No visible weapons once we're outside of the shuttle.'

They disembarked into the sterile environment of the landing bay. The air smelled faintly of ozone and some-thing sweeter…like citrus blossoms. A single figure awaited them, tall and slender in flowing white and blue robes that shimmered with subtle patterns that seemed to move of their own accord.

'Sarhaan,' Tirexion called, his voice stronger than it had been in days.

The Theo stepped forward, her pale features arranged in an expression of serene welcome that didn't quite reach her eyes. Bache had occasionally seen Theos before, but always at a distance. Up close, her otherworldly beauty was almost unsettling…skin like polished alabaster, eyes a deep violet that seemed to shift hue as she moved and hair so pale it appeared white in certain light.

'Tirexion Loftt,' she replied, her voice melodic and precise. 'It has been many spins.' Her gaze shifted to Bache. 'And this must be your son. The resemblance is striking.'

'This is Bache,' his father confirmed. 'And our colleagues, Specialist Zaphir Mye and Commander Riccs.'

Sarhaan inclined her head slightly.

'Welcome to Oasis Seven. Please, follow me.'

She led them through empty corridors of gleaming white material that Bache couldn't identify. Their footsteps echoed in the silence, the only sound apart from the soft hum of environmental systems.

'Your city seems…quiet,' Bache ventured.

'Indeed,' replied Sarhaan, quietly.

Tirexion caught Bache's eye and gave a little shake of the head.

Sarhaan led them into a vast circular chamber unlike anything Bache had seen before. The room's ceiling soared at least thirty metres overhead, composed of some transparent material that allowed the binary stars' light to pour through. Intricate patterns were etched into the walls, seeming to shift and change as he looked at them.

'This is our primary research laboratory,' Sarhaan said, gesturing to the empty workstations that ringed the chamber. 'Or at least, it was.'

Bache noticed the thin layer of dust on some of the consoles, evidence of abandonment that contrasted sharply with the otherwise immaculate environment. 'Where is everyone?' he asked.

Sarhaan's violet eyes saddened. 'Gone. Dead or evacuated.' She turned to Tirexion. 'Your warning came too late, old friend.'

'What warning?' Bache asked, looking between the two.

His father's face had drained of colour.

'The message I sent before they took me. About the infiltration.'

'Indeed.' Sarhaan's melodic voice hardened. 'Three days after receiving your transmission, we detected unusual energy signatures throughout our communication systems. By the time we isolated them, seven of our researchers were already dead.'

She moved to a central console and activated it with a wave of her slender hand. A holographic display materialised above it, showing microscopic images of what appeared to be neural tissue riddled with thread-like filaments.

'This technology doesn't merely interface with our systems,' she explained. 'It interfaces with us. These filaments were found in the brain tissue of the deceased researchers.'

Bache felt his stomach turn.

'They were…infected?'

'Controlled,' Sarhaan corrected. 'The technology establishes a direct neural link. It begins with headaches, then progresses to auditory hallucinations. Eventually, the host becomes a conduit…conscious but unable to resist the impulses transmitted through the filaments.'

Riccs stepped forward, his size seemingly out of place among the delicate Theo architecture.

'Like Hollander…he claimed to hear voices.'

'Precisely.' Sarhaan's gaze shifted to the commander. 'The most disturbing aspect is the selection criteria. The technology appears to target specific genetic markers. Only certain individuals are susceptible.'

'Selective infiltration,' Tirexion muttered, leaning heavily against a console. 'That's why they've been able to remain undetected for so long. They don't need to control everyone…just key personnel in strategic positions.'

Bache's mind raced through the implications.

'The modified drives…they're not just communication nodes. They're transmission vectors.'

'Yes,' Sarhaan confirmed. 'The resonance frequency doesn't merely carry information. It carries the infection. Each time a susceptible individual works near an active drive, they risk exposure.'

Zaphir had moved to examine the holographic brain scans more closely.

'So let me get this straight,' she said. 'This can not only manipulate an infected person, but can kill them at any given time?'

'Indeed,' Sarhaan confirmed. 'When they found out we had discovered what they were doing, they managed to murder seven of my researchers before we were able to neutralise it.'

Bache withdrew the chip from his pocket and handed it to Sarhaan.

'We need to be able to turn this Nkris shit off too, as soon as possible.'

'Oh!' exclaimed Sarhaan, her purple eyes opening wide in surprise. 'This isn't the Nkris,' she said. 'You shut down their threat a couple of spins ago.'

'Well…who's doing all this to us then?' Riccs asked, getting the question in before anyone else.

'It's designed to look like the Nkris,' said Sarhaan. 'I didn't know you hadn't realised. It's actually…'

Her mouth was open to continue, but she adopted a puzzled expression and began to shake uncontrollably. She grabbed Bache's wrist as she began convulsing even more. It hurt she squeezed so hard.

'Lay her down,' shouted Zaphir, fumbling for the medical kit in her backpack.

Bache lowered her down gently and prised her fingers off his wrist before she crushed his implant. Her frightened eyes were searching as her limbs flailed about. Riccs knelt down and grabbed her legs, pinning them down. Zaphir snatched out the auto syringe and programmed it for a strong sedative.

Sarhaan let out a sigh, she went still and her eyes disappeared up inside her skull as blood dripped from her mouth and ears.

'Too late,' said Bache, glancing up at Zaphir, his expression one of absolute fury.

29

The central medical suite, *Katadromiko 2*, orbiting
Paradeisos

Captain Whipper slammed his fist against the wall of the
medical bay, his face flushed crimson with rage.

'Explain to me again how we managed to lose the one
person who could tell us who's really behind all this?' he
demanded, his voice dangerously low.

Bache stood rigidly beside the examination table where
Sarhaan's body lay beneath a sterile field. The Theo
woman's once luminous features were now waxy and still,
the violet of her eyes hidden forever behind closed lids.
His throat felt raw, as if he'd been screaming for hours,
though he hadn't uttered a sound since they'd rushed her
body back to the ship.

'She was about to tell us,' he said, the words scraping

against his throat. 'Then whatever was inside her activated. It happened in a split second.'

'And the Theo authorities are howling for explanations,' Whipper continued, pacing the length of the medical bay. 'I've got their orbital control centre demanding we surrender her body and threatening to bring up planetary defences if we don't comply within the hour.'

Dr Renn looked up from her preliminary examination, her expression grim.

'Captain, these neural filaments are unlike anything I've ever seen. They've completely infiltrated her cerebral cortex. When they activated, they caused catastrophic neural collapse.'

'Remote execution,' Tirexion murmured from where he sat in the corner, his face ashen. 'Someone knew she was about to reveal their identity and triggered a kill switch.'

Whipper's nostrils flared as he inhaled deeply, clearly struggling to contain his fury.

'So we're dealing with someone who can monitor conversations on a supposedly secure Theo research facility, and remotely kill people when they become inconvenient?'

'It gets worse,' Dr Renn added, gesturing to her diagnostic display. 'The filaments are dissolving. In another hour, there will be no evidence they were ever there.'

'Self-erasing evidence,' Riccs growled from his position by the door. 'Clever and convenient.'

Bache stared at Sarhaan's still form, his mind racing.

'We need to stall the Theo authorities,' he said suddenly. 'If we return her body now, they'll never discover what really happened. We need time for a proper autopsy.'

Whipper nodded curtly.

'I'll handle the Theos. You focus on extracting whatever information you can from that chip she was going to programme for us.' He turned to Tirexion. 'Do you have any idea what she was about to say? Any theory about who could be behind this if not the Nkris?'

Tirexion shook his head slowly. 'There are possibilities, but without more data...' He trailed off, his gaze distant but thoughtful.

Bache watched as his eyes became unfocused as if searching through memories. The silence in the medical bay stretched uncomfortably while the gentle hum of medical equipment provided the only sound.

'There were always rumours,' Tirexion finally said, his voice barely above a whisper. 'Whispers about old ancient races that predated even the Klatt. Species that might have survived from extinction many millennia ago.'

Dr Renn looked up from her scanner with a furrowed brow. 'The neural structure of these filaments is remarkably sophisticated. They almost seem to have been designed specifically for Theo physiology.'

'That would require intimate knowledge of Theo biology,' Zaphir added, leaning against the wall beside Bache. 'Knowledge that very few outside their world would possess.'

Bache felt a cold sensation creep up his spine as he looked down at Sarhaan's lifeless form. Just moments ago, she'd been about to reveal everything. Now their best lead was gone, and they were left with more questions than answers. His shoulder throbbed, not as bad now, but a persistent reminder of everything they'd been through.

'The chip,' he said, patting his pocket to confirm it was still there. 'Whatever's on this might still help us, even without Sarhaan to implement it.'

He noticed his pocket became warm against his leg as he patted it.

'That's weird,' he said, pulling the chip out to discover it was glowing, flicking through multiple colours and emitting a low hum.

Tirexion's eyes widened and he pointed at the chip.

'That's what they do when they're activated,' he said.

'I thought only a Theo could do that,' Riccs said, leaning in.

Whipper nodded sharply.

'Whatever it's doing, Loftt…get on with it. I need to deal with the Theo authorities before they decide to start firing on my ship.' He turned to leave, then paused at the door. 'And another thing, Loftt…find me something concrete. We can't fight an enemy we can't identify.'

After the captain left, Bache noticed the chip had quietened again. He turned to his father. 'What would make it wake like that? You said you've worked with Theo technology before? All I did was pat my pocket like this and…'

He'd brought his arm over to touch his pocket again and as he passed the chip in his other hand it glowed again.

'It's your hand,' exclaimed Zaphir. 'Why would your left hand do that and not your right?'

'It's not my hand,' said Bache, the realisation slapping

him in the face. 'It's my dermal data chip in my wrist. She grabbed me there just before she died…it got really hot.'

'Wow,' said Tirexion. 'She transferred her biometric signature over to you.'

Bache stared at his wrist and slowly brought it up to the chip. It instantly woke up and began its colourful display, but this time Bache held it there, feeling the chip's warmth against his palm. He concentrated on the modified Xephoni drives, the neural filaments, the resonance amplifier they'd destroyed. The chip grew hotter, almost uncomfortably so, and the humming intensified.

A beam of light projected from his fingers, forming a holographic display in the air above his hand. Complex diagrams appeared…schematics for a device unlike anything Bache had seen before.

'That's it…the resonance neutraliser,' Tirexion breathed, leaning forward. 'Designed to disrupt the specific frequency the filaments use to communicate.'

Bache studied the schematics, noticing elements of his father's design philosophy interwoven with unmistakably alien technology.

'We need to construct one and test it quickly,' said Bache.

'Would we be able to track the source?' Riccs asked. 'To find and destroy the other two crystals?'

'Without a doubt,' nodded Tirexion. 'But we will need another friendly Theo to help us.'

Bache ran a hand through his hair, frustration building in his chest.

'We can't exactly request another one, not after what just happened to Sarhaan.'

His father's eyes suddenly brightened.

'Perhaps we can. There's one more Theo I know who might help us. Valent Kir. He worked with Sarhaan and me years ago, before the Theos began their isolation policy.'

'Where would we find him?' Bache asked.

'Last I heard, he was conducting research on Meridian Station. It's in neutral space, at the boundary between GDA and Klatt territories.'

Bache felt a flicker of hope. 'That's only a couple of jumps from here.'

'It's worth a try,' Zaphir said, straightening up. 'It's not like we have a bucket full of other options.'

Riccs nodded his agreement. 'I'll inform the captain once he's finished bullshitting the Theos.'

Bache's tablet chimed with an incoming message from the bridge. He glanced down to watch Captain Whipper's notification.

'The Theo authorities have granted us six hours to complete our examination before we must surrender Sarhaan's remains. Make it count, Loftt,' he said and the message ended.

'Six hours,' Bache repeated, passing the message to his father. 'Not much time to build a resonance neutraliser from scratch.'

Tirexion studied the holographic schematics still hovering above Bache's palm. His thin fingers traced the air around one particular component, causing the display to zoom in automatically.

'We can modify one of the *K2*'s sensor arrays,' he said, his voice stronger now. 'The base structure is similar enough. The main challenge will be calibrating the resonance frequency without Sarhaan's expertise.'

Dr Renn looked over from her examination of the body.

'Before you two rush off to engineering, there's something else you should see.' She beckoned them closer to the diagnostic display. 'These neural filaments…they're not just dissolving. They're transmitting.'

Bache leaned in, squinting at the microscopic view of the dissolving structures. Tiny pulses of energy flickered through them at regular intervals.

'She's still connected to whatever network killed her,' he muttered, feeling a chill crawl up his spine.

'Which means…' Riccs said from the doorway. '…whoever's on the other end might be listening to us right now.'

The realisation hit Bache like a physical blow. He quickly closed his hand around the Theo chip, cutting off the holographic display.

'We need to move this conversation somewhere secure. Somewhere they definitely can't eavesdrop.'

'The gunship,' Zaphir suggested immediately. 'The one we used for the rescue mission. It's still in maintenance bay four, completely powered down except for basic life support.'

Tirexion nodded.

'Perfect. No active communications systems, no connection to the *K2*'s network.'

Bache helped his father to his feet, trying not to show his concern at how frail the older man appeared to be.

'Dr Renn, keep monitoring those filaments. If anything changes…'

'I'll alert you immediately,' she promised, turning back to her instruments.

Twenty minutes later, they'd gathered in the cramped confines of the gunship. Bache sat in the pilot's seat, the chip once again projecting its schematics across the darkened cockpit. Riccs had performed a thorough sweep for any surveillance devices before sealing them inside.

'If we're going to build this neutraliser,' Bache said, studying the complex diagrams, 'we need to understand exactly what it does.'

Tirexion leaned forward, his face illuminated by the hologram's shifting colours.

'It's designed to disrupt the specific frequency the neural filaments use to communicate with their control nodes. Once activated, it should sever the connection permanently.'

'And potentially reveal the source of the signal, I'm hoping,' said Riccs.

'So am I,' said Bache. 'So am I…best we crack on.'

30

Engineering bay 3, *Katadromiko 2*, orbiting Paradeisos

SIX HOURS LATER, Bache stood in engineering bay three, staring at their hastily assembled prototype. The resonance jammer looked nothing like he'd expected...a jumble of modified *K2* components surrounding a pulsing crystalline core they'd synthesised using the ship's molecular fabricator. His hands were covered in burns from soldering and his shoulder had woken up again, but a fierce sense of accomplishment pushed any pain aside.

'Will it work?' Captain Whipper asked, circling the device with a sceptical expression.

'In theory,' Bache replied, adjusting a final connection. 'We've calibrated it to the exact frequency pattern we found in Sarhaan's neural filaments. If we're right, it should disrupt any similar signals throughout the ship.'

Tirexion sat nearby, his face drawn with exhaustion but eyes bright with purpose.

'The resonance pattern is distinctive. Once activated, the jammer will create a localised field that should sever any active connections.'

Dr Renn entered the bay, her medical whites stained with blood.

'Autopsy's complete,' she announced, her voice heavy. 'And the Theo authorities are demanding we return her body immediately. Their patience has run out and a shuttle is on the way.'

'What did you find?' Bache asked, looking up from the final calibrations.

'The filaments had almost completely dissolved, but I managed to preserve tissue samples showing their integration pattern.' She handed Bache a data tablet. 'They weren't just monitoring her...they were controlling her central nervous system with microscopic precision. Whoever designed this technology has an understanding of neural architecture far beyond our current capabilities.'

Whipper nodded grimly.

'And the body?'

'Being prepared for transport now. It'll be ready when their ship gets here.'

Bache felt a pang of frustration. They were sending Sarhaan back to her people with more questions than answers.

'Did you identify any markers that might tell us who's behind this? Anything distinctive about the technology?' he asked.

Dr Renn shook her head.

'Nothing conclusive. The composition includes elements I can't even identify. But there is one thing...' She hesitated, glancing at Tirexion. 'The filaments showed signs of adaptive evolution...they were specifically tailored to Theo physiology. This wasn't some generic infiltration technology, it was designed specifically for them.'

Tirexion's expression darkened.

'That narrows the list of suspects considerably. Very few outside the Theo scientific community have such detailed knowledge of their neural structure.'

'We should activate the jammer,' Riccs suggested from his position by the door. 'If there are any other compromised personnel on this ship, we need to know.'

Bache exchanged a look with his father, who gave a slight nod.

'Everyone stand back,' Bache warned, reaching for the activation sequence. 'We don't know exactly what the energy field might do to sensitive equipment. So we're about to find out.'

He input the final sequence, holding his breath as the device hummed to life. The crystalline core began to pulse with an eerie yellow light, the frequency increasing until it became a steady glow. For a moment, nothing seemed to happen. Then a high-pitched whine filled the air, rising in pitch until it hovered just at the edge of human hearing.

Bache felt a strange pressure building behind his ears, not quite painful but distinctly uncomfortable.

'Did anyone else feel that?' he asked, blinking away the momentary disorientation.

Zaphir nodded, rubbing her temple.

'Like someone was jet washing inside my head.'

The jammer's light pulsed once more, then stabilised into a steady glow. Bache checked the readings on his tablet, his heart rate accelerating as the data streamed in.

'It seems to be working,' he said, unable to keep the excitement from his voice. 'The device is currently detecting and disrupting nearby resonance patterns.'

Tirexion leaned forward, his eyes widening as he studied the tablet's display.

'Look at that,' he said, pointing to a series of fluctuating patterns. 'The jammer isn't just disrupting the signals…it really is tracing them back to their source.'

Riccs moved closer, casting a shadow over the device.

'Can you pinpoint the location?'

Bache manipulated the display, expanding the signal trace map. A red line stretched out from their position, winding through space towards a specific point.

'It's not precise yet,' he admitted. 'But it's narrowing down. The signal is coming from somewhere in the dead Dimioi sector.'

Whipper's expression darkened.

'That's right at the edge of charted space. Nobody's been going there since the end of the Extermination War. There's been no GDA presence anywhere near there for a thousand years.'

'Too much old extermination era ordnance floating about,' said Riccs. 'The place is a fucking death trap.'

'Perfect place to hide something you don't want found,' Zaphir observed.

A sudden alarm blared from the jammer, startling them

all. The yellow glow intensified, pulsing rapidly as new data flooded the display.

'What's it doing now?' Whipper demanded, taking an involuntary step back.

Bache's fingers flew across the controls, trying to make sense of the unexpected readings.

'The jammer's picking up multiple signals,' he explained, his voice tight with concentration. 'Not just from the Dimioi sector, but from…here. On this ship.'

'Someone on the *K2* is infected?' Riccs straightened, his hand instinctively moving towards his weapon.

'Not just someone,' Bache replied, his stomach dropping as he expanded the display. 'According to this, there are seventeen active neural connections on board.'

The momentary stunned silence that followed felt heavy enough to crush bone.

'Seventeen,' Whipper repeated, his face draining of colour. 'How is that possible without us noticing?'

Bache stared at the display, the red dots scattered throughout the ship's schematic making his blood run cold. Each one represented a crew member…someone they worked with, ate with, trusted…they'd been compromised without anyone realising it.

'The filaments are designed to remain dormant until activated,' Tirexion explained, leaning heavily against a console. 'The infected individuals might not even know they're carrying them.'

Riccs had already drawn his weapon, checking the charge with cold proficiency.

'We need to identify and isolate them immediately.'

'Wait,' Bache said, holding up his hand. 'If we start

rounding people up, whoever's controlling them will know we've discovered the infiltration. It'd be a death sentence for them all.' His mind raced through the possibilities, calculating risks against dwindling time. 'We need to track these signals to their source first, then neutralise them all simultaneously.'

The jammer pulsed again, its yellow glow intensifying as it processed more data. Bache watched the signal trace narrowing, coordinates becoming more precise with each passing second.

'We're getting there,' he murmured, excitement mingling with dread in his chest. 'The trace is converging on a specific location in the Dimioi sector.'

Whipper leaned over his shoulder, studying the coordinates.

'That's the Sarcophagus Nebula. Nothing's supposed to be out there except radiation and debris from the Extermination War.'

'Perfect cover,' Riccs growled. 'Who'd look for advanced technology in a radioactive graveyard?'

The ship's comm system chimed, interrupting their discussion.

'Captain to the bridge,' came the urgent voice of the first officer. 'Theo shuttle has arrived for transfer of remains.'

Whipper straightened, jaw tight.

'I'll go and handle this. Loftt, keep working on that trace. I want precise coordinates when I get back.' He turned to Riccs. 'Commander, discreetly identify those seventeen compromised crew members. No confrontations, just surveillance.'

After the captain left, Bache turned to Zaphir.

'We need to miniaturise this jammer. Something portable that we can use to protect ourselves when we go after the source.'

'When we go after it?' She raised an eyebrow. 'You're planning an away mission to a radioactive death zone?'

'Do you see any other options?" Bache gestured towards the display showing the infected crew members. 'We can't trust our own ship anymore can we?'

His father nodded slowly, eyes fixed on the pulsing jammer.

'I can help with the miniaturisation. We'll need at least three portable units…one for the away team, one for the bridge, and one backup.'

Bache's shoulder picked this moment to grumble as he bent over the workstation, but he ignored it, focusing instead on the task at hand.

31

GDA shuttle, Meridian Station, Klatt border neutral zone

MERIDIAN STATION HUNG against the backdrop of stars like an enormous mechanical spider, its eight docking arms extending from a central hub. Bache gazed out the front screen as the shuttle approached, taking in the hodgepodge of architecture that characterised the neutral trading post. Unlike the sleek military precision of GDA facilities or the elegant curves of Theo design, Meridian was a chaotic fusion of a dozen different construction styles, each section added as needed over centuries.

'Quite the eyesore, isn't it?' Tirexion commented beside him, his voice stronger than it had been in days. The journey from Paradeisos had done him good, giving him time to recover further under Dr Renn's care.

'I've never actually been here before,' Bache admitted, studying the patchwork of hull plating and the hundreds of small vessels clustered around the docking arms. 'It's…a busier place than I expected.'

'That's neutral territory for you,' Riccs said from behind them, filling the doorway to the shuttle's cockpit. 'No extradition treaties, minimal security, and a blind eye turned to most activities as long as the station fees get paid. Perfect place to disappear if you want to.'

The shuttle slowed as it approached one of the outer docking arms, revealing the true scale of the station. What had appeared modest from a distance was actually enormous, housing tens of thousands of beings from across the galaxy. Advertisements in a dozen languages scrolled across exterior displays, hawking everything from luxury goods to mercenary services.

'How do we even begin to find one Theo in all of this? It's enormous,' Bache said, the scale of their task suddenly hitting him.

Tirexion's lips curled into a small smile.

'Fortunately, Valent has particular…requirements. He conducts sensitive research that needs specific environmental conditions. If I remember rightly, there is only one section of this station that would accommodate his work.'

The shuttle docked with a gentle thud and a whining as the clamps engaged. When the airlock cycled open it released the distinctive smell of Meridian Station – overly recycled air tinged with cooking odours, oil, and the unmistakable musk of too many species living in close proximity. Bache wrinkled his nose as they disembarked.

'Lovely,' Zaphir muttered, adjusting the small pack containing one of their portable jammers. They'd managed to miniaturise the technology into three units, each about the size of a standard back pack. The devices hummed softly against their bodies, creating a protective field that would prevent any neural filaments from establishing connections.

Captain Whipper had remained on the cloaked *K2* a few million kilometres back, coordinating with Riccs to monitor the seventeen compromised crew members. The infected personnel had been discreetly assigned to non-critical duties while Whipper maintained the illusion that nothing was amiss. If whoever controlled the filaments realised they'd been discovered, those seventeen lives would be forfeit.

'Section fourteen on deck eighty-six,' said Tirexion.

They made their way through the crowded corridors of Meridian Station, weaving between merchants hawking exotic wares and travellers from hundreds of different worlds. The station's artificial gravity felt slightly heavier than the *K2*'s and the air grew progressively staler as they moved deeper into the residential sectors.

'How well do you know this Valent Kir?' Zaphir asked, keeping her voice low as they passed a group of Klatt traders arguing over the price of some unidentifiable technology.

'Well enough,' Tirexion replied. 'We collaborated on several projects before the Theo isolation began. He was always…unconventional by Theo standards. More willing to engage with outsiders.'

Bache noticed his father's pace had slowed, his breathing becoming more laboured. Despite Dr Renn's treatments, Tirexion was still far from recovered. The older man caught his concerned glance and straightened his posture with visible effort.

'I'm fine,' he muttered. 'Just need to catch my breath occasionally.'

'Stay close,' Riccs murmured as they approached a bank of lifts. 'This station has sixteen different security jurisdictions, and most of them don't talk to each other.'

The glass lift was cramped and smelled of something pungent that made Bache's eyes water. As they ascended through the levels, the character of the station changed. The commercial chaos gave way to more orderly corridors, the lighting shifting from the garish colours of the market levels to a more clinical white.

'Section fourteen is one of the few regulated areas,' Tirexion explained, his voice low. 'Scientific research requires a certain…predictability that the rest of Meridian lacks.'

When they reached deck eighty-six, Bache was struck by the contrast. The corridors were clean, almost sterile, with security checkpoints visible at regular intervals. Laboratory doors lined the hallway, each marked with cryptic designations and warning symbols.

'Valent's lab will probably be at the far end,' Tirexion said, leading them forward. 'Assuming he hasn't moved since I last talked to him.'

They approached a door marked with Theo script and a molecular symbol Bache didn't recognise. Tirexion paused before it, drawing a deep breath before pressing the communication panel.

'Identify,' came a melodic voice, similar to Sarhaan's but deeper.

'Tirexion Loftt,' his father replied. 'With my son, Bache, and colleagues. We need to speak with you, Valent. It's about Sarhaan.'

A long silence followed, during which Bache fought the urge to press the panel again. The jammer on his back felt suddenly heavier.

The door slid open suddenly with a soft hiss, revealing a Theo male standing in the entrance. Like Sarhaan, he possessed the ethereal beauty characteristic of his species…alabaster skin, eyes of shifting violet, and hair so pale it seemed to glow under the laboratory lights. But where Sarhaan had projected serenity, Valent radiated a nervous intensity.

'Tirexion,' he said, his voice betraying no emotion. 'It has been many rotations.' His gaze shifted to the others in the group.

His eyes lingered on Bache for a moment longer than the others, as if measuring him against some internal standard.

'You'd better come inside,' Valent said, stepping back to allow them entry. 'These corridors have ears.'

The laboratory beyond was unlike any Bache had seen before. Unlike the sterile uniformity of GDA research facilities, Valent's space was a chaotic blend of cutting-edge technology and what appeared to be ancient artefacts. Crystalline structures similar to the one they'd destroyed at the mining facility stood in transparent containment fields, though these pulsed with blue light rather than green. Holographic displays floated at various workstations, showing molecular structures rotating slowly in three dimensions.

'You mentioned Sarhaan,' Valent said, securing the door behind them with a complex series of commands. 'What's happened?'

Bache exchanged a glance with his father, who nodded slightly.

'She's dead,' Bache said, the words still painful to voice. 'Murdered through neural filament activation while helping us.'

Valent's alabaster features remained impassive, but his violet eyes darkened to almost indigo.

'I suspected as much when I couldn't reach her. The connection patterns changed three days ago.' He moved to a workstation and tapped a sequence into a console. 'Who else knows you're here?'

'Just our captain,' Riccs answered, positioning himself near the door. 'We're travelling under communications blackout.'

Valent nodded approvingly.

'Wise. The network is extensive.' He turned to Tirexion. 'You were right all along, old friend. About everything.'

'I wish I hadn't been,' Tirexion replied, lowering himself into a seat with a grimace. 'We've identified seventeen compromised crew members on our ship. And we've tracked the control signal to somewhere in the Dimioi sector.'

'The Sarcophagus Nebula,' Valent said, not a question but a confirmation. 'Yes, that makes sense. The radiation interference would mask their presence from casual scans.'

Bache stepped forward, removing the miniaturised jammer from his pack and placing it on the table. 'We've developed this based on Sarhaan's design. It disrupts the neural connections and prevents new ones from forming.'

Valent's eyes widened slightly as he examined the device.

'Impressive adaptation. But it won't be enough, not for what you'll face in the nebula.'

'What exactly will we face?' Zaphir asked, her voice tense.

Valent glanced at each of them in turn before his gaze settled on Tirexion.

'She was about to tell you, wasn't she? Before they killed her?'

Tirexion nodded grimly. 'She said it wasn't the Nkris. That we'd defeated them only a few years ago and this particular operation has been running for decades. She was about to name who was really behind it all when...' He trailed off.

'No,' Valent agreed, moving to a spherical console at the centre of the room. 'Not the Nkris. Though they really want you to believe that.' He activated the device, and a holographic display of the galaxy materialised in the air. Certain areas glowed with an ominous red light, forming a pattern that resembled a web stretching right across the galaxy.

'What you're seeing is the infiltration network,' Valent explained, manipulating the display to zoom in on one particular sector. 'Each point represents a node of influence...modified drives, compromised personnel, resonance amplifiers and so on.'

Bache studied the pattern, his engineering mind automatically searching for the underlying structure. The web was densest around key GDA installations and trade routes, but tendrils extended into Klatt space and even beyond into unaligned territories.

'This is far more extensive than we realised,' he murmured, counting several major nodes.

'Indeed,' Valent agreed, his violet eyes reflecting the holographic light. 'They've been building this network for nearly eight centuries, patiently expanding their influence.'

'Eight hundred years?' Riccs's voice carried a tone of disbelief. 'That's impossible. No operation could remain hidden that long.'

'It can when the architects live for thousands of years,' Valent countered, his voice dropping to barely above a whisper. 'When they have the patience to place agents and influence events across generations.'

Tirexion leaned forward, his face pale in the red glow of the hologram.

'The Dimioi,' he said softly. 'It's the Dimioi again, isn't it?'

Valent's expression remained neutral, but he inclined his head slightly.

'Yes and no,' he said. 'The Dimioi were as good as wiped out more than a millennium ago in the Extermination War. Or so everyone believed.'

Bache's mind raced, trying to recall what little he knew of the ancient species from his history lessons. The Dimioi had been a technologically advanced race that had attempted galactic domination, triggering the devastating Extermination War. Every historical record indicated they had been completely wiped out.

'You're saying some survived?' he asked.

'Not survived as much,' Valent corrected. 'More evolved. When they were faced with extinction, a small fraction of Dimioi leadership uploaded their consciousness into a hybrid technological-biological matrix. They abandoned their physical forms and became something else entirely.'

'What does that even mean?' Zaphir asked, her eyes wide at the revelation.

Valent moved to another console and activated a secondary display. This one showed microscopic images of neural tissue infested with the now-familiar filaments.

'These aren't merely control mechanisms,' he explained. 'They're extensions of the Dimioi consciousness itself. Each filament carries a fragment of their collective mind. When they infect a host, they don't just control them…they partially merge with them.'

Bache felt his stomach turn as the implications sank in.

'The voices Hollander claimed to hear…'

'Would've been real,' Valent confirmed. 'The whispers of ancient Dimioi consciousness filtering through the neural network. They call themselves the Omada.'

32

Valent's laboratory, Meridian Station, Klatt border neutral
zone

BACHE'S MIND RACED, connecting pieces that had seemed
disparate before.

'The modified Xephoni drives, the resonance amplifiers,
the selective targeting of key personnel…they're building a
network of agents throughout GDA space,' he said.

'And beyond,' Valent confirmed. 'The Klatt Empire
has been similarly infiltrated. The Omada don't recognise
political boundaries.'

Zaphir folded her arms, her expression sceptical.

'If they've been at this you say for centuries, why
haven't they succeeded already? Why the sudden accelerated timeline now?'

Valent's eyes darkened.

'Because something changed. The Nkris threat united the galaxy in ways that hadn't happened before. New alliances formed, technologies were shared…and the Omada saw an opportunity in the ensuing chaos.'

He manipulated the display again, and the image shifted to show what appeared to be a massive crystal similar to the one they'd destroyed, but exponentially larger.

'This is their primary resonance node,' Valent explained. 'Hidden deep within the Sarcophagus Nebula. From here, they coordinate their entire network. The two remaining more localised nodes…'

'We're tracking those now,' said Bache, interrupting.

'You've found the other nodes already?' Valent's eyes widened with surprise. 'That's impressive.'

'One appears to be in the Auriga system, probably on one of the outer moons,' Bache explained. 'The other's signal is harder to pin down, it's…'

'In Klatt territory,' said Valent. 'That would be a tough one to get to.'

Valent nodded, his expression turned grave as he manipulated the holographic display again. The image shifted to show a detailed cross-section of what appeared to be the main resonance node.

'This is what you'll face in the nebula. The structure is heavily defended, not just with conventional weapons, but with neural interfaces that can attack your mind directly. Your jammers will provide some protection, but they'll need modifications to withstand the concentrated assault you'll encounter there.'

Bache studied the schematics, his engineering mind already cataloguing the necessary adjustments.

'Can you help us upgrade them?'

'I can do better than that.' Valent moved to a storage unit at the far end of the lab and pressed his palm against its surface. The unit hummed briefly before sliding open, revealing a set of sleek, silvery devices. 'These are advanced neural shields…Theo technology combined with what I've learned about Omada resonance patterns. They'll provide almost complete protection from infiltration attempts.'

Riccs stepped forward, examining the devices with a suspicious eye.

'How do we know these will work? Or that we can trust you?'

Valent's face remained impassive, but Bache noticed a slight tightening around his eyes.

'A fair and justified question,' the Theo acknowledged. 'Sarhaan trusted me with her research after the first attacks on our people. I've been working independently ever since, developing countermeasures.' He turned to Tirexion. 'Your father can vouch for me. We've collaborated for several decades.'

Tirexion nodded slowly.

'Valent has always been…unconventional by Theo standards, but his work is impeccable. If he says these will protect us, they will.'

Bache's shoulder twinged as he shifted his weight. 'These shields…will they allow us to approach the main node without detection?'

'They'll prevent neural infiltration,' Valent clarified. 'But conventional sensors will still detect your ship. You'll need another advantage to reach the node undetected.'

'The *K2* has cloaking technology,' Zaphir said.

Valent shook his head.

'The radiation in the nebula will interfere with standard cloaking fields. And the Omada will have sensors calibrated specifically to detect GDA drive signatures.'

Bache frowned, considering their options.

'What about a smaller vessel? Something with a different drive signature?'

'That might work,' Valent agreed. 'Especially if it's something they wouldn't expect.' He hesitated, then added, 'I have a small ship. Modified Theo design with a hybrid drive.'

Riccs stepped closer, eyeing Valent. 'Everything sounds a bit convenient and easy. What's the catch?'

Valent's violet eyes darkened.

'The catch, Commander, is that someone needs to physically place a device at the heart of their primary node and activate it manually. The Sarcophagus Nebula is probably defended, and the radiation will interfere with any attempt at a remote detonation.'

Bache felt a chill run down his spine.

'I'll go,' he said without hesitation.

'We'll go,' Zaphir corrected, stepping beside him. Her eyes met his, challenging him to argue.

Valent shook his head.

'Not alone you won't. I'm coming with you. The device requires Theo biometric authentication to activate, and I'm the only one who can provide it now that Sarhaan is gone.'

Tirexion started to rise from his seat.

'I should be the one who…'

'No,' Bache interrupted, placing a hand on his father's shoulder. 'You're still recovering. I have Sarhaan's biometrics on my data chip here. I will go alone.'

'Don't you fucking dare,' Zaphir spluttered. 'It's suicide.'

'I'm not intending to die,' he said, giving her shoulder a squeeze and turning back to Valent. 'Would it be possible to construct a time delay to the device?' he asked.

Valent sucked on his bottom lip for a moment, as he turned and stared at one of his holographic designs.

'It's possible I think,' he said, finally.

'That's settled then,' said Bache, holding up both hands to thwart any more objections.

Zaphir huffed and glared at Valent.

'You'd better make the delay long enough for him to escape,' she hissed.

'I will do my utmost to ensure his safety,' the Theo scientist said, already moving to a workbench covered with intricate components. 'Assuming the device isn't damaged during placement, I can create a delay sequence of approximately ten to fifteen minutes.'

Bache nodded, satisfied with the answer.

'That should be sufficient.'

Riccs's expression remained sceptical. 'The captain won't approve this mission without proper planning and backup. We need contingencies.'

'Then let's make some,' Bache replied, stepping closer

to examine Valent's ship schematics. The vessel was sleek and compact, clearly built for speed rather than combat. Its hybrid drive configuration was unlike anything he'd seen in GDA vessels, with crystalline components integrated directly into the power matrix.

Tirexion pushed himself to his feet, his movements slow but determined.

'If you're going to attempt this, you'll need to modify the jamming frequency to account for the increased power at the primary node.'

Valent nodded in agreement.

'The resonance will be exponentially stronger there. Standard jammers would be overwhelmed within minutes.'

Bache's mind was already racing through the technical adjustments they'd need to make. The basic principles were sound, but the scale would require significant recalibration.

'How soon can we have the ship and jammers ready?' he asked.

'Eight hours for the modifications,' Valent replied, his slender fingers dancing over a holographic display. 'The neural shields are ready now, but integrating them with your existing technology will take some time.'

Zaphir stepped closer to Bache, her voice dropping to ensure only he could hear.

'This is bloody reckless, even for you. There has to be another way.'

'If you have a better suggestion, I'm all ears,' Bache replied, keeping his voice equally low. 'But right now, this is our best chance to cut off the Omada at their source.'

Her eyes held his for a long moment before she sighed in resignation.

'Fine. But I'm coming with you. You'll need someone to watch your back.'

'We'll discuss that with the captain,' Bache said, not wanting to argue the point further. He turned back to Valent. 'What kind of defences should we expect at the node?'

The Theo scientist's expression grew more severe.

'Automated defence systems, certainly. Possibly some form of biological guardians...the Omada have been known to create hybrid organisms to protect their installations. But the most dangerous threat will be the resonance itself. Even with protection, prolonged exposure could have...unpredictable effects.'

'Define unpredictable,' Riccs demanded.

'Hallucinations, disorientation, temporary neural pathway disruption,' Valent listed, his tone clinical. 'In extreme cases, permanent cognitive damage.'

Bache felt a chill at the scientist's words but pushed the sensation aside.

'How soon can you prepare the ship?' he asked Valent.

'The ship can be ready in three hours,' Valent said, his long fingers manipulating the display to show the vessel's specifications. 'It uses a modified Theo drive that produces minimal resonance signatures. The Omada's sensors will have difficulty distinguishing it from background radiation.'

'And the device?' Tirexion asked, his voice strained despite his obvious effort to appear strong.

'I've been working on it for years,' Valent replied,

moving to another section of his lab. He pressed his palm against a seemingly blank wall, which shimmered and disappeared to reveal a secure chamber beyond.

Inside sat an object that made Bache's breath catch. It resembled a crystalline sphere about the size of his head, but the interior swirled with colours that seemed to defy the normal spectrum…shifting between hues that his mind couldn't quite recognise.

'This is a resonance inverter,' Valent explained. 'When activated at the heart of their primary node, it will create a cascading disruption throughout their entire network. Every neural filament, every modified drive, every resonance amplifier will be severed simultaneously and cause the nodes to explode violently.'

'What about the infected personnel?' Bache asked, thinking of the seventeen crew members on the *K2*.

'The disruption should sever the connection without harming the hosts,' Valent said, though Bache detected a slight hesitation in his voice. 'The neural filaments will dissolve harmlessly.'

'Should?' Riccs questioned, his expression darkening.

'There are no guarantees when dealing with technology this advanced,' Valent admitted. 'But our tests on isolated neural tissue have shown promising results.'

Bache felt the weight of responsibility settling on his shoulders. Seventeen lives on the *K2*, most likely thousands more throughout GDA space, and perhaps the fate of multiple civilisations…all depending on this mission's success.

'I'll take that risk,' he said firmly. 'Riccs…we don't have a choice.'

Tirexion reached out and gripped his arm, his fingers surprisingly strong despite his weakened state.

'Be careful, Bache,' he said, his eyes searching his son's face.

'I will,' Bache promised, squeezing his father's arm reassuringly in return.

33

The bridge hangar, *Katadromiko 2*, Meridian Station, Klatt
border neutral zone

WITHIN HOURS, they'd loaded Valent's sleek vessel into the
K2's main hangar bay, securing it with magnetic clamps.
Bache supervised as engineering crews helped transfer the
scientist's equipment, including the resonance inverter,
which remained sealed in its protective case. The crystalline device seemed to pulse with an inner light even
through its containment, making Bache uneasy every time
he glanced at it.

Valent moved efficiently around the hangar, directing
the placement of his equipment with precise gestures. For
someone who'd supposedly spent years in isolation, he
adapted quickly to the military environment of the *K2*.

'Careful with that,' the Theo scientist called as two
crew members struggled with a large crystalline compo-

nent. 'The alignment must remain perfect or the calibration will be lost.'

Captain Whipper approached Bache, his expression grim.

'I don't like this plan,' he said without preamble. 'It's too risky, too dependent on variables we can't control.'

'Do you have a better option, sir?' Bache asked, watching as Valent's ship was securely anchored. The vessel's sleek lines and unusual configuration stood out starkly against the utilitarian design of the *K2*'s hangar.

'No, I don't,' Whipper admitted with obvious reluctance. 'But I'm not sending you in alone. Specialist Mye and a small tactical team will accompany you to the edge of the nebula. They'll remain at a safe distance but close enough to extract you if things go to shit.'

Bache nodded, relief washing through him despite his earlier insistence on going alone. The thought of facing whatever waited in the nebula without backup had been weighing on him more than he'd admitted to himself.

'Thank you, sir.'

Whipper's eyes narrowed as he studied Bache's face.

'There's to be no heroics, Loftt. This is a tactical operation. You get in, place the device, and get out. No improvisation, no last stands. Clear?'

'Crystal, sir.'

The captain nodded sharply before turning to watch Valent's equipment being transferred.

'How much do you trust this Theo?' he asked, lowering his voice.

Bache followed his gaze.

'My father vouches for him. That's enough for me.'

'Let's hope so,' Whipper muttered. 'Because we're betting a lot on his intel and technology.'

The final preparations moved quickly. Valent worked alongside Bache and the engineering team to calibrate the neural shields and integrate them with the *K2*'s systems. The modified jammers would protect the ship during their approach into the nebula.

'That's the last of it,' Zaphir announced, checking items off a digital manifest. She'd barely spoken to Bache since his decision to undertake the mission alone, her disapproval evident in the tight set of her jaw.

'Thank you,' Bache replied, hoping to thaw the tension between them. 'This wouldn't be possible without your help.'

She met his eyes briefly before looking away. 'Just make bloody sure you come back.'

Before he could respond, Riccs approached, his military boots clunking across the hangar floor.

'Captain wants you to follow him up to the bridge. We're ready to depart.'

Bache nodded, taking one last look at the Theo vessel that would carry him into the heart of the Omada network. It seemed impossibly small for such a momentous mission.

The bridge was humming with activity when Bache arrived. Whipper stood on his raised dais, studying the navigational display with intense interest. The image showed their planned route to the Sarcophagus Nebula…a series of jumps through increasingly remote sectors, avoiding major shipping lanes and monitored space.

'Right, Chief Engineer,' Whipper said, not looking up. 'Your Theo friend's equipment is secured?'

'Yes, sir. Everything's locked down and ready for transit.'

'Good.' Whipper straightened, addressing the bridge crew. 'Set course for the Sarcophagus Nebula. We depart in ten minutes.' He turned to face Bache directly. 'This is our one chance to cut off the Omada at their source. Make it count.'

'I will, sir,' Bache replied, his throat dry.

The journey to the edge of the nebula took nine days, each jump bringing them closer to the radioactive graveyard that had once been the front line of the Extermination War. Bache spent most of his days with Valent, making final adjustments to both the neural shields and the resonance inverter. The Theo worked with meticulous precision, his long fingers moving over the crystalline components with confident familiarity.

'The radiation will interfere with standard communications,' Valent explained as they calibrated the ship's systems. 'Once you're inside the old war zone, you'll be on your own.'

Bache nodded, focusing on the control interface. The Theo vessel's systems were unlike anything he'd piloted before…it had a masculine sentient computer that annoyed Bache no end, with his tediously vexatious sense of humour.

'What do I call you?' Bache asked, staring up at the ceiling.

'Valent calls me Tyche.'

'Where does that name come from?'

'It's an ancient Ellinika word for luck.'

'Well, let's hope you are just that.'

Valent arrived through the airlock carrying the inverter.

'How close will I need to get to place that?' Bache asked.

Valent placed the box carefully in the corner of the cockpit before answering.

'In the central chamber. You'll know it when you see it…a crystalline structure much larger than the one you destroyed, pulsing with green-gold light. The inverter must be hidden directly beneath it, so no one can move it before the event.'

'And the time delay is?'

'Twelve minutes and about forty seconds,' Valent confirmed. 'It should be sufficient for you to clear the immediate blast radius.'

'Should be,' Bache repeated under his breath.

The Theo scientist paused, studying him.

'Having second thoughts?'

'No,' Bache said firmly. 'Just making sure I understand the parameters.'

On the morning of the ninth day, Bache stood in the observation deck, watching as the *K2* dropped out of its final jump. The nebula spread before them, a vast cloud of dust and radiation glowing with an eerie blue-green luminescence. Lightning-like discharges flickered through the gases, creating brief, spectacular flashes that illuminated the debris field beyond.

'Beautiful in a terrifying way,' Tirexion said, joining

his son at the viewport. His father looked stronger now, though still far from his normal self.

'Dad, I...'

'Don't,' Tirexion interrupted, placing a hand on Bache's shoulder. 'Whatever you're about to say, save it for when you return.'

Bache nodded, swallowing the lump in his throat. 'I'll be careful...I promise.'

'I know you will.' His father's eyes were bright with emotion he rarely displayed. 'You've become more than I ever could have hoped for, Bache. Just remember what I taught you...there's always more than one way to skin a Deelataynian river rat.'

The final briefing took place in the tactical operations room. Captain Whipper stood before a holographic display of the nebula, the swirling gases casting an eerie glow over his stern features. Bache took his place among the assembled team, feeling the weight of every glance. Zaphir stood beside him, her earlier anger seemingly replaced with grim determination.

'This is what we're facing,' Whipper said, manipulating the display to zoom in on a particular region of the nebula. 'Somewhere in this sector lies the Omada's primary node. The radiation makes precise scanning impossible, but Valent's calculations put it approximately here.' He indicated a darker region where the nebula's gases seemed more concentrated.

Bache studied the display, committing the approach vector to memory. The path would take him through massive fields of debris...remnants of ancient warships destroyed in the Extermination War.

'Once you're inside...' Riccs continued, stepping forward, '...standard communications will be compromised. We'll establish a retrieval point at these coordinates.' He highlighted a position just outside the densest part of the nebula. 'Specialist Mye and her team will maintain position there, ready for extraction. Both vessels will have an emergency jump plotted at all times. The blast radius might be bigger than you expect.'

Zaphir nodded, her face set in stone.

'We'll be monitoring for your exit signal. Don't keep us waiting.'

'The neural shield should protect you from direct infiltration attempts,' Valent added, his violet eyes reflecting the holographic glow. 'But prolonged exposure to the resonance field may cause disorientation. You must place the inverter and exit quickly, before you lose your way.'

Whipper's gaze locked with Bache's.

'Remember your primary objective. Place the device and get out. Nothing else matters.'

'Understood, sir.'

The briefing concluded with final equipment checks and contingency planning. As the others filed out, Whipper held Bache back with a hand on his arm.

'Your father tells me you've always had a tendency to improvise,' he said, his voice low. 'Not this time, Loftt. I want you back on my ship in one piece.'

'I'll do my best, sir.'

'Hmm,' grunted Whipper. 'See that you do.' He released his arm. 'Launch in thirty minutes.'

The Theo vessel hummed with energy as Bache completed his pre-flight checks. The cockpit was designed for a single pilot, its crystalline controls responding to touch with subtle pulses of light. The neural shield sat behind him, its soft blue glow casting strange shadows across the console.

'Systems all tickety-boo,' Tyche announced, his voice carrying that irritating lilt Bache had come to dread. 'All parameters within acceptable coolness. Though I must say, for a suicide mission, you seem remarkably calm.'

'It's not a bloody suicide mission,' Bache muttered, adjusting the navigation settings. 'And I'd appreciate less commentary and more navigation assistance.'

'All right, keep your pants on,' Tyche replied, sounding almost hurt. 'Though I feel obligated to point out that the radiation levels in our destination will be a tad high and your suit will barely cope.'

Bache sighed and rolled his eyes as he prepped the ship for flight.

34

Valent's ship, entering the Sarcophagus Nebula

THE SARCOPHAGUS NEBULA LOOMED AHEAD, a swirling mass of irradiated gases stained blood-red and sickly green from a millennium of warfare. Bache guided Tyche through the outer boundary, feeling the small ship shudder as it penetrated the radioactive barrier.

'Shields holding at eighty-seven percent,' Tyche announced. 'Radiation levels elevated but within tolerance.'

'Any sign we've been detected?' Bache asked, his eyes scanning the sensor display.

'Negative. The nebula's interference is masking our approach as anticipated,' Tyche answered. 'Beware, multiple wrecks dead ahead.'

Bache nodded and was pleased Tyche was behaving a little more seriously now they were operational.

The viewport filled with the ghostly remnants of ancient warships, their twisted hulls frozen in the moment of their destruction. Massive dreadnoughts drifted alongside smaller frigates, all bearing the scars of weapons that had turned metal to slag. Some had been cleft nearly in half, others showed the distinctive honeycomb pattern of molecular disruptors that had been outlawed for centuries.

'This really is a massive graveyard,' Bache murmured, navigating around the blackened carcass of what might have once been a Klatt warship.

'The final battle of the Extermination War occurred right here,' Tyche informed him. 'Over three thousand vessels were destroyed in less than six hours.'

A flash of blue-white light erupted to port, and Bache yanked the controls, narrowly avoiding a tendril of plasma lightning that arced between two derelict hulls. The ship rocked violently as the energy discharge passed within metres of their hull.

'Warning,' Tyche announced, its masculine voice maddeningly calm. 'Plasma discharge detected. Recommend maintaining minimum safe distance of five hundred metres from all derelict vessels.'

'Thanks for the timely advice,' Bache muttered, sweat beading on his forehead as he adjusted course. Another flash illuminated the cockpit, casting harsh shadows across the controls. This time the lightning struck a nearby wreck, sending the lump of ancient hull spinning past Tyche's front screen.

The debris field grew denser as Bache pushed deeper into the nebula. He threaded the nimble ship through gaps barely wider than its hull, wincing each time a piece of wreckage scraped against their shields. The neural jammer hummed, its protective field making his skin tingle with static electricity.

'Energy signature detected,' Tyche announced. 'Bearing zero-three-five, range eighty-four kilometres. Profile matches Valent's description of the primary node.'

He adjusted course, only to curse as another plasma discharge erupted directly in their path. He cut power, slowing again to allow the discharge to dissipate. He turned to sweep wide around more dead hulks. Some were recognisable as early GDA designs, others bore the distinctive architecture of the Dimioi...angular and threatening even in destruction.

'Detecting elevated radiation levels,' Tyche warned. 'Shield integrity at seventy-seven percent.'

A massive shadow loomed suddenly to port...the broken spine of what must have been a Dimioi dreadnought, its hull still bearing the scars of whatever had finally killed it. Bache banked sharply to avoid it.

The wreckage continued to spin in the nebula's currents, forcing Bache to make a series of rapid course corrections. He gripped the unfamiliar controls tightly, his knuckles whitening as another piece of debris scraped against their shields.

'Shield integrity at seventy-two percent,' Tyche announced, sounding almost bored. 'Primary node now forty kilometres and closing.'

Bache squinted through the viewport, trying to make out anything beyond the swirling gases and floating debris. The eerie glow of the nebula cast everything in sickly shades of green and blue, making distance and size difficult to judge. His eyes stung from the strain of the constant wide-eyed staring.

'Can you filter out some of this interference?' he asked, adjusting the sensor display. 'I would love a clearer view of what's coming up ahead.'

'I'll have a bash,' Tyche replied. 'But don't expect miracles.'

The display flickered, then sharpened slightly. Through the haze, Bache could now make out a larger structure ahead…not a derelict, but something deliberate and intact. His pulse quickened as he leaned forward.

'That's gotta be it,' he whispered.

Rising from the nebula haze like some ancient monument was a massive crystalline structure, its surface faceted like a geometric nightmare. Green-gold light pulsed from within it, sending waves of energy rippling through the surrounding gases. Unlike the resonance amplifier they'd destroyed before, this was exponentially larger…at least the size of a small space station.

'What remarkable engineering that is,' Tyche commented. 'The crystalline lattice appears to be self-repairing. No wonder it's survived in here for all those centuries.'

Bache circled the structure slowly and cautiously, searching for a way in. The neural shield hummed more intensely now, the protective field straining against the powerful resonance waves emanating from the node.

His headache intensified as they drew closer, a pressure building behind his eyes that made him squint. The neural shield was working, but something was still getting through…a subtle influence that made his thoughts feel sluggish and heavy.

'Any signs of automated defences?' he asked, scanning for weapon emplacements.

'None detected, but that doesn't mean they're not there,' Tyche replied. 'The radiation could be masking them.'

As if on cue, a beam of energy lanced out from the structure, narrowly missing their port side. Bache yanked the controls hard to starboard, sending the ship into a tight spiral.

'What was that about no defences?' he snapped, fighting to stabilise their course.

'I said none detected,' Tyche corrected primly. 'My sensors struggle in this soup.'

Three more energy beams cut through the nebula gases, creating ionised trails that lingered in the murk. Bache dove beneath one, rolled over another, and skimmed perilously close to a derelict hull to avoid the third.

'Analysing defence pattern,' Tyche announced. 'They appear to be automated and have problems with targeting here in this soup. Recommend reducing power output.'

He throttled back to a crawl just as Tyche spoke again.

'Warning,' he announced, a new urgency in his voice. 'Detecting directed energy scan. We are being probed.'

Bache's heart hammered against his ribs. 'Can they actually see us?'

'Unknown. The neural shield is interfering with their scan, but they seem to be aware something is present.'

He swallowed hard and adjusted course, aiming for what appeared to be a docking structure extending from one of the crystalline arms. The resonance inverter sat in its container beside him, humming softly in response to the massive node's energy.

'Taking us in,' he said. 'Prepare for landing.'

As they approached, Bache noticed movement around the structure…small, dart-like objects that moved with unnatural precision. They resembled no vessels he'd ever seen, their surfaces shifting and flowing like liquid metal.

'Sentinels,' Tyche warned. 'Automated defence units. They are converging on our position.'

'How many?'

'Eight…nine now,' Tyche corrected as another sentinel appeared from behind a crystalline spire. 'They appear to be scanning for our neural signature.'

Bache gripped the controls tighter, his mind racing through possible approaches. The sentinels moved with unnatural fluidity, their metallic surfaces rippling as they changed direction.

'I need a blind spot,' he muttered, scanning the structure. 'Some way to approach without them detecting us.'

He banked sharply, diving beneath the main structure where the crystalline arms met in a complex geometric pattern. The headache intensified, pressure building behind his eyes until his vision blurred at the edges. He blinked hard, trying to clear it.

'The radiation is higher here and affecting the shield integrity,' Tyche warned. 'Sixty-three percent and dropping. Recommend limiting exposure time.'

Bache circled beneath the structure, looking for any opening. The sentinels had lost track of them temporarily, their dart-like forms hovering above the main structure in a search pattern.

'There,' he whispered, spotting what looked like a maintenance access point where two of the crystalline arms joined. 'Can we fit through that gap?'

'Barely,' Tyche replied. 'But it's your best option unless you fancy taking on nine sentinels with our non-existent weapons systems.'

Bache guided the ship towards the opening, powering down all non-essential systems to minimise their signature. The vessel slipped between the crystalline structures with barely centimetres to spare on either side, the hull vibrating as their shield scraped against the sides.

'Shield integrity at fifty-eight percent,' Tyche reported. 'The resonance is intensifying. Your neural shield is experiencing considerable strain.'

The pressure in Bache's skull increased. A high-pitched whine filled his ears, like the sound of stressed metal about to fracture. He gritted his teeth and pushed forward, guiding the ship deeper into the structure's interior.

The passage opened suddenly into a vast central chamber that took his breath away. A massive crystalline core hung suspended in the centre, pulsing with the sickly green-gold light. Energy arced between it and smaller crystals arranged in a complex three-dimensional pattern around the chamber.

'That's what we're looking for,' he breathed, the pain in his head momentarily forgotten. 'The primary node's core.'

Below the floating core was a platform that appeared

to be designed for maintenance access. Bache guided the ship towards it, fighting against the disorientation that threatened to overwhelm him. The neural shield hummed frantically against his back, struggling to maintain its protective field.

'I'll need to set down there,' he said, indicating the platform. 'Can you maintain position while I place the inverter?'

'I can, though I must point out that radiation levels on that platform exceed safe exposure limits for humans. You'll have approximately eighteen minutes before cellular damage becomes lethal.'

'The delay's set for twelve minutes and forty seconds,' Bache replied, checking the environmental readings on his suit. 'I'll have more than enough time to get back out.'

He flared the ship, turned and landed, feeling the slight jolt as the struts made contact with the platform. The resonance inverter felt heavier than he remembered as he lifted it from its container, the weight of it straining against his injured shoulder.

'Beginning countdown when you exit the airlock,' Tyche informed him. 'Remember, the radiation shielding in your suit is minimal. Eighteen minutes maximum.'

Bache secured his helmet, checking the seal twice before cycling the airlock. The moment the outer door opened, he felt it…a wave of pressure that seemed to push against his mind rather than his body. The neural shield strapped to his back vibrated against his spine, working overtime to protect him from the invisible assault.

He stepped onto the platform, his boots connecting with a surface that felt oddly organic beneath his feet. The massive crystalline core hung above him, pulsing with hypnotic rhythm, tendrils of energy arcing between it and the surrounding structure. Up close, the scale of it was overwhelming…easily thirty metres in diameter, its surface etched with patterns that seemed to shift when he wasn't looking directly at them.

'Sixteen minutes remaining,' Tyche's voice crackled through his comm. 'The sentinels are still searching the exterior. You remain undetected in here for now.'

Bache moved carefully towards the centre of the platform, directly beneath the core. Each step felt like wading through thick mud, the resonance creating resistance that wasn't physical but somehow affected his movements anyway. His headache intensified, vision blurring at the edges as he fought to maintain focus.

The platform contained what looked like maintenance stations, crystalline consoles arranged in a circle around the central point. None of them resembled any technology he recognised, their surfaces flowing like liquid even as they maintained solid form.

He reached the centre and knelt down, placing the inverter on the platform in the middle of the consoles. His fingers felt thick and clumsy as he activated the device, watching as its surface shifted from inert crystal to the same swirling patterns as the core above. The moment it activated, the pressure in his head doubled, a spike of pain driving through his temple that made him gasp.

'Fourteen minutes,' Tyche reminded him. 'Radiation exposure at twenty-two percent of maximum safe dosage.'

Bache pressed his wrist against the inverter's authentication panel, feeling the burn as Sarhaan's biometric signature transferred from his implant. The device vibrated, its inner light shifting from blue to violet as it accepted the authentication.

'Countdown initiated,' he confirmed, watching the timer begin its backward march. 'Twelve minutes forty seconds to detonation.'

He stood, turning back towards the ship, when movement caught his eye. At first, he thought it was just another tendril of energy from the core, but this was different... more deliberate. A ripple moved across the platform's surface, heading towards him with disturbing purpose.

35

Inside the primary node, the Sarcophagus Nebula

THE RIPPLE SURGED TOWARDS HIM, a fluid-like disturbance in the platform's surface. Bache back-pedalled, nearly losing his balance as the neural shield on his back vibrated violently against his spine.

'Tyche, what the hell is that?' he hissed into his comm.

'Unknown entity approaching your position,' the AI responded, its usually glib tone now sharp with urgency. 'Strongly recommend immediate withdrawal.'

'No shit,' he said, continuing to back away.

The ripple stopped about two metres away, then rose from the surface. The material of the platform twisted upward, forming a column that gradually took shape… humanoid, but wrong in several ways Bache couldn't immediately process. Its proportions were slightly off, limbs too long and thin, head too large and oddly angular.

'Twelve minutes remaining,' Tyche reminded him. 'Radiation exposure increasing.'

The figure's surface solidified, revealing what appeared to be a Dimioi…or at least, what the historical records suggested they looked like. Its skin was silver-grey, with darker patterns etched across its surface that pulsed with the same sickly green-gold light as the core above.

'You should not be here, human,' it said, its voice resonating directly in Bache's mind rather than through his ears. The neural shield screamed in protest, the pitch rising to an almost unbearable level.

Bache's hand moved instinctively towards his sidearm, but stopped halfway. The inverter was counting down behind him. He just needed to stall this creature.

'I could say the same to you,' he replied, fighting to keep his voice steady despite the pounding in his head. 'The Dimioi were supposed to be extinct.'

The figure's face rippled, features rearranging in what might have been amusement.

'The Dimioi you knew are gone. We are Omada now. Beyond flesh, beyond death.' It tilted its head, studying him with eyes that were simply empty voids in its face. 'You carry Theo technology. Interesting. We thought we had eliminated that particular threat.'

The pressure in Bache's skull intensified. His vision blurred momentarily, dark spots dancing at the edges. He blinked hard, forcing himself to focus.

'Eleven minutes,' came Tyche's voice, now distorted through the comm. 'Entity is attempting to breach your neural shield.'

The figure took a step forward, its movements unnaturally fluid, as if its joints followed different rules of physics.

'Your primitive barrier will not hold,' it said. 'Already your mind begins to fracture. Soon you will join us, another consciousness in our collective.'

Bache felt something warm trickling from his nose… blood, he realised. The neural shield was failing. He needed to get back to the ship.

'I don't think so,' he said, slowly backing towards Tyche. 'I'm not staying for the party.'

The figure's arm suddenly extended, stretching impossibly across the space between them like a liquid whip, aiming straight for Bache's throat. He ducked and rolled sideways, the movement sending a spike of pain through his shoulder. The creature's arm slumped down into the platform where he'd been standing, the impact creating ripples across the surface.

'Ten minutes,' Tyche warned. 'Radiation exposure now at thirty-one percent.'

He scrambled to his feet, drawing his weapon and firing at the Omada entity. The energy bolt passed straight through its fluid form, leaving a momentary hole that closed almost instantly.

'Conventional energy weapons are ineffective against our current form,' the creature said, its voice echoing painfully inside Bache's skull. 'We are beyond physical harm.'

The neural shield on Bache's back shrieked, the pitch rising to an unbearable level as the creature's influence pressed against it. More blood trickled from his nose, the metallic taste reaching his mouth and tongue. His vision swam, the chamber seeming to distort around him.

'Nine minutes,' came Tyche's increasingly distorted voice. 'Radiation exposure approaching critical.'

The Omada entity flowed towards him, its form rippling and changing as it moved. Bache backed towards the ship, keeping his eyes on the creature while trying to maintain his footing on the vibrating platform.

'Your opposition is admirable but completely futile,' the entity said. 'The device you've placed is already being neutralised.'

Bache risked a glance back at the inverter. To his horror, tendrils of the platform's material had begun to wrap around it, attempting to smother its glow.

'Shit,' he hissed, firing again at the creature to buy himself seconds. He lunged back towards the inverter, his body screaming in protest as radiation seared through his protective suit.

The Omada entity anticipated his move, its form splitting into two distinct shapes that flanked him. Bache skidded to a halt, trapped between them as they slowly converged.

'Eight minutes,' Tyche reported. 'Multiple entities detected approaching your position.'

Bache's mind raced through his options, each one worse than the last. The inverter was being smothered, and without it, the entire mission would fail. Millions would remain under Omada influence, including the seventeen crew members on the *K2*.

A desperate plan formed in his radiation-addled mind.

'Tyche, can you move closer to my position? I need to reach the inverter.'

'Affirmative, though can I point out this is extraordinarily reckless.'

'No, you can't.'

The ship's engines whined as it lifted slightly and began moving towards him. The Omada entities turned towards the new threat, momentarily distracted.

Bache seized the opportunity, diving between them towards the inverter. His fingers closed around the device, tearing it free from the platform's grasping tendrils. The moment he touched it, a shock wave of energy pulsed through him, knocking him back with its intensity. His neural shield wailed in protest, the device straining against the overwhelming resonance.

'Seven minutes,' Tyche called, the ship now hovering just metres away, airlock open. 'Radiation reaching dangerous levels. Your cellular structure is showing signs of damage.'

The two Omada entities flowed towards him with terrifying speed, their forms merging into a single wave that rose above him like a tsunami of living material. Bache clutched the inverter to his chest, its heat searing through his suit, and sprinted for the ship.

'No.' The unified voice of the entities thundered inside his skull, bringing him to his knees as blood now flowed freely from his nose and ears. 'You will not take that, it must be eliminated.'

Bache's vision narrowed to a tunnel, the edges darkening as radiation poisoning and the neural assault combined to overwhelm his systems. The ship was so close, just metres away, the open airlock beckoning.

'Six minutes,' Tyche announced. 'Your neural shield is failing. I detect multiple breaches in its protective field.'

With a final surge of desperate strength, Bache lunged towards the airlock, the inverter clutched against his chest. The Omada wave crashed against him, its substance flowing around his legs, trying to drag him back. He kicked frantically, feeling the alien material trying to seep through his suit at the joints.

His fingers caught the edge of the airlock, and he hauled himself inside, the inverter scraping against the frame as he pulled it in with him. The Omada substance still clung to his legs, flowing up his body with horrifying purpose.

'Close the airlock.' he screamed, unable to reach the control panel from the floor.

The outer door began to slide shut, severing the Omada substance that still reached for him. The material writhed and pulsed before falling inert, its connection to the main entity cut off.

'Five minutes,' Tyche said as the airlock cycled. 'Recommend immediate departure from the node.'

Bache crawled into the cockpit, blood streaming down his face and his vision fading in and out. The neural shield had fallen silent, its protective field completely overwhelmed. He slumped into the pilot's seat, the inverter still clutched against him.

'Get us up high,' he gasped, his voice barely audible even to himself.

The ship lifted. The crystalline structure around them

began to pulse more rapidly, the green-gold light shifting towards a deep crimson.

'Four minutes,' Tyche reported. 'The node appears to be initiating some form of defensive protocol. Detecting energy build-up throughout the structure.'

Bache struggled to focus on the controls, but his hands wouldn't respond properly. The radiation poisoning was progressing rapidly, his muscles beginning to spasm.

'Three minutes.'

'I can't...can't pilot,' he said, blood bubbling from his lips.

'I have control,' said Tyche.

'Just keep us away from anything threatening,' Bache called. 'Be ready to fly underneath the node.'

'Two minutes.'

Bache threw himself back down onto the cockpit floor and with the inverter pushed out in front of him, he began crawling back towards the airlock.

'One minute.'

'Tyche...be ready to jump when I say,' he croaked. 'And open the airlock.'

'Are you insane?' Tyche replied, but the airlock door slid open anyway. 'What exactly are you planning to...'

'Fly under the node, NOW,' Bache shouted, clutching the inverter with trembling hands as he dragged himself towards the open doorway. Pain lanced through every cell in his body, radiation poisoning making his muscles spasm uncontrollably.

The ship banked sharply, and Bache had to grab the doorframe to avoid sliding back into the cockpit. Through the opening, he could see the massive crystalline structure looming above them, its surface now pulsing an angry crimson.

'Thirty seconds to detonation,' Tyche announced, his voice strangely solemn.

Bache positioned himself at the edge of the open airlock. The platform swirled below, radioactive gases illuminated by the node's ominous glow. His vision blurred, consciousness threatening to slip away entirely.

'Twenty seconds.'

Forcing himself to focus, Bache raised the inverter. The device was burning hot in his gloves, its surface shifting through impossible colours as the countdown approached zero.

'Fifteen seconds.'

He thought he was going to throw up, but forced the bile back down.

'Lower. Get us directly under the centre,' Bache shouted, blood spraying from his lips onto the inside of his visor with each word.

The ship dropped, positioning itself directly beneath the massive crystalline core. Bache could feel the resonance vibrating through his bones, threatening to tear him apart from the inside.

'Ten seconds.'

With his last ounce of strength, Bache pushed the inverter out the airlock door, watching as it tumbled away beneath the node. For a moment, it seemed to hang suspended, as if caught in some invisible current.

'Close the airlock,' he screamed, collapsing backward onto the deck. 'Jump now, Tyche...JUMP.'

The airlock hissed shut as Tyche engaged the jump

drive. Reality twisted around them, the familiar disorientation of a jump amplified a hundredfold by the nebula's distortion field. Bache's vision went white with pain, his consciousness wavering with the overwhelming trauma.

The inverter had activated, causing the massive node to detonate with planet-busting violence at the exact time of the jump.

The shock wave caught the envelope as they jumped, sending the ship tumbling. Alarms blared as systems tried to make sense of why the vessel was spinning out of control. Bache was momentarily thrown against the bulkhead like a rag doll until the inertial dampers regained some form of normality. Something cracked in his chest, a fresh agony adding to the symphony of pain already consuming him.

'Navigation systems reloading,' Tyche announced, his voice somewhat distorted. 'Jump sequence compromised. Attempting to restabilise and establish location.'

Bache couldn't respond. His body had finally reached its limit, consciousness slipping away into blessed darkness

36

Observation deck, *Katadromiko 2*, bordering the
Sarcophagus Nebula

THE *K2* HUNG IN SPACE, its massive bulk silhouetted
against the swirling gases at the edge of the Sarcophagus
Nebula. Twenty-four hours had passed since the detonation, a cataclysmic explosion that had rippled through the
nebula with such violence that the shock wave had been
visible from the extraction point. The *K2*'s sensors had
recorded the event in remarkable detail…a brilliant flash
of light followed by an expanding sphere of energy that
had obliterated everything in its path.

Zaphir stood at the viewport on the observation deck,
her fingertips pressed against the cold transparent alloy as
she stared out into the void. Her eyes burned from lack of
sleep, her uniform was rumpled from the hours spent waiting. The space beyond was empty. No sign of Bache, of

Tyche, no emergency beacon, no debris field they could identify as the remains of the Theo vessel.

Nothing.

She pressed her forehead against the viewport, closing her eyes momentarily. A single tear running down her cheek. The persistent ache in her chest had grown worse with each passing hour. Twenty-four hours of scanning, searching, waiting. Twenty-four hours of increasingly desperate hope giving way to cold dread.

'Any change?' Tirexion's voice came from behind her.

She straightened, composing herself before turning to face Bache's father. The older man looked even more haggard than she felt, his face drawn with exhaustion and worry.

'No,' she said, the word scraping against her throat. 'Not a thing.'

Tirexion nodded slowly, his eyes carrying a weight that made Zaphir look away. She couldn't bear to see her own desperate sadness reflected there, magnified through a father's perspective.

'Captain Whipper is extending the search another twelve hours,' he said, his voice steady despite everything. 'Commander Riccs has three gunships mapping the debris field.'

'They won't find anything,' Zaphir said, the words bitter on her tongue. 'The blast radius was...extensive. So much bigger than we had anticipated. If he was anywhere near it...' She couldn't finish the sentence and turned away as she succumbed to a sob.

The observation deck door hissed open again, and Valent entered, his pale features sombre in the dim lighting. The Theo scientist had been working with the medical team to treat the seventeen infected crew members. With the complete annihilation of the primary node, the neural filaments had dissolved harmlessly, just as he had predicted.

'The last of the crew has been cleared,' Valent announced, his melodic voice subdued. 'No trace of the filaments remains. The Omada's influence has been completely severed.'

'Thanks to Bache,' Tirexion said quietly.

An uncomfortable silence fell between them. Zaphir turned back to the carbon glass window, unable to face their expressions. The nebula's gases seemed to mock her with their beauty, swirling clouds of blue and green illuminated by distant stars. Somewhere in that vastness, Bache had succeeded in his mission and likely paid the ultimate price.

Riccs entered, his heavy footsteps announcing his arrival before his voice did.

'Initial scans of the blast wave front indicate no evidence of Theo debris,' he said.

Zaphir straightened but didn't turn around. 'It doesn't surprise me, he would've been too close.' The words felt like broken glass in her throat.

'Captain's called another meeting.' Riccs's voice was gentler than she'd ever heard it. 'Ten minutes.'

She nodded, not trusting herself to speak again. When everyone had left, she allowed herself one moment…just one…where her shoulders sagged and her eyes squeezed shut against the burning sensation that threatened to overwhelm her. She screamed and kicked the wall as the tears came.

The tactical room felt smaller than usual, the air heavy with unspoken fear. Captain Whipper stood at the head of the table, his face drawn with exhaustion. Tirexion sat beside him, looking frail and hollow-eyed.

'It's been more than twenty-four hours,' Whipper began without preamble. 'Our sensors confirm the massive detonation occurred at the coordinates of the primary node. The blast radius exceeded our projections by a factor of three.'

'The inverter worked,' Valent said from his position near the door. 'The resonance cascade seems to have severed every neural connection in the Omada network simultaneously as expected.'

'At what cost?' Tirexion's voice was barely audible.

Zaphir clenched her fists under the table. The mission was, by any objective measure, a complete success. Except for one critical detail.

'We need to consider the possibility…' Whipper said carefully, '…that Chief Engineer Loftt didn't make it out in time.'

'No.' The word escaped Zaphir before she could stop it. All eyes turned to her. 'The Theo ship had jump capabilities. Bache would have calculated the blast radius. He would have gotten clear.'

'The radiation levels in the nebula would have interfered

with standard jump calculations,' Valent said, his violet eyes showing something that might have been sympathy. 'And the blast wave could well have disrupted the jump envelope.'

'So what are you saying?' Zaphir demanded. 'We just give up? Declare him dead and just walk away?'

Whipper's jaw clenched, the muscles in his face tightening visibly.

'I'm not suggesting we abandon him, Specialist. But we need to be realistic about our options.' He tapped the holomap, bringing up a projection of the nebula's current state. 'The blast has altered the entire structure of the region. Radiation levels have spiked beyond our ability to safely navigate. Even our most shielded vessels would be compromised within minutes.'

Zaphir stared at the projection, refusing to accept what she was seeing. The beautiful swirling gases had been transformed into a chaotic maelstrom of radiation and debris. If Bache was somewhere in that mess...

'Sorry to interrupt, Captain,' said the first officer, his image appearing next to the holomap. 'We've detected unusual energy signatures at the far edge of the nebula. They don't match any known vessel configuration.'

'Omada survivors perhaps?' Whipper asked.

'Unclear, Captain,' he replied. 'The readings are inconsistent. Could just be debris caught in some kind of resonance loop, just thought you'd want to know.

A sudden chime from the communications officer startled everyone. The officer's voice came through, tense and with urgency.

'Captain, we're receiving a transmission. Weak signal, unknown origin.'

Whipper frowned.

'Put it on.'

The speakers crackled with static, the sound rising and falling like waves on a shore. Zaphir held her breath, straining to hear anything recognisable through the interference.

'...ych...K...do...ead...' The voice faded in and out, distorted beyond recognition.

'Clean that up,' Whipper ordered, his knuckles white as he gripped the edge of the table.

The static receded slightly, and a voice...distinctly artificial but somehow familiar...broke through more clearly.

'Tyche to *Katadromiko 2*. Do you read? Situation rather dire. Require immediate assistance. Coordinates follow.'

Zaphir's heart leapt into her throat.

'That's Tyche. Bache's ship.'

Whipper was already moving.

'Lock onto that signal. Riccs, prep a rescue team. Full radiation protocol.' He turned to Zaphir. 'You're with me.'

Twenty minutes later, Zaphir stood in the hangar bay beside Commander Riccs, encased in a heavy-duty radiation suit. Her hands trembled slightly as she checked her equipment one final time. The rescue gunship loomed before them, its hull reinforced against the radiation they would encounter.

'Remember,' Riccs said, his voice muffled through the suit's comm system. 'We have a thirty-minute exposure window. Not a second more.'

Zaphir nodded, unable to trust her voice. The past day had drained her completely, hope and despair warring within her until she felt hollowed out. Now, with this faint glimmer of hope, she felt almost afraid to believe.

'Incoming transmission,' announced the *K2*'s navigation officer through the hangar speakers. 'Coordinates received and locked.'

The gunship's engines hummed to life as the pilot ran through the pre-flight sequence. Zaphir climbed aboard, her extreme radiation spacesuit making her movements clumsy. She took her position near the rear hatch, where she'd be first out when they reached the Theo ship.

'Radiation shielding at maximum,' the pilot reported as the hangar doors began to slide open. 'Departure in thirty seconds.'

The journey to the coordinates seemed to take an eternity. Zaphir stared at the status display, watching as they approached the edge of the nebula. The swirling gases had been transformed by the explosion, creating eddies of radiation that glowed with unnatural brilliance. The gunship's shields flared repeatedly as they penetrated the outer boundary, alarms chiming softly as radiation levels climbed.

'Ten minutes of safe exposure remaining,' the pilot announced, her voice tense. 'Signal source two kilometres ahead.'

Zaphir stretched up to peer through the front screen, straining to see through the murk. At first, there was nothing but swirling gas and debris, but then she spotted it…a glint of metal reflecting the nebula's eerie light.

'There he is,' she pointed.

The gunship slowed as they approached. Tyche was

barely recognisable. The once-sleek Theo vessel was now a battered hulk, its once smooth hull cracked and scorched. One entire section had been sheared away, exposing the interior to space. It tumbled slowly, adrift in the nebula's currents.

'Life signs?' Riccs demanded.

The pilot checked her sensors. 'One human life sign detected. Extremely weak but present.'

Zaphir's heart hammered against her ribs. Alive. He was alive.

'Docking will be impossible with that damage,' the pilot warned. 'We'll need to tractor it out to the *K2*.'

'Eight minutes of safe exposure remaining,' the suit's automated system reminded them.

'Do it,' said Riccs.

The small gunship manoeuvred as close as possible to the damaged vessel, its thrusters firing in short bursts to match Tyche's erratic tumble. Zaphir watched as the pilot activated the tractor and stabilised both vessels, before heading back towards clear space as quickly as possible.

It took fourteen minutes to get the two ships back into one of the *K2*'s hangars. A full radiation shield had been initiated, sectioning off the hangar from the rest of the ship.

The gunship, once it had dropped the Theo vessel gently down onto the deck, turned and landed beside it. Anti-radiation crews immediately began spraying both ships with an absorbent isofoam. Everyone on board the gunship was sprayed and washed down as they emerged.

Zaphir and Riccs both dived towards the Theo ship as

soon as they were done and began forcing open a damaged airlock with a plasma cutter.

It took eleven minutes to remove the outer door. They gave the still glowing hinges a wide birth as they entered the ship.

The vessel's interior was dark, emergency lighting casting eerie blue shadows across the cramped space. The air was bitterly cold as life support systems had clearly failed at some point. Condensation had frozen in delicate patterns across every surface. They'd had to enter via the rear airlock, as the two front ones were badly twisted.

'Tyche?' Zaphir called out. 'Where is he?'

Tyche responded, his voice distorted and fading in and out.

'Cock…pit. Radiation…exposure…critical. Sys…tems failing, so sorry.'

They moved forward, Riccs taking point as they navigated through the narrow passage towards the cockpit. The deck beneath their feet was buckled in places, evidence of the violent forces that had battered the vessel during its escape.

The cockpit door was jammed partially open. Riccs forced it wider with a grunt of effort, the metal groaning in protest. Zaphir squeezed through behind him.

And there he was.

Bache lay slumped in a corner, his body limp and still. His face was a mask of dried blood from his nose and ears, his skin deathly pale beneath the crimson-stained faceplate. The neural shield lay shattered on the floor beside him, its protective field long since failed.

Zaphir rushed forward, her radiation suit feeling unbearably bulky as she checked for vital signs. His pulse was rapid and thready, his breathing shallow and irregular.

He was alive, but for how long?

37

Hangar 228, *Katadromiko 2*, bordering the Sarcophagus
Nebula

'HE IS ALIVE,' Zaphir confirmed, her voice breaking. 'But
barely.'

Riccs stepped over and was already calling for the
medical team on standby.

'Prepare for immediate evac. Critical radiation poisoning. Multiple traumas.' He carefully lifted Bache up from
the floor, noting with alarm the amount of dried blood over
and around him.

They were just manoeuvring him out of the airlock
when a commotion erupted behind them as the medical
team burst through the hangar doorway. Valent was at the
front, his pale features taut with concentration as he
directed the medics pushing a large, grey device Zaphir
had never seen before. The machine hummed with energy,

its inner workings glowing with a red luminescence that pulsed slowly.

'Move aside,' Valent commanded, his melodic voice carrying an unusual urgency.

Riccs lowered Bache gently to the floor as the Theo scientist knelt beside him. Valent's violet eyes narrowed as he assessed Bache's condition, his slender fingers working with scientific precision to remove his suit.

'Lift him in,' he said, nodding at the strange machine.

'What in the ancients is that thing?' Zaphir asked, refusing to step back despite the medics trying to create space around Bache.

'An autonurse,' Valent replied, not looking up as his fingers danced across the icon controls. 'Theo medical technology. I brought it from Meridian Station. It can neutralise the radiation poisoning and begin cellular repair.'

The machine extended gossamer-thin beams of light that reminded Zaphir uncomfortably of the neural filaments they'd been fighting. These, however, glowed with a gentle red and white light rather than the sickly green.

'Will it work?' Riccs demanded, looming over them.

Valent's expression remained focused as he calibrated the device. 'It must. His radiation exposure is beyond what conventional medicine can treat. This is his only chance.'

The beams flashed over Bache's body, creating a web-like pattern that pulsed in time with his weakening heartbeat. Where they touched his skin, the ugly radiation burns began to fade, the damaged tissue visibly regenerating.

'That's incredible,' one of the medics whispered.

Bache's eyelids fluttered, a soft groan escaping his

bloodied lips. His body convulsed suddenly, back arching as the autonurse intensified its efforts.

'Come on, you stubborn bastard,' Zaphir whispered. 'Don't you dare die on me now.'

The machine's hum deepened to a resonant tone that vibrated through the deck plates. The web of beams intensified, glowing brighter as they penetrated deeper into his ravaged body. His breathing, which had been shallow and erratic, gradually steadied.

'It's working,' Valent announced, relief evident in his voice. 'The radiation poisoning is being reduced and the cellular damage reversed. His vital signs are on the up.'

Bache's hand moved weakly, his fingers brushing against Zaphir's wrist. His eyes opened, bloodshot and unfocused, but searching until they found her face.

'Did it…work?' he croaked, his voice so faint she had to lean closer to hear him.

'Yes,' Zaphir said, her voice breaking. 'You destroyed the node. Their entire network is gone.'

A ghost of a smile touched his cracked lips before his eyes fluttered closed again. The autonurse continued its work, the beams pulsing with increasing intensity as they repaired damage at the cellular level.

'We need to move him to medical,' Valent instructed, adjusting settings on the device. 'The autonurse will continue treatment, but he needs to be in a controlled environment and not a smelly hangar.'

The medics carefully helped wheel the autonurse out to a tube train that rushed him up to the central medical centre. Zaphir stayed close, unwilling to let him out of her sight after coming so close to losing him.

As they moved through the corridors towards the medical bay, she noticed the crew members they passed stopping to watch. Word had spread quickly about Bache's return and the success of his mission. Some saluted as the stretcher passed, others simply stood and bowed their heads in respectful silence.

Tirexion was waiting outside the medical bay, his face lighting up with desperate hope as he caught sight of his son. He fell in step beside the stretcher, reaching out to gently touch Bache's arm.

'How is he?' he asked Valent.

'The autonurse is working,' Valent assured him. 'His cellular structure is already showing signs of regeneration.'

'Will there be lasting damage?' Tirexion asked, his tone tight with concern.

Valent's expression remained neutral.

'Too early to tell. The radiation exposure was extreme, but Theo medical technology can repair damage that would be permanent with conventional methods. We have a lot of experience with radiation.'

They entered the medical bay, where Dr Renn was waiting with her team. Her eyes widened at the sight of the autonurse, but she adapted quickly, directing the medics to position Bache in the central position and having the awaiting GDA bed whisked away to make room.

'I've never seen anything like this,' she murmured, studying the autonurse's operation.

'Few outside Paradeisos have,' Valent replied. 'It's not technology we typically share.'

Zaphir stood back as the medical team worked around Bache, monitoring his vital signs as the autonurse continued its treatment. The blood had been cleaned from his face, revealing skin that was pale but no longer had the grey cast of radiation poisoning. His breathing had steadied, though each inhale still seemed to cause him pain.

Captain Whipper entered the medical bay, and his normally stern expression softened with relief as he saw Bache.

'Status, doctor?" he asked Dr Renn.

'Stabilising is the best I can do at the moment,' she replied, studying her monitors. 'The radiation damage is being reversed at an extraordinary rate though.'

'Good,' said Whipper. 'Keep me informed.'

Bache opened his eyes again, then immediately squeezed them shut against the harsh light above him. His entire body felt wrong…lighter somehow, as if he were floating just above the surface of his skin. The pain he expected wasn't there, replaced instead by a peculiar numbness that worried him more than agony would have.

'He's conscious,' someone said. Valent's voice he thought, but distorted as if travelling through water.

He tried opening his eyes again, more carefully this time. Blurry shapes gradually resolved into faces hovering above him…Valent's pale features, Zaphir's dark eyes wide with concern, and behind them, his father's haggard expression.

'Did it…' His voice rasped painfully, throat feeling like he'd swallowed broken glass. 'Did it work?'

Zaphir smiled as he obviously didn't remember asking

her that question before. Her hand found his, squeezing gently.

'Yes it worked. The Omada network is completely destroyed. You did it, you crazy idiot.'

Memory flooded back in fragments…the nebula, the massive crystalline node, the Omada entity forming before his eyes, the desperate race to escape the blast. He remembered tossing the inverter from the airlock, screaming at Tyche to jump.

'Tyche?' he managed.

'Still functional, though rather put out about his current condition,' Valent replied. 'The ship sustained significant damage, but his core memory and systems remain intact.'

Bache tried to sit up, but his body refused to cooperate. His muscles felt disconnected from his commands, responding with sluggish reluctance.

'Easy,' his father said, placing a hand on his shoulder. 'This amazing machine is still repairing your neural pathways. Movement will be difficult for a while.'

'What the hell is this?' Bache asked, glancing down at his body, noticing for the first time the web of red-white light that encased him like a cocoon, the gossamer strands pulsing gently.

'Theo medical technology,' Valent explained. 'It's repairing the cellular damage from radiation poisoning. You were exposed to nearly three times the lethal dose.'

Bache swallowed painfully. 'How long was I out there?'

'Thirty-eight hours in total,' Zaphir answered, her voice catching slightly. 'We thought you were…' She didn't finish the sentence.

The weight of what he'd accomplished settled over him. The Omada – the entity that had posed as the Nkris, that had infiltrated countless minds across the galaxy – was gone. Destroyed by the inverter he'd placed beneath the primary node.

'The crew members,' he said suddenly remembering. 'The seventeen infected personnel. Are they...'

'All fine,' his father assured him. 'When the primary node collapsed, the neural filaments dissolved harmlessly, just as Valent predicted.'

Relief washed through him, followed immediately by a wave of exhaustion so profound it made his eyes feel impossibly heavy. He fought against it, trying to focus on the faces around him, but his consciousness was already slipping away. The last thing he saw was Zaphir's relieved smile as darkness claimed him once more.

38

Central medical centre, *Katadromiko 2*, en route to the
Klatt border

DAYS PASSED in a blur of semiconsciousness. Bache drifted
in and out of awareness, sometimes opening his eyes to
find the medical bay empty save for the monitoring staff,
other times surrounded by visitors. Captain Whipper came
several times, his stern countenance mellowed with what
might have been approval. Riccs visited once, awkwardly
standing at the foot of Bache's bed before gruffly acknowl-
edging his "acceptable performance under extreme
duress".

Throughout it all, the autonurse continued its work, the
webs of light gradually fading as his body healed. By the
fifth day, Bache could sit up without assistance, though the
effort left him trembling with exhaustion.

'The cellular regeneration is proceeding at an optimal

rate,' Valent explained during one of his frequent visits to check the device. 'Another three days and you should be able to return to light duties.'

'Three days?' Bache croaked, his voice stronger now but still rough. 'That's impossible. Radiation poisoning at that level would take months to recover from, if at all.'

Valent's violet eyes sparkled with something that might have been amusement.

'With your primitive medical technology, perhaps. The autonurse operates at the quantum cellular level, restoring damaged DNA and accelerating mitotic reproduction without the risk of mutation.'

'I don't understand what you just said, but it sounded pretty good.' Bache looked down. 'Where did you get this thing anyway?' He asked, studying the strange grey device more carefully now. Its inner workings pulsed red with rhythms that seemed to match his heartbeat perfectly.

'It's not where, but when,' Valent replied cryptically. 'This technology has existed on Paradeisos for a long time, but we rarely share it beyond our borders.'

Bache frowned, remembering something his father had said about the Theos' technology being more advanced than they typically revealed.

'Why advertise you have it now? Why help me?'

Valent's expression grew serious.

'Because you risked everything to stop the Omada. Their infiltration affected all species, including mine. The Theo Council is…reconsidering our policy of isolation in light of recent events.'

On the seventh day, Dr Renn finally declared Bache fit enough to receive more visitors. His father had been a constant presence, of course, but now others were allowed in for longer periods. Clunk burst into the medical bay like a hurricane, his boisterous energy filling the sterile space.

'There he is, Mr save the fucking universe,' Clunk laughed, hopping from foot to foot.

'Are you still here?' said Bache, shaking his head.

'I am…my ship's getting a thorough upgrade,' he said, with a grin.

'Why? What was wrong with it?'

'Oh, nothing really…just wanted something to occupy your engineers while you were pissing around with aliens.'

Bache snorted a laugh which made his broken ribs hurt.

'How d'you feel now?'

'Like I've been trampled by a herd of Dasonian calloppes,' he croaked, his voice still raw. 'But better than being dead.'

Clunk pulled up a chair and spun it around, straddling it backwards. 'So what was it like? Meeting one of those Omada things face to face?'

'Like having someone reach inside your skull and start rearranging the furniture with a hull plate hammer.' Bache shuddered at the memory. 'It wasn't just talking to me…it was trying to bulldoze inside my head. If the neural shield hadn't held…'

'Well, you're a lucky bastard,' Clunk said, tapping his fingers against the chair back. 'The *K2*'s been buzzing with stories. Half the crew thinks you're some kind of hero now.'

'And the other half?'

'Think you're a reckless fucking idiot who got lucky.' Clunk grinned. 'I'm a bit in both camps, personally.'

Bache laughed, wincing as his ribs protested again. The autonurse pulsed brighter for a moment, its red-white beams intensifying around his chest.

'Captain's been in a weird mood since you got back,' Clunk continued. 'Almost…cheerful. It's bloody disturbing.'

'Mr Whippy, cheerful? Now I know you're lying.'

The medical bay doors slid open, and Zaphir walked in. She was wearing a fresh uniform, her dark hair straight for once and half way down her back. Dark circles lingered under her eyes, but her face brightened when she saw Bache awake.

'I'll leave you two alone,' Clunk said, standing up with exaggerated slowness. He winked at Bache before sauntering out.

Zaphir took the vacated chair, turning it around properly before sitting. For a moment, neither spoke. The soft hum of the autonurse filled the silence between them.

'You do look terrible,' she finally said, taking his hand, her voice softer than Bache expected.

'You should see the other alien,' he tried but the joke felt weak even to him.

'I did, remember? Or what was left of it after you blew it to atoms.'

'Did you call me a stubborn bastard, or did I dream that?'

'Yeah…among other things.' A small smile flickered across her face. 'I thought I'd lost you.'

'For a while there, so did I.' He reached out, his hand

finding hers. Her fingers were warm against his still-cold skin. 'Thank you. For coming back for me.'

'Like I had a choice.'

The medical bay doors slid open, and Captain Whipper strode in. Bache tried to sit up straighter, wincing as his ribs protested.

'At ease, Chief Engineer,' Whipper said, his expression unusually warm. 'You've earned the right to relax.'

'Thank you, Captain,' Bache replied, settling back against the pillows. 'Any word on the condition of the other two nodes?'

'That's actually why I'm here.' Whipper pulled up a holographic display above Bache's bed. 'The Auriga node self-destructed shortly after the primary explosion. It seems they were linked as Valent predicted.'

'And the one in Klatt territory?'

Whipper's mouth tightened. 'That's where things get interesting. The Klatt are reporting unusual activity in their region. They've actually requested GDA assistance in investigating.'

'They what?' Bache couldn't hide his surprise. The Klatt Empire rarely requested assistance from anyone, especially the GDA.

'It appears the destruction of the Omada network has created a power vacuum there,' Whipper continued. 'Various factions are scrambling to fill it... Well, you know what the Klatt are like.'

Zaphir slid her chair closer to Bache's bed, her eyes finding his. 'The president has requested you specifically for the mission.'

'Me?' Bache frowned. 'I'm no bloody diplomat and I'm not exactly in fighting shape.'

'Not immediately,' Whipper clarified. 'Once you've recovered. The Klatt representative was quite insistent that the "destroyer of the false Nkris" be present for negotiations.'

Bache sank back into his pillows, processing this new development. The thought of another mission so soon after nearly dying made his whole body ache.

'I don't really have a choice, do I?' Bache asked, already knowing the answer.

Whipper's mouth quirked in what almost passed for a smile.

'Not really, no. The president was quite clear on that point.'

Bache sighed and immediately regretted it as pain lanced through his chest. The autonurse pulsed brighter, sending waves of healing energy through his damaged ribs. He'd never been to Klatt territory before…few GDA had. The militaristic empire kept mostly to themselves, aggressive and territorial. The fact that they were asking for help, specifically his help, was unprecedented.

'When?' he asked finally.

'Four weeks, assuming your recovery continues at this rate,' Whipper replied. 'The *K2* will have all the Omada stuff removed by then. We've been ordered to escort you personally.'

Zaphir squeezed his hand. Her fingers were warm against his skin, reminding him how cold he still felt despite the autonurse's efforts.

'I'll be going with you,' she said, her voice leaving no

room for argument. 'Someone needs to make sure you don't get yourself killed properly this time.'

'The specialist will be joining the diplomatic team, yes,' Whipper confirmed. 'Along with your father, once he's fully recovered too. His expertise with the Omada systems will be invaluable.'

Whipper cleared his throat and straightened his uniform.

'That's not all. I received another direct communication from the president only an hour ago.'

Bache tensed, suddenly alert despite his exhaustion. The captain's demeanour had shifted subtly…shoulders back, chin raised, the slight formality that came with official business.

'The president was impressed with your actions against the Omada,' Whipper continued. 'So impressed, in fact, that he's issued a presidential order for an immediate field promotion.'

Bache blinked, not comprehending.

'Sir?'

'Congratulations, Captain Loftt.' Whipper's face broke into a rare genuine smile as he extended his hand. 'You're now the youngest ship's captain in GDA history.'

The words hit Bache like a physical blow as he shook the captain's hand. His mouth opened, then closed again as he struggled to process what he'd just heard.

'I…what? That's not…I'm an engineer, not a…'

'The president was quite clear,' Whipper continued. 'Once you're recovered, you'll be taking command of the *Tromos*. She's one of our newest destroyers, fresh out of the Jagnorite shipyards.'

Zaphir's grip on his hand tightened to the point of pain. When he glanced at her, her eyes were wide, her expression caught between shock and delight.

'The *Tromos*?' Bache's voice came out as a croak. 'But that's a premier command. There are dozens of officers with more experience who…'

'None of whom single-handedly infiltrated and destroyed the most significant threat to the GDA in centuries,' Whipper interrupted. 'The president believes, and I reluctantly agree, that your…unconventional thinking is exactly what we need right now.'

The autonurse pulsed brighter around Bache's chest as his heart rate spiked. Captain. Him. Of a destroyer. The idea was simultaneously terrifying and exhilarating. His father had spent decades working his way up to chief engineer, and now Bache was leapfrogging past that position entirely.

'When does she arrive?' he managed, his throat suddenly dry.

'Nine days. She'll rendezvous with us just before the Klatt mission. You'll have a couple of days to get acquainted with her systems before taking command.' Whipper's expression softened slightly. 'Consider the Klatt mission your trial by fire. Some of the crew are already aboard, so they'll help you find your feet. The remainder are for you to choose.'

'Oh…right,' he said, his mind already racing as to who he would want with him on his first command. He ran a hand through his hair, wincing as his ribs protested the movement. 'My father…does he know?'

'Not yet. I thought you might want to tell him yourself.'

The medical bay suddenly felt too small, the air too thin. Captain Loftt. The title echoed in his mind, foreign and ill-fitting. He was an engineer, not a ship commander. He solved problems with tools and calculations, not tactics and diplomacy.

'I don't know what to say,' Bache admitted.

'That's a first,' said Zaphir, squeezing his hand again.

'Thank you, Captain,' he managed finally.

'When you're fit, go and see my quartermaster and he'll sort you out with your uniform requirements,' said Whipper.

Bache nodded, exhaustion washing over him in a sudden wave. His eyelids felt impossibly heavy. The autonurse hummed, adjusting its output as his vital signs fluctuated.

'I think that's enough for today,' Dr Renn said, appearing at his bedside with perfect timing. 'He needs a lot of rest over the next couple of weeks.'

Whipper nodded and turned to leave. 'We'll discuss the details later, Captain Loftt. For now, focus on healing and who you'll want as your senior officers.'

Zaphir lingered a moment longer, her eyes searching his face. 'Don't worry, you'll do just fine. You'll make a great captain and don't fret about the Klatt either,' she said quietly. 'We'll figure that out together.'

Bache managed a weak smile. 'Like we always do, eh!'

After she left, he stared at the ceiling, his mind racing despite his exhaustion. He was a captain now. The dangers of the Klatt. Had the third node been destroyed. Whatever waited for them there deep in Klatt territory would be precarious…the Klatt weren't renowned for their hospitality. But right now, all he wanted was sleep.

As his consciousness began to fade, he thought he heard Tyche's irritating voice emanating through the autonurse.

'Don't worry, Lofty. I'll be coming too. Wouldn't miss it for all the beer on Panemorfi.'

Bache groaned. Perfect. Just bloody perfect.

EPILOGUE

Observation deck, *Katadromiko 2*, en route to the Klatt
border

NINE DAYS LATER, Bache stood on the observation deck of
the *K2*, watching the sleek black silhouette of the *Tromos*
glide into position alongside them. His new command. The
destroyer's lines were predatory and elegant, its hull
absorbing rather than reflecting the light of the distant
stars. His heart hammered against his ribcage as he imagined himself at her helm.

'Impressive, isn't she?' Zaphir said, joining him at the
viewport.

'Terrifying is more like it,' Bache admitted, running a
hand through his hair. The autonurse had completed its
work a week ago, and physically he felt strong. Mentally,
however, he was a storm of doubt and anticipation. 'I still

can't believe this is happening, it seems only yesterday I was a junior lieutenant.'

'Well, you'd better start believing. The official handover ceremony is in thirty minutes.'

Bache adjusted his new captain's uniform for the tenth time that morning. The collar felt too tight, the triple gold bands on his cuffs too heavy. He'd spent the past three weeks studying every technical specification of the *Tromos* he could access, trying to prepare himself for a position he'd never imagined holding.

'I've been meaning to ask you something,' he said, turning to face Zaphir. 'I need a first officer. Someone I can trust. Someone who isn't afraid to tell me when I'm being an idiot.'

Zaphir raised an eyebrow and grinned. 'That's a full-time job then?'

'I'm serious. I want you as my XO.'

Her expression shifted, surprise giving way to something more complex. 'Me? I'm not even in the command track.'

'Neither was I until three weeks ago.' He gestured towards the *Tromos*. 'She's the most advanced destroyer in the fleet. I need someone who can think outside the regulations when necessary.'

'You're really offering me the promotion to XO?' Her voice was carefully neutral, but Bache caught the flicker of excitement in her eyes.

'Effective immediately, if you accept.'

She laughed, the sound unexpectedly light. 'You really are insane. But yes. Of course I'll accept.'

Bache felt a knot of tension release between his shoulders. 'Good. That's…very good.'

The door to the observation deck hissed open, and Ash strode in, her usual scowl firmly in place. The engineer had been one of the few personnel to treat Bache exactly the same after his return from the nebula…with grudging respect tinged with perpetual irritation.

'There you are,' Ash grumbled. 'Captain Whipper's looking for you. Something about final transfer protocols.'

'Thanks, Ash,' Bache said. 'Actually, while you're here…I've been reviewing personnel files for my engineering section.

Ash folded her arms. 'And?'

'And…I want you as my ship's engineer.'

The scowl deepened. 'What? Have you forgotten I'm a civilian engineer?'

'No…you would be a contractor. This is not an uncommon occurrence. I would be prepared to sponsor you to study too.'

'Study what?'

'To be a fleet officer.'

'Really?'

'Yes…but only if that's what you'd like.'

Ash grinned for the first time.

'I like,' she said. 'You've just got yourself a ship's engineer.'

Zaphir glanced down as her tablet chimed.

'Transport shuttle's ready, Captain,' she said, the corners of her mouth twitching upward as she emphasised his new rank. 'Valent's already aboard with his…gift.'

Bache groaned.

'Don't remind me.'

The "gift" in question was Tyche…or rather, what remained of the Theo ship's sentient AI core. Valent had somehow managed to salvage the personality matrix and central processors from the wreckage, and had spent the past weeks rebuilding them into a portable unit. The Theo scientist had announced his intention to return to Paradeisos, but not before presenting Bache with the refurbished AI as a parting gift.

'It'll be nice having a reminder of our adventure,' Zaphir teased, falling into step beside him as they headed towards the tube train to the hangar bay.

'That's one word for it,' Bache muttered. 'I'm just worried he'll drive me insane before we even reach Klatt space.'

The shuttle ride to the *Tromos* was brief but significant. As they approached the smaller destroyer, Bache felt the weight of responsibility settle more firmly on his shoulders. Forty crew members would soon be looking to him for leadership.

As the shuttle landed in the destroyer's small hangar, Bache felt his stomach tighten. The airlock cycled open with a soft hiss, revealing a formal reception line of officers standing at perfect attention.

'Looks like they've rolled out the welcome mat,' Zaphir murmured beside him.

Bache swallowed hard and straightened his uniform one last time. He stepped through the airlock onto the polished deck of his new command. The ship was immaculate, every surface gleaming under the bright lights. The assembled crew snapped to even more rigid attention as his boots touched the deck.

A sharp voice called out, 'Captain on deck.'

The sound of forty sets of boots coming together in unison echoed through the hangar. Bache fought the urge to look behind him for the actual captain before remembering that was now him.

A tall, lean officer with close-cropped silver hair stepped forward.

'Captain Loftt, Commander Tera Voss, acting captain of the *Tromos*. I hereby relinquish command to you, sir.'

Voss handed him a small data tablet...the ship's authentication codes and command protocols. As his fingers closed around it, the tablet glowed briefly, recognising his biometric signature.

'Thank you, Commander. I accept command of the *Tromos*.'

Voss's eyes were evaluating him with military precision.

'Permission to introduce the senior staff, Captain?'

'Granted, Commander,' Bache replied, finding his voice growing steadier with each word.

Voss led him down the line, introducing each officer by name and position. Bache shook hands with the tactical officer, navigation chief, and weapons specialists, trying desperately to commit each face and name to memory.

'And this is our current chief engineer, Lieutenant Marris,' Voss said, stopping before a stocky woman with burn scars on her forearms.

'Lieutenant,' Bache nodded. 'I've read good things about your work on the propulsion system.'

Marris looked surprised.

'Thank you, sir. I didn't realise you'd reviewed our technical specifications already.'

'First thing I did,' Bache admitted. 'Old habits die hard. I was an engineer before…all this.' He gestured vaguely at his captain's insignia.

A small smile broke through Marris's professional demeanour.

'That explains why our maintenance logs were accessed at 0300 this morning.'

'Guilty,' Bache said. 'I hope you don't mind that I've brought another engineer along.' He gestured to Ash, who stood awkwardly behind him. 'Ms Ash Stevns will be joining your department.'

Marris nodded. 'We can always use more hands, sir.'

Bache's head swam with names and faces, but he maintained his composure, acutely aware that every eye on the ship was on him.

A young lieutenant stepped forward, offering another salute.

'Lieutenant Rao, sir. If you'll follow me, the early shift bridge crew await your arrival.'

Bache nodded, following the lieutenant with Zaphir and Ash trailing behind. The *Tromos* was significantly smaller than the *K2*, but what it lacked in size it made up for in cutting-edge technology. Every surface seemed to gleam with newness.

'They certainly rolled out the red carpet,' Zaphir murmured close to his ear. 'I don't think I've ever seen such a formal welcome.'

'Makes you wonder what they've heard about me,' Bache whispered back.

'Oh…only that you single-handedly saved the galaxy,' Ash snorted from behind them. 'Nothing major.'

They entered a lift that whisked them upward towards the bridge. Bache used the brief journey to compose himself, to push down the doubt that kept threatening to surface. He wasn't just an engineer anymore. He was Captain Loftt now, and these people needed to see confidence.

The bridge doors slid open to reveal a compact, gleaming command centre that took Bache's breath away. Unlike the sprawling bridge of the *K2*, the *Tromos*'s bridge was designed for efficiency, every station within a few steps of the central command chair. The lighting was subdued but precise, illuminating each console without creating glare.

The bridge crew rose as one, snapping to attention as Lieutenant Rao announced, 'Captain on the bridge.'

Bache took a moment to scan the faces before him…all watching him with expressions ranging from curiosity to barely concealed excitement. This was his crew now. His responsibility.

'At ease, everyone,' he said, his voice steadier than he expected.

He moved towards the command chair positioned at the centre of the bridge. It sat on a slightly raised dais, providing a clear view of every station. Bache hesitated for just a heartbeat before lowering himself into it. The synthetic leather creaked slightly beneath his weight. His hands found the armrests, fingers curling around the edges where control interfaces were subtly integrated into the design.

'Status report,' he said, the words feeling foreign.

The navigation officer, a young woman whose name badge read "Lt Karit", turned from her station.

'All systems operational, Captain. Pre-departure checks complete. Awaiting your orders.'

Zaphir moved to stand at his right side, her presence a steadying influence. She gave him the smallest of nods…a silent reassurance that he belonged in that chair.

Bache straightened his back and made his decision.

'Plot a course for the Klatt border,' he ordered, his voice carrying across the bridge with an authority he didn't entirely feel. 'Standard approach through the Narol sector. We'll rendezvous with our diplomatic escort at the designated coordinates.'

'Course plotted, sir,' Lieutenant Karit responded, her fingers dancing across her console. 'Estimated arrival at Klatt border in forty-seven hours at standard cruise.'

'Tactical status?' Bache asked, turning slightly towards the weapons station.

A broad-shouldered lieutenant with a scar across his jawline responded immediately.

'All defensive systems at full capacity, Captain. Weapons systems in standby mode as per diplomatic protocol.'

Bache nodded.

'Communications, notify *Katadromiko 2* of our departure and intended course.'

'Aye, Captain,' came the crisp response from his left.

He took a deep breath, aware that every eye on the bridge was watching him, waiting for the final command.

'Execute,' Bache ordered, feeling a surge of adrenaline as the *Tromos*'s engines powered up, the deck vibrating subtly beneath his feet.

The holomap showed the *K2* falling away as they manoeuvred out of formation. Whipper would follow in the much bigger cruiser.

'Jump in five seconds,' the helm officer announced.

Bache relaxed back in his chair and grinned.

AFTERWORD

I wanted to say a huge thank you for choosing to read *The Engineer.* I sincerely hope you enjoyed the fourth adventure in the *Bache Loftt* series.

If you did enjoy this novel, it'd be fantastic if you could write a review. It doesn't have to be long, just a few words, but it is the best way for me to help new readers discover my writing for the first time. I use the best and most imaginative reviews in my marketing too.

If you'd like to buy my ebooks direct from me, or stay up to date with what's going on, you're welcome to join my reader group at my website www.nickadamsbooks.com You'll receive a free short story (The Architect Fold), a bi-monthly newsletter and advance notice of new releases and cover reveals. I will never share your email address and you can unsubscribe at any time.

You can also contact me via Facebook, Instagram, or by email. I love hearing from readers...I read every message and try to reply to everyone personally.

Thanks again for your support.
Nick Adams